ZigZag

Also by Ellen Wittlinger

Razzle
The Long Night of Leo and Bree
What's in a Name
Gracie's Girl
Hard Love

ZigZag

BY ELLEN WITTLINGER

SIMON & SCHUSTER BOOKS FOR YOUNG READERS
NEW YORK LONDON TORONTO SYDNEY SINGAPORE

SIMON AND SCHUSTER BOOKS FOR YOUNG READERS
An imprint of Simon & Schuster Children's Publishing Division
1230 Avenue of the Americas, New York, New York, 10020

This book is a work of fiction. Any references to historical events, real people, or real locales are used fictitiously. Other names, characters, places, and incidents are products of the author's imagination, and any resemblance to actual events or locales or persons, living or dead, is entirely coincidental.

Book design by Dan Potash
The text for this book is set in Berling.
Manufactured in the United States of America
2 4 6 8 10 9 7 5 3 1
Library of Congress Cataloging-in-Publication Data
Wittlinger, Ellen.
Zigzag / Ellen Wittlinger.
p. cm.
Summary: A high-school junior makes a trip with her aunt and two cousins, discovering places she did not know existed and strengths she did not know she had.
ISBN 0-689-84996-6
[1. Automobile travel—Fiction. 2. Vacations—Fiction. 3. Cousins—Fiction. 4. Aunts—Fiction. 5. Interpersonal relations—Fiction.] I. Title.
PZ7.W78436 Zi 2003
[Fic]—dc21 2002002145

For my mother, Doris Wittlinger,
and for my second parents, John and Mary Pritchard.

With grateful thanks to my editor, David Gale; his assistant, Ellie Bisker; my agent, Ginger Knowlton; and to Pat Lowery Collins, Anita Riggio, and David Pritchard for their help and advice on the manuscript.

Special thanks also to the Fine Arts Work Center in Provincetown, Massachusetts, for time and space in which to work.

Chapter One

The party was to celebrate my boyfriend Chris's high school graduation, no occasion for rejoicing as far as I was concerned. As usual, the Melvilles had gone overboard for their one and only son, putting up a big white tent in their overly landscaped backyard and having the food catered by Biscuit, the hot new restaurant in Iowa City.

I'd already been forced to talk to the high school principal, two Spanish teachers, and Chris's next-door neighbors; my smile was sagging like Custer's mustache. All anybody could come up with to say to me was, "Just think, Robin, next year you'll be graduating!" Whoopee. Sure couldn't wait for my big fabulous future to start.

I found Chris scarfing down shrimp at the buffet table. "Having fun?" he asked between mouthfuls.

"Fun might be too much to aim for," I said, hooking my thumb in the armhole of my dress to try and stretch it a little. It really was too tight this year. "You think we can leave soon?"

"I don't know." He grimaced. "It's my party. I can't just . . ."

"I know, but it's been going on all afternoon already. I thought we could . . . you know . . . have our own celebration." I tried to look innocent and loving, rather than the way I actually felt—bored and bummed.

Chris slipped an arm around my waist and kissed my hair just above my ear. "I can't wait," he said. "You know, you look gorgeous in that dress."

I gave him a skeptical look. "This dress is a hundred years old."

"It is not, and anyway, I like it on you. Don't you believe me?"

Big sighs from both of us.

We'd argued about this more than once—that when Chris compliments me I disagree with him or say it's not true. He says I don't value myself enough, but I think I'm just being realistic. I look okay, but my hair's too thin, and my boobs aren't very big, and I never have anything to wear he hasn't seen a million times already. Chris always says my eyes are beautiful, but eyes are a pretty small percentage of a person. No, the only thing special about me is Chris.

A beefy hand on the end of a long arm divided the air space between us.

"Christopher! The young man with the big future!" I looked up at the tall, bald-headed guy connected to the arm and recognized Dr. Ransom, fellow surgeon and friend of Chris's dad. Chris's mother is a doctor, too, a pediatrician here in town. The party was lousy with medical types; I'd already been introduced to two cardiologists, a neurologist, and an obstetrician. My mother is a nurse, so I've heard enough about doctors over the years that I'm not that impressed by a string of letters tacked on behind a name.

Where was Franny, anyway? There weren't many high school kids there because most of Chris's friends were seniors, and their parents were throwing parties for them, too. Franny was a junior, like me. The only reason she'd agreed to come was because she'd never been inside the Melvilles' house and she wanted to "check it out." I just hoped she wouldn't get caught by one of the good doctors nosing through their closets or taking inventory in the kitchen cabinets.

Dr. Ransom was practically shouting at Chris. "Best years of your life, son! You're going to have a wonderful time at Georgetown. When I was at Hopkins—stop me if I've told you this already . . ."

Blah, blah, blah. The guy loved bouncing his big voice off Chris, but Chris didn't mind. He'd have a conversation with a rock if you painted a face on it. I gave Chris a smile and pulled away. Georgetown University, a thousand miles from Iowa, was not my favorite topic of conversation.

I was headed across the lawn to see if Franny was inside when I was intercepted by Dr. Melville. The female one.

"Robin, dear, could you do me a huge favor?" She tipped her head over toward one shoulder to show me how sorry she was about asking someone who wouldn't dare refuse her.

"Sure, Dr. Melville. What do you need?"

"The caterers have left to do another party. They'll be back to clean up, of course, but meanwhile they've left several platters in my kitchen, which are too large for me to manage in these heels. I *hate* to ask you, but . . ."

But there was no one else she'd dare ask. She was probably thinking I looked like I ought to be working for the caterer anyway.

"No problem," I told her.

The Melvilles' house is large by any standards, but in Thunder Lake, Iowa, it's a mansion. In order to get to the kitchen you have to walk across a big screened sunporch filled with wicker chairs and flowery cushions. Then the kitchen opens up in front of you, an enormous black-and-white room in which everything sparkles, from the faucet handles to the china cat food bowls. In our house the faucets are lucky to have handles, and the cats live in the barn where they nosh on filet of mousie.

The hors d'oeuvre platters were lined up on the island between the kitchen and the family room, and there, sitting on a stool, picking at olives, was Franny.

"There you are," I said. "You deserted me."

"I think you're confusing me with your boyfriend." She swallowed a hunk of cheese and reached for more. "Besides, it's hotter than hell out there."

"No kidding. And I have to take these trays out. The caterer left."

Franny's jaw fell. "Jesus, why don't they get the Prince to do it?"

"He's busy fending off jerks. Help me, okay?"

She sighed. "Okay, but I'm not putting my shoes back on. Let's leave one tray inside, so we can come back in and have our own party."

We each took two trays, wobbled down the steps and across the grass to the tent. Chris was still on the other side of the table laughing at some old guy's jokes.

"Thank you, girls," Dr. Melville said as she swept by the table on her way to greet more guests.

Franny gave a low bow. "Your wish is our command."

I elbowed her. "Careful, she has *no* sense of humor."

"Really? Can't she *buy* one? A sense of humor is more useful than most of those other senses if you're going to get through life in one piece."

Franny is an expert on getting through life in one piece. The year I met her, the year we started middle school, Franny's life was in half a dozen large chunks. Her parents had just begun the most publicly bitter divorce Thunder Lake had ever seen. They blamed each other for their own problems, and for "ruining the kid." By the time I met her, they were both demanding their right to the money, the house, the cars, and Franny.

It got so bad they'd each show up after school and stand in

front of the building literally pulling her back and forth between them. A few times Liz, her mom, was pretty drunk. Several times the principal tried to stop their arguments, and once the police were called.

Franny was just about nuts from the whole thing. Her grade school friends were scared of the whole situation and totally deserted her. She'd show up in class wearing big black boots and short shorts, with black eyeliner circles drawn around her eyes so she always looked surprised. The first time I saw her, she had a shaved head. To me she seemed like the most interesting person in the whole school. Her life was high drama while mine was still a *Nickelodeon* cartoon. Within weeks we were inseparable.

Franny's stories were riveting. When she told me her mother had had a boyfriend before she divorced her father, I was horrified.

"What did he do when he found out?" I asked her.

"Got drunk, as usual."

"But, I mean, did he scream or hit her or anything?"

"No, he usually hits me. He's afraid of Liz so he just smacks me instead."

"Franny, that's awful! You can't live with him anymore!"

Whenever I said things like that, Franny would smile at me, as if she was really sorry to have to tell me what a crappy world it was. "It just seems awful to you because your mom is so normal. I'm used to having crazy parents."

But I refused to agree. "It *is* awful, Franny. You're just used to it so you don't see how bad it is."

I couldn't imagine living with a man who got drunk and hit me when he was mad at my mother. In fact, I could barely imagine living with *any* man. My dad had left us right after my first birthday; I saw him only a few times a year.

When I was younger I'd get so excited waiting for him to come over to take me out for lunch, I'd sometimes get sick to my stomach and Mom would have to call him and put it off for another time. Just having him standing in our living room made me nervous. It made the whole house feel different, as if Mom and I were cats and here this dog—a totally different *species*—had walked into our house, and even though he *seemed* friendly, I didn't really know any other dogs. How were you supposed to act around a dog? I didn't even *speak* dog.

By the time the day was over and he dropped me off at home again, I'd just be getting used to him. I'd be starting to purr a little bit. Just in time to start missing him and his big barky voice.

Franny had been living with her mom in one of those developments where all the houses look the same. Her dad had gotten an apartment in Iowa City, where he worked, and he wanted her to live there with him instead, which would have meant changing schools. While they argued about it, they kept dragging her back and forth between Thunder Lake and Iowa City, until finally they started battling it out in court.

Franny got furious with both of them. "If I'm already *ruined*, why do they even want me? I'm not going to live with either one of them! I'm running away to Chicago."

I felt bad for her, having to put up such a brave front. But the day she showed me the bus ticket, I got scared. "You can't go there alone! Where will you live?"

"I'll get by," Franny said, lighting up a cigarette and trying to look tough without inhaling.

"I'll go with you," I announced, hoping it wouldn't come to that.

But she refused my company anyway. "Your mother would miss you too much. And you'd miss her." Which was true.

"But you can't leave, Franny!" I begged. "You're my best friend!" We cried a little over how much we'd miss each other. I hated to see Franny cry; once she started, she often couldn't stop, and I knew she wasn't crying over me. She'd cry until the eyeliner ran down her cheeks and smudged my bedspread.

So I came up with a plan. Franny would run away to *my* house. Mom and I lived in a small apartment in town then, but Mom's bedroom was downstairs and mine was upstairs with its own bathroom. We figured whenever Mom came upstairs Franny would just climb in the bathtub and pull the curtain. We had such elaborate plans; we thought we were geniuses.

It worked for two days. By then the police had been called in and Franny's parents had plastered the whole town with posters that had her picture under the headline: MISSING! I suppose, under the circumstances, my mother thought it was peculiar that I ate a hearty dinner and then asked for an extra pork chop and baked potato to take upstairs for a "snack." She followed me up and there stood Franny trying on my sweaters.

When Mom told her she had to call her parents immediately, Franny popped her gum and shrugged. "I was getting bored up here, anyway." I already knew she only lied like that when she felt really hopeless. I hugged her even though I knew she wouldn't hug me back in front of my mother.

While Franny was on the phone, I told Mom some of the details of Franny's home life. "How can she go back there? We have to help her!" I begged.

So Mom made us cocoa and explained to Franny that she was welcome in our house anytime. "*Anytime,*" she repeated. "And if you ever need help, you call me right away."

Franny didn't say anything, but she listened. Before long our house was as much her home as mine. It turned out that neither of her parents wanted her with the *other* parent, but they didn't particularly want her themselves either. Sometimes she'd call late at night because Bill had come by to declare his rights again, or Liz was passed out under the kitchen table, or she was alone and scared. No matter what time it was, we'd drive over and rescue her.

That's what Franny always called it: a rescue mission.

She's been living with her mother for the past two years now and things aren't as bad as they were. I can't remember the last time we did a rescue mission. But Franny's not the same kid anymore who cried all over my bedspread. Sometimes she seems about twenty years older than me and done with crying for good. She definitely has a sense of humor about her life, though, even if not everybody gets the joke.

After restocking the buffet table we went back inside the Melvilles' house; Franny headed straight for the refrigerator. "What do they have to drink?"

"There's soda outside."

"I'm not going back out *there* again. Ooh, lemonade—that's good." She brought out a large blue-and-white pitcher.

"Be careful with that. Dr. Melville loves that thing—it was her mother's."

"Didn't I tell you? I'm old enough to pour my own juice now."

"Do you think you should drink that? I mean, it wasn't put out for the guests."

"It's only lemonade. I don't think they'll miss it."

She stuck the pitcher back in the fridge, picked up the remaining tray of food, and walked toward the family room. "Let's sit down where it's comfortable."

"No! You can't take food in there!" I said. "Dr. Melville doesn't let anybody eat on that carpet. And besides, they just recovered the couch."

"Oh, for crapsake!" Franny turned around, slapped the tray down on the counter and sank onto a stool. "This place is a torture chamber. You can't touch the china, you can't eat the food, and you can't sit on the furniture. Are you allowed to pee in the toilets or does Dr. Melville have rules about that, too?"

"I'm sorry. I just don't want her to get mad at me, that's all."

"Why? You think all of a sudden, after two years, she's going to change her mind and decide she's so crazy about you that the Prince can stay here and go to the University of Iowa so you won't be separated? Yeah, that'll happen." She stuffed an artichoke heart in her mouth.

"I can't afford to antagonize her, that's all. And stop calling Chris, *the Prince.*"

She shook her head. "Is he really worth all this gloom and doom? You've never even gone out with anybody else."

"You wouldn't understand, Franny." She hates when I say that, because she's never had a boyfriend. But it's true.

She built up a little temper over it. "Oh, get over yourself, Cinderella! He's just a guy."

"No, he isn't . . ."

"Yes, he is! There's nothing so damn special about—"

"Yes, there is!" I shouted at her. "He *is* special!" And then the bawling started. Didn't even see it coming this time. I guess Franny didn't either.

"Oh, Jesus. Come on, Robin. Don't start this again. Please!"

"I can't . . . help . . . it."

"Okay, he's *special* already. *Really* special. Stop crying!"

It had all been so easy with Chris, right from the beginning. He was the perfect boy and he chose *me.* I knew I didn't deserve him, but I had him anyway. Except now he was leaving and I couldn't stand it. I couldn't imagine what my life would be like without him.

When I heard the footsteps coming up the porch stairs I tried to sniff the tears back, breathe deeply, look normal. But it was obvious what had been going on—my face was blotchy and slick with moisture, and Franny was handing me a tissue. Chris stopped abruptly just inside the kitchen door and his smile faded.

"Oh, Robin," he said. "Not *again.*"

Again.

Chapter Two

"I'm not leaving you—I'm just going to college! Why can't you believe that?"

I shrugged. "Call it what you want. I'm just being realistic, Chris."

"You're just being pessimistic, as usual." He paced around, kicking through the weeds, but I stayed sitting, twirling my hand in the water.

We were down by the pond on our farm. It was always my favorite place to go when I felt crummy, even back when Grandad owned the farm and Mom and I lived in town.

Chris took off his jacket and tie, unbuttoned the first couple of buttons on his shirt, and rolled up his sleeves. There were sweat circles under his arms and what I could see of his chest looked shiny, too. Which made me love him even more. It was all part of who he was, his body, his being, his life, which I sometimes had a hard time distinguishing from *my* body, *my* being, *my* life. When he came back toward me, I put up my hand and grabbed his; he let me pull him down beside me.

"I don't want to make you mad," I said.

"I'm not mad—I'm just frustrated." He ran his fingers through my hair and goose bumps scampered down my arms.

"It's just that I love you so much, Chris, and I don't know what I'm going to do when you're gone." I liked looking at his face when I told him I loved him. It got very soft and seemed to glow.

"Oh, Robin. I love you, too—you *know* that." He bent close and kissed me, like I knew he would.

"Why don't you take that shirt off?" I said. "You must be boiling." I started to unbutton the rest of the buttons.

"I am," he said, smiling. "I just didn't want to get you all turned on."

"Too late," I said, kissing the salty, blond hair on his chest. When the shirt was off, I pulled his head down onto my lap, dipped one hand in the pond, and let my cold, wet fingers run across his chest. His head rolled back in pleasure as I caressed him.

Sometimes I think I wasn't even alive until I met Chris. Not that I knew it then, of course. But when I look back, the time before Chris seems gray. It's like the difference between home movies and Steven Spielberg. Or trading in your oatmeal for Cherry Garcia. Once you know your life can be in color how can you go back to black and white?

We didn't say anything for a few minutes, and then Chris whispered, "I don't want to leave you either."

"Then why are you?" I said, not for the first time. I guess I don't know when to shut up.

Chris was quiet for half a minute, then said, "You know why."

The thing is, every time I think of him leaving, I feel like I just went over a waterfall without a life jacket. The end is near, and I'm drowning already. "I *don't* know why," I said. "I'd never leave you. I wouldn't."

Chris rolled off my lap and got to his knees. "Don't start this again, Robin. You *know why.*"

"I know the University of Iowa has courses in international

relations. I don't see why you need to go so far away."

His face tightened. "Because Georgetown is a great school, and it's in Washington, D.C., where international relations are actually *taking place.* Not to mention that it's been my first-choice college practically my whole life."

"Only because your dad talks about it all the time."

"He does not!"

I sighed. "Admit it. Your parents were dying for you to go to school someplace far away from me."

He shook his head. "I know I'll never convince you that they like you, Robin, but they do. They just think we're too young to be so serious."

"They wouldn't be so worried if my parents were doctors, or if I was a *Georgetown* girl."

Chris stood up and grabbed his shirt, shoving his arms through the sleeves. "I'm really tired of arguing about the same stuff again and again, Robin. Aren't you? Why do you want to ruin our last summer together?"

"Our *last summer*? Since when?" I jumped to my feet so I could see his eyes.

"I don't mean last summer *forever* . . . I just mean . . ."

"It sure sounds like you mean forever. That's what *last summer* means!"

Chris ran his hands through his hair. "You're making me crazy, Robin!"

"Chris, this is the worst thing that's ever happened to me! Can't we even talk about it?"

"All we *do* is talk about it!"

"Well, all I do is think about it! Unlike you, I'm not going off to some exciting new place in three months. Or ever, for that matter. What am I supposed to think about?"

"Think about *yourself* for a change!"

He looked so aggravated, I started to cry again. He put his arms around me and hugged me tightly to him so that my tears ran down his neck. When I really thought about it, I knew I wouldn't be the only girl Chris Melville ever loved. How could I be that lucky? I just wanted to hold on to him as long as I possibly could.

I sniffled and looked up at his face. "My mom's on the late shift again," I said.

"She is?"

I nodded and kept looking into his eyes until he leaned down to kiss me.

"Guess we better go inside then, before the mosquitoes have us for dinner," he said. We walked back to the house, all tangled around each other, and went up to my bedroom. This was what I'd been hoping for all day, ever since I put the new sky blue sheets on my bed that morning.

When Mom works three to eleven she doesn't get home until almost midnight, but Chris had orders to be home by ten so his parents could give him their graduation gift after everybody left. He was thinking it was a new computer, but I figured they'd probably bought him a brand new girlfriend, one with two parents, a decent wardrobe, and a merit scholarship to Harvard.

We got up about nine so I could make scrambled eggs and bacon before Chris left. He stood behind me at the stove, his arms around my waist.

"Don't forget your secret ingredients," he said. I threw in some oregano and turned the pepper mill over the eggs until they were polka-dotted. Since Chris's mother rarely cooked anything, he was awed by my ability to wield a spatula.

I piled the eggs onto two plates and put the tray of bacon on the kitchen table while Chris poured us cups of coffee. We sat across from each other, but neither of us dug right in.

"What would your mom say if she knew we were sleeping together? Would she be upset?"

I shrugged. "I don't think it would come as a big shock to her. When she first started working the late shift we had a big talk about how she knew it would be tempting for you and me to have an empty house to come to, and she hoped we wouldn't feel we had to take advantage of it. But she never said *don't*. That's not her style."

"Yeah, your mother's pretty cool."

"I'm not saying she'd be thrilled about it. I'm sure I'd get the whole safe-sex lecture for the forty-second time."

Chris nodded, and we both started in on our eggs. "I can't imagine what my mother would do. She thinks I'm so perfect."

"Well, she's right about that," I said.

Chris didn't smile, though; he just picked up several pieces of bacon at once and bit off a mouthful. "I wish you didn't think so," he said finally.

I was so surprised I spilled coffee on my bathrobe. "What?"

"I wish you didn't think I was perfect. Nobody is."

I smiled. "Well, let's just say you come closer to it than most people."

"I don't think I do, though. It scares me sometimes that I might not be able to live up to your expectations. Yours or my mother's."

I didn't like the sound of that—what did I expect that he couldn't live up to? "You just have to be you, Chris. That's all I want." I broke off a section of the orange I'd been peeling and held it up to his lips until he took it from my fingers, kissing them lightly.

When we were lying together between the sky blue sheets,

barely space for dust between our two bodies, I'd promised myself I was going to stop messing up all our good times by worrying about what was coming next. I always felt better about us after sex because being together like that made it seem that Chris was really mine. That no one could ever know me the way Chris did, and no one could ever know him the way I did.

After Chris left I lay down on the couch and fell asleep. There was a nice breeze coming in the living room windows and, for the moment, I felt content. School was out, my stomach was full, and Chris loved me. What else mattered?

Instead of a banging door waking me, I woke up gradually to the sound of my mother's voice speaking to someone outside. I couldn't make out any of the words—she was talking softly—but her laugh surprised me. I could sometimes make Mom laugh, but there weren't many other people who could. She was usually too serious to get giggly.

"Who were you talking to?" I asked her once the door closed.

"Oh!" She jumped and turned toward me. "Goodness, Robin, you scared me to death! I thought you'd be up in bed by now."

"Sorry. I fell asleep on the couch."

"Well, why don't you go upstairs. You'll probably fall right back to sleep." She headed for the kitchen to make herself a cup of tea before bed, her nightly ritual.

I followed her. "Who were you talking to just now?"

"Oh, that." She was making an unusual amount of racket putting the teapot on the stove and finding herself a cup and didn't seem to want to look at me. "Well, you won't believe this. I had to get a ride home. I couldn't get Rupert to start again—something in the starter mechanism, I think. I hope I can get somebody down at the Texaco station to take a look at it tomorrow, although I don't know who'll be there on a Sunday—"

"So who drove you home?"

She was ransacking the tea boxes in the cupboard now, as if there might suddenly be some new kind in there. "Well, I could've gone back in and looked for Esther. She was getting ready to leave, too, and even though it's out of her way, she would have driven me. Or I could even have called a cab, although Arnie's charges an arm and a leg to come way out here. So I was just sitting there grinding on the starter . . ."

Something was up. My mother *never* talks this much. "So, *who* brought you home?"

She poured the barely hot water over a chamomile tea bag, splashing water all over the countertop, then finally looked me in the eye. "A man by the name of Michael Evans."

I waited for the rest of the explanation, but now she was evidently done talking.

"Do I know who Michael Evans is?" I finally asked.

"I doubt it. I just met him this week myself." She squeezed her tea bag between her fingers and tossed it in the trash.

"You met him at the hospital?"

"Yes."

"Does he work at the hospital?"

"No."

"Is this twenty questions? Why are you being so weird?"

She sighed deeply. "Because I thought I'd have tonight to think this over before I had to talk to you about it."

"About *what?*"

She swallowed and stuck her chin out. "Michael Evans has been at the hospital this week with his sister who was in a car accident and has numerous broken bones. I've been taking care of her and we've . . . gotten acquainted."

"And he gave you a ride home," I prodded.

"Yes, he did. He happened to be coming out just when I was sitting there . . ."

"Grinding Rupert's starter. I know."

"Yes." She smiled a strange little smile. "And . . ."

"And?"

"And . . . he asked me to go out with him. Tomorrow night."

I have to admit, that was the last possible way I would have bet on that sentence ending. My jaw must have hit the linoleum.

"*You're* going on a *date*?"

"Well, thank you, Robin. That boosts my self-confidence." She took a drink of tea and her glasses fogged up.

"No, I didn't mean that. Not that he shouldn't have asked you or anything. Just that . . . I didn't even think you *liked* men."

She gave a little puff of annoyance. "What?"

"Not that I thought you liked women much either."

"Just what are you saying? I'm antisocial?"

"I'm sorry, Mom, it's just that you don't do things with people very much. You go to work and maybe you go to a tag sale with Esther once in a while, but that's about it. I mean, you're kind of a loner."

She leaned against the sink, sipping from her cup. "Well, maybe I'm getting tired of being a loner. You're not going to be around forever, you know. I might like to have some company after you leave."

I was shocked. As far as I knew, my mother had had only one boyfriend, Jerry Daley, in college. They'd gone together for a few months, she got pregnant with me, and they got married, briefly. He moved out before I was a year old. All Mom would ever say about their marriage was, "We were too young." Hence, the birth-control lessons she'd been giving me since I was ten. Of course, she was always careful to make sure I understood that she didn't regret having me. She repeatedly told me she couldn't imagine life without me, but I had a feeling she *might* have imagined it from time to time. Jerry Daley didn't have to imagine it—he saw less of me over the years than my dentist.

"Well, I think it's nice that he asked you out. I mean, do you like him?"

She banged her teacup down on the counter and put one hand up to hold on to her head. "How should I know? It's been a hundred years since I've been asked out on a date. To tell you the truth I feel sort of sick to my stomach." She looked up at me then and we both started sputtering with laughter.

"That's a good sign!" I said.

"Oh, Robin, I don't think I can go! When he comes, will you tell him I'm sick?"

"I'll tell him you had a desperate need to wash your hair." We were leaning against each other in silly hilarity.

"Oh, goodness," she said, wiping tears out of the corners of her eyes. "I don't need to find a new companion, do I? You're not really leaving me, are you?"

"Leave Thunder Lake? Unimaginable. I'm a mere child of seventeen."

"Going on thirty." She put an arm around my waist and we headed for the stairs. "Wait till you see this guy. He looks like . . ." She began to giggle again. "Ernest Hemingway!"

I stared at her. "What . . . you mean like *Great White Hunter*?"

She nodded. "He's quite large and he has a very big beard. He's even got tiger-striped seat covers in his Jeep!"

We were lucky we made it up the stairs.

Chapter Three

When Chris came by to pick me up about noon, I knew right away something was wrong. He was smiling, but he wouldn't look at me. Mom had come outside, too, to give him her graduation present. It was no big deal, just a gift certificate to the bookstore in town, but Chris went on about it like it was a gold watch. Or like he was in no hurry for my mother to go back inside and leave us alone.

Mom kept on jabbering, too, I guess because she was nervous about her big date. Finally she said, "You'll be back before seven, won't you?"

"Why? So I can meet Ernest?" I asked.

"Don't call him that! You'll forget and slip up when he's here! His name is Michael."

"Okay, Michael. We'll be back in time," I promised.

Once we drove off I had to explain to Chris about Mom having her first date in about two decades.

"Wow, that's cool. I hope it works out."

"What do you mean, works out?"

"You know, that they get along and like each other and . . . whatever happens next."

"Don't get ahead of yourself. Mom will be lucky to survive one date. This won't be a long-term thing."

"You never know," he said, his grin turning down oddly at one corner.

"What's wrong with you today?" I asked him.

He gave me a quick glance. "Wrong?"

"Something is funny." I sat back and stared at him, trying to figure it out. He kept his eyes on the road, but his Adam's apple was bobbing up and down like a great deal of swallowing was being required. What could have happened between last night and this morning? The only thing . . .

Then I remembered something. "What was their gift? Your parents. What did they give you?"

Chris sighed. "I can't tell you while I'm driving. Wait'll we get to the lake—"

"Tell me now. You're acting funny. I want to know!"

When you're out on a rural route in Iowa you don't have to be all that careful about the other traffic. Chris pulled his car over to the side of the road next to miles and miles of cornfields. I sat up sideways, on my knees, ready to leap down his throat, but he kept staring out the windshield, his eyes glazed over as if he was looking inside himself instead of out at the world.

"I don't know how to tell you this, Robin. You won't like it."

"Yeah, I was already pretty sure of that. Tell me."

"My parents gave me . . . a trip to Rome."

The breath I'd been holding exited slowly as I thought that over. "Rome? Like a vacation? Are they going, too?"

"No, just me."

"So, that's another couple of weeks out of our summer," I said grumpily, but actually I was kind of relieved. I'd been expecting worse news than that by the look on his face.

But Chris shook his head. "It's a summer program. I'll be

taking courses in history and government at a university in Rome for six weeks—then all the kids on the program travel around Italy for another four weeks."

I did the math. "Ten weeks? That's the whole summer!"

Finally he turned and looked at me, his green eyes sparkling. "Robin, please don't be upset. This program is so amazing. I'll get college credit for the courses I take and I'll get to travel all over Italy! I've never been anyplace like that before!"

"Yes, you have! You went to Mexico with your parents last year. And you've been to Barbados, too. You've been a million more places than I have." As if that would stop him from going.

"But I've never been to Europe," he said, his face all lit up and excited. "And this is such a great opportunity. Can you imagine studying ancient history in Rome?"

When I didn't answer him, he took my hand in his. "I know what you're thinking . . ."

"What am I thinking?"

"That my parents did this just to separate us."

"And you *don't* think that?"

"No, I don't. They heard about this program through somebody Dad works with and it sounded perfect for me—which it is—so they just went ahead and signed me up for one of the last spaces and decided to surprise me with it as a graduation present."

"That's what you think happened?"

"It *is* what happened. Why do you hate my parents so much?"

"Why do they hate *me*, Chris? They can't wait to get you away from me." Tears again, only this time they were angry tears—scalding and miserable. "Do you *have* to go? Are they *making* you go?"

He sighed heavily. "It would really hurt their feelings if I didn't go. And besides, this is too good to pass up. It's not like I won't miss you. I'll think about you all the time, and I'll write to you . . ."

"You want to go away for the whole summer? Our whole *last* summer together?"

He looked at me guiltily, the answer quite obvious. All of a sudden I felt like I'd just made the whole thing up, that the past two years had never even happened. Chris had never loved me. I had to get out of that car and away from his eyes.

"Don't follow me," I commanded as I flung myself out the door and stumbled down the culvert by the roadside. "I need to be alone a few minutes." When I reached the field I started thrashing through the cornstalks, which were sharper than I thought they'd be. I'd gotten about twenty feet in when I noticed the slices on my arms were starting to bleed, so I just sat down right there in the field, little corn ears swaying above me, and licked at one of the wounds on my arms. I used to do that a lot as a kid—I liked the salty taste of the blood. But then one day at school somebody saw me doing it and called me a vampire, so I stopped. I guess when you're losing the best boyfriend in the world you turn into a little kid again, needing to know what's inside you.

It was obvious to me, sitting there in my little cornstalk home, that Chris did not love me as much as I loved him. Probably he was tired of me, tired of all my whining lately, and he figured why put up with it for the whole summer when he could just get rid of me right now. How could this be happening? We weren't like other high school couples who argue, break up, and then get back together a few days later. We argued once in a while, sure, but there was no question of us breaking up, not ever. We only wanted to be with each other. "I love you," we said, back and forth, over and over. It had seemed like a totally original idea, as if no one else had ever said it before.

Now I wondered what the words even meant. How did we decide this was love anyway? People talk about love as if it's a big mystery nobody can explain. *You'll know it when you feel it.* Franny got mad when I said that to her. Maybe she's right, maybe it's not the same thing to everybody. All you know for sure is what *you* feel. I *know* I love Chris, but I don't know if he loves me. When people say they love you, you just have to decide to believe them, because you'll never know for sure.

To me, love is when you want to be with someone all the time, you miss him when he's gone, and he shows up in your dreams. But sometimes I think it must be more than that and I just don't know yet what more there is. Maybe if I *really* loved Chris I'd be happy for him that he gets to go on this trip.

I wish people could take a love test. Sort of like a lie detector test, only you'd find out if the person was really in love with you *before* you went ahead and fell totally in love with him. Before you handed him your life and he broke it in half.

Finally I walked back to the car. Chris was sitting behind the wheel with his eyes closed, but when he heard me coming, he leaned over and opened the passenger door from inside.

"You okay?" he asked.

I nodded, even though it wasn't true.

"So, we still going to the lake?" he asked.

I closed the door and looked at him. "When do you leave?" I asked. "When do you go to Rome?"

"Um, well. On Thursday." He swept his eyes over cautiously to locate mine.

"*This* Thursday?"

"Yeah."

"That's four days from now!"

"The orientation starts Friday."

"You know what?" I said. "Take me home."

Chris let his head hang back. "Robin, come on. Don't be mad at me again."

"I'm not mad. I just want to go home. I don't feel like listening to you tell everybody your big news."

He was quiet for a minute. "Okay. Maybe tomorrow we can go to the lake?"

I shrugged. "If you want."

"Of course I *want*! I want to see you as much as possible before I leave!"

Why bother? is what I thought. *This is torture. If you're going, just go.*

Chapter Four

Mom was on the phone in the kitchen when I came back into the house. She looked up and interrupted her conversation for a moment. "Forget something?" she asked.

"Nope," I said. We both listened to Chris's car peel out of the driveway. I was not going to fall apart, go ballistic, or lose my mind. Not right this minute anyway. I would discuss it with Mom when she got off the telephone.

"What's wrong?" she called in.

"Finish your phone call," I said, sitting carefully on the edge of the couch. I picked up a copy of the University of Iowa Alumni Bulletin from the coffee table and pretended to look at it while I eavesdropped on my mother's conversation. There were only a few people in the world she could be talking to—it shouldn't be hard to figure out which one this was.

"She and Chris must be arguing again," Mom told the caller. "You know, about his going to school so far away."

It was someone who knew me pretty well. Not, for example, Mr. Hemingway. Must be Esther, although Esther doesn't like to hang on the phone either.

"I know, it would be great if the kids could see each other more often."

I sat forward. Could it be Dad? But why would he be calling now—I just talked to him on my birthday last month. I hadn't seen him in three years, not since he got remarried and moved to Arizona with his wife. They had a two-year-old son I'd never seen either: David, my half brother. I was barely fourteen when Dad left—he doesn't even know what I look like anymore.

But, no. Mom seemed too at ease to be talking to Dad. Not that they were unfriendly, not anymore, but their limited conversations were kind of formal, and Mom always seemed to be faking cheerfulness.

"I *will* ask her, but I don't think you should get your hopes up. You and the kids could stop at the farm on your way west anyway, couldn't you? You haven't been here since Dad died."

Okay, I got it. I should have guessed by the tired sound of her voice that she was talking to her sister, Dory, a labor-intensive job. Aunt Dory is Mom's younger sister by two years, her only sibling, and the one who did everything right, according to Grandad. Didn't get pregnant until she was married and done with college. Married Allen Tewksbury who made a lot of money. Had two children instead of only one. Didn't get divorced. But Grandma and Grandad died before they could see Dory's perfect life begin to unravel. Last year Allen was hit by a car and killed in downtown Chicago, walking back from a business lunch talking on his cell phone. So, I guess even if you do things "right" it doesn't necessarily mean you're safe forever.

"Listen, I should go, Dory. Let me talk to Robin and I'll get back to you in a few days. Okay. Love you, too. Give my best to the kids." She hooked the phone back onto the wall and sighed. "Poor Dory. She's so high maintenance, and now there's nobody around to take care of her."

"What? You mean Iris and Marshall aren't a big help?" Sarcasm was the most pleasant tone I could muster.

"Don't be mean." Mom came into the living room shaking her head. "I feel bad for the kids. They were both very close to Allen."

I didn't, at the moment, feel like extending my sympathies to my cousins. Sure, it was terrible when their father died; they were like zombies at the funeral last fall. But those two have never really warmed the cockles of my heart. Iris is probably thirteen by now, and I guess Marshall is ten or so, but I never really thought of them as kids. They're just no *fun*. The few times we visited them in Chicago all they wanted to do was show me their expensive belongings. Of which there were many. I knew they looked down on me because I lived in the country. They go to private schools and they think they're *très* sophisticated, especially Iris.

I don't think they got that from Aunt Dory, though. I always liked Dory, even though she's high-strung and nervous sometimes. She and Mom are so different you can hardly believe they're sisters.

Mom brought in a dust cloth and started wiping down the mantelpiece, removing each picture frame and then setting it back in exactly the same place. "So, why are you back already? Surely you couldn't have had an argument in this short a time. You've only been gone half an hour."

I intended to tell her the whole story, in a calm, rational manner, but I barely got the first sentence out before meltdown occurred.

"The Melvilles' graduation gift to Chris was a trip to Rome on some kind of summer program. He's leaving *Thursday* and he'll be gone for the *whole summer* and I'll hardly ever *see* him again!" Full-fledged crying. "They just *hate* me and they couldn't *wait* to get us apart!"

Mom stopped dusting and sat down next to me. For a minute

she was quiet, her hand rubbing my back. Then she said, "It was only a matter of a few weeks until Chris left anyway, honey."

"But they were *our* weeks! We had *plans*! Now everything is *ruined*."

"I know this is upsetting to you, Robin, but you were going to have to face it sooner or later. And I'm sure the Melvilles don't hate you—they just worry because the two of you are awfully young to have such strong feelings for each other. I have to admit, it's worried me, too."

"*Why*? Chris is the best thing that ever happened to me!" I was choking on tears now, my voice contorted with hiccups and sobs.

She nodded. "You were lucky to meet such a nice boy, yes. But there are other interesting people in the world, and other people you'll come to love."

"How do you *know* that? You never met anybody else after Dad!"

She chewed her cheek. "I wasn't looking for anybody else."

"I don't even *want* to feel this way about another person! I just want *Chris*!"

"Oh, Robin, you're so young—"

"So what if I'm young! Don't you get it, Mom? I *need* him! I'm nobody without Chris! I'm *nobody*!" The truth of it hit me like a wrecking ball and I slumped over onto the arm of the couch.

Mom pulled her arm away from me and sat forward so she could see my face. The look on hers was a cross between shock and horror.

"I hope you don't really believe that!"

"It's *true*! I was nobody before I met Chris and when he leaves I'll be nobody again! I don't know what to *do* without Chris!"

Mom didn't say anything for a while then. She got the tissue box and sat next to me and let me bawl until finally I was sick and tired of it and just stopped. Little spasms made me shiver and breathe raggedly, but I sat up and blew my nose.

"Maybe you should do something this summer, too," Mom said finally. "Something different."

"I'm working at the Tastee-Freez," I reminded her.

She shook her head. "No, I think you should get out of this town for a while. See something new."

I gave her a sideways look. "Yeah? You wanna send me to Rome?"

"No, but Dory has a proposition for you—that's why she called this morning. I didn't think you'd be interested, but now that Chris won't be around, I don't see why you shouldn't do it. It's an opportunity."

I sniffed and coughed a few more times. "What kind of an opportunity?"

"She and the kids are taking a car trip this summer—from Chicago to Los Angeles, kind of a zigzag route, stopping along the way to see the sites and the countryside. She'd like you to go with them, to help her drive, but also to keep the kids company."

"*Me,* in a car with Iris and Marshall all summer? I don't think so."

"Why not?"

"Because I don't like them. I'm sorry, Mom, I know Dory is your sister, and she's okay, but her kids are the biggest brats going. Besides which, I have nothing in common with them."

"You've hardly spent any time with them, a few visits to Chicago and that one time they came here."

"Thank God! No, Mom. I'll be miserable enough this summer without being trapped in a moving vehicle with those two!"

"It would be a chance to do some traveling—except for Chicago you've never been any place but Iowa. You don't know what this country looks like."

"I've seen pictures."

"Wouldn't you like to see the West?"

I rolled my eyes. "What's in the West? Cowboys?"

"Dory would pay for everything—food, hotels, all of it—just to have the help. I can't afford to give you a trip like that, Robin. I hate to see you pass up an opportunity."

Mom had always wished we could afford to take vacations. She'd gone to New York City once with a girlfriend before she got married, and she often talked about what a great trip that was. Maybe *she* should help Dory drive to California and I could stay home and be wretchedly depressed by myself.

"Just think about it, will you?" Mom said as she stood up. "It would be good for you to see a wider world."

"I don't need a wider world," I said. "I just need Chris."

She sighed and went back to her dusting, running the cloth over the tops of all the books on the shelf. I imagined myself looking out the window of Dory's minivan for hour after hour, day after day, Kansas, Colorado, Arizona, whatever else is between here and California. What a living hell that would be. Except . . . wait a minute. *Arizona.*

"If I *did* go, do you think Dory would stop in Arizona for a few days? So I could see Dad and my . . . brother?" *Brother.* It was weird to imagine that I even had one.

Mom smiled. "I think there's a good chance."

Watching Mom get ready for her date was at least comic relief. After her shower she puffed on enough talcum powder to choke herself and anyone who came near her. She was so shaky with the razor she sliced one of her knees open and needed a large Band-Aid to staunch the blood flow.

"Well, that looks lovely," she said. "I'll guess I'll wear a long skirt."

Thank God she didn't have a big wardrobe because the woman tried on every last thing in her closet.

"I don't *have* any nice clothes!" she said.

That was pretty much true. She wore uniforms to work and jeans around the farm. The few times she went anywhere that required a dress she wore an old green one she'd had for several decades.

"Where's he taking you?"

"Some restaurant in Iowa City. I think it's fancy." She was tossing clothing onto the floor. "Most of this should go straight to the Salvation Army. Why did I say I'd go out with this man? I'm too old and weird to be dating."

"What about the skirt you bought for Allen's funeral?" I suggested.

"It's black! You don't wear black when it's this hot." If she kept fuming around she'd have to take another shower and re-powder herself.

"People wear black all the time," I said. "It's hip."

She stared at me. "Is it? Anyway, I'm too old to be hip."

"Mom, put on the black skirt."

Between the two of us we managed to make her look presentable: the skirt, my cream-colored silk blouse, the turquoise earrings Chris gave me for my birthday last year, a silver necklace she'd had since college, my black sandals, a size too big for her but better than her eight-year-old Birkenstocks.

She was still cursing her hair when the doorbell rang. Seven on the dot—the guy was punctual. Mom's eyes grew huge and dark. "I'm going to throw up," she said.

It was amazing to watch my calm, reasonable mother turn into a puddle of goo over one little date.

"Mom, you've been talking to the guy all week. All you're doing is eating in a restaurant with him, not running off to Mexico."

I went downstairs to let him in. With the Hemingway image in mind, I was expecting a large man with a bushy beard, but

Michael Evans was even larger and bushier than I'd been led to believe. He was a Hemingway and a half.

"You must be Robin," he said, extending a humungous hand. I hesitated, then put mine out to be engulfed and possibly smothered, but his handshake was very gentle. "I'm Michael Evans. Is your mother ready?"

"Come on in. She's almost ready," I said. "Would you like to sit down?"

Michael Evans ducked his head to get through the doorway. Then he and I looked over at our ancient sofa and armchairs, left over from the days Grandma and Grandad lived here, and I think we both had the same thought: Mr. Evans could do a lot of damage to those old springs. It wasn't that he was fat exactly—that is, the fat wasn't all collected in his belly like it usually is with large men. He was just big all over. Even his beard, black with a few gray stripes, was longer and fuller than any I'd ever seen, except maybe in old pictures of Woodstock or something.

"I'll just wait here," he said, then smiled at me. "Too nervous to sit down, anyway."

I glanced up the stairs to see if my equally apprehensive mother was on her way. No sign. What do you say to a guy who's picking up your mother for a date? *Have her home by midnight*. I didn't think so.

"So, do you live in Iowa City?" I asked him.

"Yes, I do now," he said. "I was offered a job in the English department at the university last year and since my sister lives here I decided to take it."

"Oh, right. Your sister was in a car accident. I hope she's okay."

"She will be. Her leg was badly broken and she'll need quite a bit of therapy. Your mother has been wonderful with her, though." His eyes got shiny.

I looked back up the stairs. "Uh-huh. She's a good nurse."

Hurry up! Finally I saw her approaching, slowly, inching her way toward the stairs. "Here she comes!" I said, thinking she might disappear again if she wasn't announced.

It was the oddest feeling watching my mother come down those stairs, like she was the child and I was the parent. She looked prettier than I'd ever seen her look, and scared, too. Michael Evans thought she looked good, too—you could tell. They didn't say much to each other in front of me, just got very smiley. Mom gave me a big hug good-bye as if she thought it might be the last time she'd ever see me, and then they were gone.

When it was nine thirty in Iowa, it was seven thirty in Phoenix, Arizona. I wasn't sure what my dad's work schedule was—he managed a small electronics store in a mall—but seven thirty seemed like a time a father should be at home. Not that I would know. He'd be surprised to hear from me; the last time we had talked was six weeks ago. Birthdays and Christmas he calls me—the obligatory days—but I almost never call him.

"Hello?" a female voice sang.

This was *why* I never called. It was awkward to talk to Dad's wife, Allison, who I hardly even knew. She seemed nice enough, but you could tell she was sort of thrown by the whole seventeen-year-old stepdaughter idea.

"Hi, Allison. It's Robin." I knew to wait a moment while she remembered who Robin was.

"Oh, *Robin*! What a surprise! How are you?"

"I'm fine. I was just wondering if my dad was around."

"He sure is. Let me go find him for you. One minute." The phone clunked down on a counter and I could hear her hollering,

"Jerry! Get the phone! It's your *daughter*!" She made it sound like there was some emergency.

I wondered what their house looked like, whether it was one of those low-slung places you saw in magazines with rocks and cactus out front instead of grass. All I really knew about Arizona was what everybody knew: very hot, lots of golf.

"Robin! This is a nice surprise! Is everything okay back there?" Obviously phoning my father was such an unusual event that both these people assumed some tragedy must have befallen me.

"Everything's fine, Dad. I just called because . . . well, I'm thinking of taking a road trip with Aunt Dory and her kids this summer. And if I do, we'd probably go through Arizona on the way to California. So I was wondering . . . I mean, I don't know if you'll be on vacation or anything, but, you know, if I *do* go with her, we'd be so close. . . ."

Finally he rescued me. "Do you want to stop and see us? Wow, that would be . . . *great*!" There was a silence while we both considered just how great it would be, then he said, "You know, our place is kind of small to handle that whole crew, but . . ."

"We can stay in a motel or something. Dory has money," I said, which I realized made it sound like Dad *didn't* have money.

"You could stay here if you wanted to, if you don't mind the fold-out couch."

"Whatever. I just wanted to see you and your . . . my . . . David."

"Well, I know he'd like to meet you, too. He's right here—I was reading to him when you called. Maybe he'll talk. . . . David! Can you say hi to your big sister? Come on, Davy, say, 'Hi Robin!'"

Davy was silent as a stone. "He doesn't like telephones much," Dad explained.

"That's okay. I don't either."

"Well, you must be related then," he said, forcing a laugh.

"So, it's okay with you if I come? If it's okay with Dory?"

"Sure, sure. We're not going anywhere with a two-year-old except maybe the zoo. When do you think you'd come?"

"It's really up to Dory—she wants to sort of wander across the country. Maybe late July or early August. I'd have to call you, say, a week ahead of time. Is that okay?"

"Of course it is, Robin. We'll look forward to seeing you."

When I hung up the phone I was shaky and out of breath. Why did it take so much energy to have a simple conversation? He was my dad, and yet he wasn't. Other kids, even when their parents are divorced, hang out with their fathers more than I ever did with mine. Even when he still lived in Iowa it was mostly birthdays and Christmas. He'd bring me a couple of presents that were too young for my current age, and then we'd go out to a kid-friendly restaurant for lunch where we'd concentrate on our French fries as though they'd been prepared by Emeril. The older I got, the harder those lunches were. By then I knew he wasn't really interested in the fact that my soccer team was second in the region, or that I was a blueberry in the school play. Not that he didn't pretend twice a year to be a real dad. He did. It's just that you can't *be* a real dad twice a year.

Mom always said not to blame him. He'd been young and scared when I was born. He hadn't known what to do with a child, so she'd "released him from his obligation." That's how she put it. Sometimes he gave us money, but Mom never asked for it—it was a point of pride with her that she raised me by herself.

Usually I don't mind at all. Mom and I have always been a pretty good team. Then twice a year I remember I'm missing something. I mean, he was *reading* to David when I called. That's what a real father does.

The thing is, *I* didn't release him from his obligation.

Chapter Five

The next week was a disaster. Even though I told myself not to screw up our last bit of time together, I was still angry with Chris. He'd started carrying an Italian phrase book around with him, and when he thought I wasn't listening, he'd greet people by saying, "*Buon giorno*!" and "*Ciao*!"

Tuesday we were at the lake. I went for a long swim and when I came back he was sitting on our blanket talking to himself. "*Mi chiamo* Chris. *E tu? Come sta? Bene. Che ore sono?*"

"What does that mean?" I asked.

He jumped. "Jeez, sneak up on a person, why don't you?"

"I wasn't sneaking—I was walking on sand. What were you saying?"

He sighed. "I said, 'My name is Chris. And you? How are you? Good. Do you know the time?'"

"What if the person says, 'None of your business—I feel crappy—who cares what time it is?'"

Chris stuck the phrase book back in his pack. "I don't think Italians are that nasty."

He had a point. Who could blame him for wanting to run away from a grouch like me? But it seemed as if the Chris I loved and couldn't bear to part with was a different person from the one who was memorizing foreign phrases for his exotic summer vacation. *That* Chris was aggravating the hell out of me.

Everywhere we went people kept asking him questions about his trip. He was so excited, I couldn't stand listening to him. Over the top of everything he said, I kept hearing a background voice singing, "And I'll be going without *her*!"

When I called to tell Franny the news, she was less than compassionate.

"I knew something like this would happen," she said. "Chris is one of the lucky ones: lots of money, no divorce, all the breaks. What's the chance he's gonna end up with somebody like you?"

"God, Franny, say what you think!"

"I don't mean because he's better or anything. I just mean, that's how it works. Face facts: Love is doomed if you're too different from each other."

"I thought you didn't know what love was," I said.

"I've observed some so-called love," she said. "You should be glad he's leaving now so you can start getting over him as soon as possible."

"Maybe I'll never get over him."

"That's just what I mean. You're *way* too attached to him. Roll with the punches a little, Robin. Chris is not actually necessary to your long-term survival."

I was pretty sure he *was*, but I didn't argue. After all, Franny knew more about long-term survival than I did.

Since I'd decided not to accompany Chris and his parents to the airport in Cedar Rapids the next day—I did not intend to descend into hell with the Melvilles *watching*—we were having dinner at our favorite place, the Fish Shack down by the lake. I kept thinking about how it was the last time I'd see him until August 20, and the catfish bones kept getting caught in my throat. Neither of us was able to look the other in the eye or come up with anything more to say than, "Good fish."

Then, when I did look up, who should be headed for our table but my mother and her giant boyfriend.

"I didn't know you two were coming here," she said. Then she got a good look at our faces and probably wished *she* hadn't come.

"Your mother says the catfish from Thunder Lake is the best I'll ever eat," Michael Evans said, beaming at her as if picking a restaurant showcased her brilliance.

"Hi, Mom. Um, Michael, this is Chris," I said, keeping the presentations brief. Chris stood up immediately and shook hands with Michael.

"Nice to meet you, sir."

"So, *you're* Chris," Michael said as though he'd been hearing about him for years.

"I'm afraid so," Chris said, smiling weakly.

"We didn't come over to interrupt you," Mom said quickly. "Our table is on the other side. We just wanted to say hello." She took Michael Evans's arm and he steered her across the room to "their" table.

Since Sunday she'd seen him every day. At the hospital on Monday, then last night they'd gone to a movie, and now they were having dinner together again. Was this getting to be a *thing* or what?And what was this "we" business? A few nights ago she was laughing at his seat covers.

"That's the guy, huh? He's twice the size of your Mom. She seems to like him though."

I shivered. "I guess. It's weird."

"Is it?"

"Yeah. I mean, she's never dated anybody before. Not since my dad, anyway."

"Long time to be alone."

"She isn't alone—I'm with her."

"You know what I mean. Most people want to get married again. Your dad did."

I shrugged. "I guess. You know, I might go see him this summer." The more I thought about the trip, the more I liked the idea. After all, if Chris was going away, why shouldn't I? It couldn't be any worse than staying here alone, squirting mushy ice cream into cones and feeling sorry for myself.

"Really?" Chris sat back in his chair and looked at me skeptically. "When did this happen?"

"Monday. My aunt Dory wants me to help her drive across the country—her and my two cousins. To California."

Chris looked surprised. "That's great! Why didn't you tell me right away?"

"I don't know. You were so excited about your trip . . ."

"Wow, I've never even been to California."

"Well, I've never been to Italy, so now we're even."

He ignored my little sting. "Are these your cousins from Chicago? Whose dad died recently? I thought you weren't too crazy about them."

"Oh, they're older now. We get along. It'll be fun!" That was highly unlikely, but it seemed like a good idea to make Chris think I had an interesting summer planned, too. That I wouldn't be spending three months lying on my bed, weeping.

A big smile spead across his face. "That is so great! California!"

"Yeah, now you don't have to feel guilty." I guess I should have worn a muzzle.

We finished our meal in silence. When I glanced over at Mom and Michael they were forking up the catch of the day and grinning like monkeys.

"I can't believe you're going to California!" Franny said, hands on her hips. "And here I was starting to feel sorry for you!"

Franny had come over to hang out with me Thursday afternoon so I wasn't sitting alone imagining the beautiful girl Chris would be seated next to on the plane.

"At least feel sorry for me a little bit longer." I looked at my watch. "He's boarding right now."

"You're pathetic."

"Besides, it's not like this California thing is much of a pleasure trip. I'll be stuck in a minivan, which probably has a bumper sticker on the back that says, '*My children are honor students at Saint Snooty's Prep School.*'"

Franny didn't look convinced.

"My cousins are creeps, and now they're probably depressed on top of it because their father just died."

"Some nerve."

"And they're rich, too."

"Hey, if you don't want to go, tell 'em I'll go. I don't mind driving, especially if I'm getting out of Thunder Lake and rich people are paying for everything." Franny had a way of boiling things down to their essence.

"At least this summer you've got a good job," I said.

"Good? What's so good about working in a video store? People complaining all the time. They *did* return *Reservoir Dogs* on time—it must be *my* mistake. They *have* to have a Mary-Kate and Ashley Olsen movie because they *promised* their seven-year-old, so I should make one magically *appear*. I hate the public."

"The public is just people."

"Yeah, they're annoying, too."

"Oh, Franny, at least it's air-conditioned in there. And you don't end up all sticky with ice cream."

"I don't end up in California either."

My watch said 2:45. Oh, God, he was on the plane and it was probably getting ready for takeoff. I closed my eyes. *Please don't let the stupid thing crash*, I prayed. *Please, please, please.*

"Hey, here's a novel idea!" Franny said. "Let's forget about Chris for five minutes and talk about *my* fascinating life for a change!"

I opened my eyes. "Why? What happened to you?"

"Nothing much," she said, giving me her most enigmatic grin.

I was supposed to guess. "Is it . . . about your mother?"

Franny looked disgusted. "My *mother*? This is about *me*."

"Well, I don't know . . . you're working at the video store, you're living at your mom's, you're not going to summer school. . . . What?"

"Those are the only things about me you think are interesting? I'm that utterly boring?"

"Franny, just tell me already!"

She walked over to the window and looked out. "Oh, look, there goes Chris's airplane!" she said.

I jumped up and then, realizing I'd been had, fell back onto the bed. "You can't tell which airplane is which."

"I'm using my imagination. Now you try using yours. Think of fifth period Spanish."

Spanish? It was the one class Franny and I had had together this year. But I couldn't think what . . . oh . . . maybe I could. "Does this have anything to do with your enormous crush on Des Sanders?"

She shrugged. "Could be."

"Really? Tell me, Franny! Come on—don't make me guess!"

She sauntered over to the bed and sat down. "He called me last night."

"He *called* you?"

"Could you try not to act like you're shocked out of your mind?"

"I'm just surprised! What did he say?"

"He asked me to go to a movie with him tonight."

I belted her on the arm. "No way! I didn't even know you *knew* him. You never even spoke to him in Spanish class."

She smiled. "Turns out he works at Mid-America Videos."

"Oh, my God." I laughed then and she laughed with me, a hard trick to pull off with Franny. "Yeah, you've really got a horrible job."

"Well, you know what my gram says. *You make your own luck.* Fortunately, this time it was *good* luck."

Franny had wanted a boyfriend for such a long time, and she could have had one, too, just not the ones she wanted. She wasn't one of those girls who'd go out with a boy just because he *was* a boy. By the time she left, I was actually a little cheered up, even though I didn't have the energy to do anything about it.

Mom waylaid me as I wandered through the kitchen looking for something to put in my mouth and imagining Chris having dinner on the airplane.

"Let's call Dory before I have to leave for work. She'll be happy to hear you're going on the trip."

"How about you call and tell her and then I'll get on for a minute. I don't feel like a big conversation right now."

As soon as Mom told her, Dory started talking so loudly I could hear her from across the room—she must have been *screaming* into the phone.

"Well, it turns out Chris has gone away for the summer," Mom explained, "so Robin is feeling a little . . . bereft." She looked at me to see if that was going too far. It wasn't.

"She has a request, though," Mom said. "She'd like to stop and visit Jerry in Phoenix for a few days. She's never seen his little boy." She listened for a minute, nodded at me, and mouthed: *no problem*. They talked a few more minutes, then Mom handed the phone to me.

"Hi, Dory."

"Sweetheart! I'm so happy! Thank you! Thank you!"

"It's okay. I mean, thank you, too."

"Oh, we're going to have *such* a good time! I'm reading up on all the sights between here and Los Angeles. We're taking the *long* route!"

Oh, crap. "Great!"

"Stopping in Phoenix is a good idea. You can see your dad and the rest of us will do the city."

"It's not out of your way then?"

"Nothing is out of our way. This is adventure travel!"

No kidding.

"Your mom says you're a perfect driver, and I know you'll be a wonderful companion for Iris. And Marshall, too, of course." Her voice seemed to be a little strained when she mentioned her kids. "Oh, here's Iris! Iris, come and talk to your cousin! She's going with us on the trip! Isn't that great?"

I could tell there was a struggle going on with the phone. Obviously Iris had no more interest in talking to me than I had in talking to her. But eventually Dory won.

"Hello." Iris sounded furious.

"Hi, Iris!" I said, pretending great cheerfulness. "It's great to talk to you!"

She grunted.

"So, are you guys getting everything ready for the trip?"

"Mom is." Two words. A record.

"I bet she is. Well, I can't wait, can you?" God, all I needed was a cardigan sweater and I'd be Mr. Rogers.

Iris's response was a deep sigh. I gave up and returned the same thing to her. The summer of my discontent was underway.

Chapter Six

By Saturday I was comatose, or at least as close to it as you could be while constantly stuffing food into your mouth. I'd woken up early, which was depressing to begin with, so I made myself pancakes with raspberry syrup. Mom had taken somebody's early shift at work so she wasn't around to help me polish them off. Then, I took a book and a bag of cookies out to the bench by the pond and tried to imagine what people in Rome did on Saturday morning. I decided they probably didn't stuff Oreos into their mouths for hours at a time. I fixed some soup around two o'clock and by four-thirty my aimless wandering brought me back to the kitchen, and what else is there to do in a kitchen except eat?

"What are you making *now*?" Mom asked. She'd gotten back from work a short time before and was sitting with a cup of tea and a magazine at the kitchen table. I guess she'd noticed the remains of my day's cooking stacked in the sink.

"Sandwich," I said.

She picked up her tea and blew on it. "You might want to hold off on that. I'm making dinner in a little while. I got some beautiful steaks at the store this week."

On closer observation I could see she was looking awfully

perky for someone who'd just put in a full day walking up and down the eighth floor. She'd changed into a pair of ironed khakis and a short-sleeved white shirt, and she had on my black sandals again instead of the tacky old slippers she usually wore after work.

"You invited what's-his-name for dinner, didn't you?" All signs pointed to yes.

She gave me a guilty smile. "Do you mind? I thought you might not like me going out every night the way I have been lately. I know it's hard on you with Chris gone . . ."

"And you think it'll be easier for me to watch my mother with *her* date?"

Her face stiffened. "I'm sorry if you don't like the fact that I'm seeing someone. I haven't been out with a man in sixteen years, you know. I think I've waited long enough."

My crappy mood bubbled to the surface. "I didn't tell you to wait! Go out, already! You don't need my permission."

"No, I certainly don't."

"You spend every day with him! I would think you'd get sick of him."

"Why? Do you get sick of Chris?"

"That's different. We're in love." As soon as I said it, I thought, *Oh, no! Now she's going to tell me she's in love with this Michael person and he's going to be my new daddy and I'll have to go throw up.*

But fortunately her face softened and she smiled. "Well, I'm not in love with Michael Evans. But I do like him a lot, and I was hoping you might like him, too, if you got to know him. He's very funny and sweet."

I shrugged. What a louse I was, begrudging my mother a few dates. She wasn't the one who sent Chris to Rome. Things were just changing too fast and I didn't like it. I wanted everything to go back to the way it had been for the past two years, but wishing wasn't going to make it so.

"Fine, I'll break bread with Michael Evans," I said. "Or break steak."

"It won't kill you," Mom assured me.

By the time Michael showed up and Mom put the steaks on the grill I was hungry again. Why does missing somebody make you feel so starved? While Michael was making moony eyes at my mother, I was making mashed potatoes. Shucking corn. Ripping up lettuce. Slicing an avocado. Mmm.

While I assembled the salad I watched the two of them out the window. In some ways they seemed just like teenagers; there was a lot of embarrassed flirting and looking for excuses to touch each other. But in other ways you could tell they were older, that they'd done this before. For instance, they weren't afraid to be quiet sometimes and just look at each other. As a matter of fact, it gave me goose bumps the way they looked at each other, like people who'd just run a marathon might look at the long white stretcher that comes to carry them off. Like they were *relieved* to see each other standing there.

Michael carried the platter inside proudly, as though he'd brought down the cow himself, or maybe it was just the Hemingway image surfacing again. Mom took off her apron and we brought the rest of the bowls into the dining room table. I couldn't remember the last time we'd eaten in there—the kitchen table was more convenient. For years the dining room had been the place to fold laundry.

It was strange to have three people at the table, especially since one of them was an enormous man I barely knew. Other than Franny—who wasn't really a guest—we hardly ever had anybody over to eat. Of course Chris had eaten here a few times, but I didn't enjoy having him at our house that much. Not that he and Mom didn't get along—they did—but there was such a difference between my house and his, (linoleum and rag rugs in mine, marble and Oriental carpets in his), between the foods we ate (meat and mashed potatoes here, curry and couscous there), and between his parents and mine (he had two, dressed by Ralph Lauren; I had one, dressed by Sears). It always made me feel slightly—I hate to admit it—slightly not good enough for him.

Which I knew was ridiculous. Chris didn't even care about money and possessions and things like that. And he certainly didn't care about couscous or my mother's bedroom slippers. I guess having him at our kitchen table just pointed out our differences more than I liked.

"These mashed potatoes are great, Robin," Michael said, smacking his lips a little too loudly.

"That's high praise," Mom said, turning to me. "Michael is quite a cook."

I tried to look interested. "Thanks. You do a lot of cooking?"

He nodded. "One of these days I plan to open a restaurant. Give up teaching and cook ribs and corn bread and hash brown potatoes. Real food."

"Well, if the meal you made for me last night is any indication, you'll be wildly successful," Mom said, blushing happily.

"You think so? Wildly?" He arched his eyebrows and they both laughed.

Gag me. I couldn't stand watching any more of this elderly mating ritual, so I forked up my steak as fast as humanly possible and retreated to the kitchen, offering to do the dishes, no need to help me, please, stay right there, I *want* to do them.

Yeah, it was sure nice to have Mom home, keeping me company and all. I scoured the pots in record time, then called in to them, "Hey, I think I'll go up to bed early."

"Already?" Mom said. "I thought maybe we'd get out the Scrabble board."

Was she kidding?

"Great idea! I *love* Scrabble!" Michael assured Mom. I suspected Michael Evans would have sworn a passion for any idea Mom came up with, from tipping cows to jumping off a bridge. He'd be there.

"You two go ahead," I said. "I told Franny I'd call her tonight."

I knew Mom was disappointed, but what did she expect? I had too much going on in my own mixed-up life to sit around making nice with her boyfriend. Franny, I knew, was out with Des Sanders again, so I crawled into bed without even taking off my clothes. It just didn't seem worth the effort.

Since Aunt Dory and the ghouls were due to arrive at the end of the week, I'd been put in charge of cleaning up the house as well as getting myself ready for the westward trek. Housecleaning was easy compared to figuring out what to take along to drive cross-country with a van full of rich snots. Dory had said to bring a sleeping bag "just in case we decide we want to camp out under the stars some night." That sounded good; I'd camped at the lake plenty of times over the years with Mom or Franny. Of course, it's no big deal to camp at Thunder Lake. I mean, you're about eight miles from home and you know everybody else who's down there. It's just an excuse to make a campfire, tell ghost stories, eat marshmallows, and sleep outside.

I didn't know about Marshall, but Iris was the last person I could imagine wanting to sleep out under the stars. She'd probably bring her hair dryer and a nonallergenic pillow. I aired my bag anyway, just in case, then rolled it up and wrapped a bungee cord around it to. Mom said to use the duffle bag we take when we go to Chicago so I got it down from the attic and aired that, too. It was so old it smelled moldy, but there was no other choice. I sprayed it with a little of Mom's Wind Song, which has a nice soapy smell, before I put anything inside.

Two pairs of jeans, some shorts and T-shirts, a jacket, and sneakers. Wear my sandals. Bathroom stuff. A few books. What else? Dory had said that the van had a CD player if I had any favorite CDs I wanted to bring, but we only have a tape player in our house and car, so I don't have any CDs.

Franny and I went into Iowa City one morning so I could buy a new pair of sneakers and some sunglasses. I also wanted some time alone with Franny, away from Thunder Lake so we wouldn't run into Des. I hadn't talked to her in days.

"So, what's the deal, anyway? Are you going with Des now?"

Big sigh from Franny. "I don't know *what* I'm doing. I swear, men are so much trouble. I don't know how you stuck with Chris for so long."

"What do you mean?

"They want so much attention all the time. It gets like *work*."

"You sound like your mother."

Franny turned to me, betrayed. She was trying on sunglasses and the price tag of the current pair dangled in front of her nose. "I do not!"

"I'm not saying you're actually *like* her. But that's her attitude: *Men aren't worth the trouble.*"

Franny was quiet a minute and took off her sunglasses. "Jesus, she *has* ruined me."

"No! Franny, that's not what I meant. I just think you should give Des a chance. You know, don't start out looking for problems."

Franny nodded. "This is why you've had a boyfriend for two years. You just let things happen. I keep wanting to force it. Like we should either be desperately in love or break up already . . ."

I reached for another pair of sunglasses—so far they all made me look like a raccoon. "Is he making a pest of himself or something?"

She sighed. "It's not that. I just can't get used to having a guy around. It's hard to be myself."

"You'll get over that. You still like him?" I tried on another pair of glasses—small and silvery—*very California,* I thought. *They might be the ones.*

"Of course I do. I've liked him for ages. You know that."

"I know, but sometimes when you actually hang out with the guy, he's not as great as you thought he would be."

She smiled. "He's *very* cool. Last night he bought two chocolate shakes and we went down to sit by the lake. So, he puts both straws in one of the cups and says, 'Let's share them, one at a time.' So we did."

How come stories about somebody else's love life always sound so ridiculous? "You're blowing my mind, Franny."

"I know. I'm blowing mine, too."

"So, what do you think of these?" I asked, tilting my head back and adjusting the sunglasses.

"Pretentious."

"Really?"

"Yeah, they're perfect."

Mom was waiting for me when I got back, in her uniform, ready to whisk Rupert away and head for work. She was holding an envelope in her hands and smiling. I knew right away.

"Is it from Chris?"

"Yes, it is."

I grabbed it from her and stood looking at the envelope—a thin blue airmail form with odd-colored stamps on it. From Italy. A place I couldn't even imagine. And there on the back was his new address: 4749 Via della Vittorio. That's where Chris *lived* now.

Not on a street anymore—on a *Via*. What did it look like on the Via della Vittorio in Rome, Italy? For all I knew about Rome, he might as well be on Jupiter.

"Aren't you going to open it?" Mom asked.

"I want to take it upstairs, okay? I'll tell you about it later, when you get home."

"Okay. When you write him back, tell him hi from me."

I ran to my bedroom and propped my pillows against the headboard so I could be comfortable while I read. But my heart was pounding so hard I could feel it in my ears. What would this letter say? I'd never gotten anything more than a note from Chris before—*see you after school*—that kind of thing. Now he'd written me a whole letter, and I was almost afraid to read it.

Finally I slit it open. His handwriting was cramped and slanted. I took a deep breath and read:

Dear Robin,

I don't know how to start to tell you about Rome—it's so amazing! I've only been here two days so I'm still totally lost and confused most of the time, but I don't even care. The first day we got here, even though we hadn't slept much on the plane, we dropped our stuff off at the dorms and started walking.

The program we're attending is located in Trastevere, an old section of Rome, which is across the Tiber River from the main downtown area. The Vatican is on our side of the river though, so we started our trek by walking there to see St. Peter's Basilica. We didn't go inside—the guide just wanted us to get a feel for where things are in the city so we can explore it later on our own.

Anyway, we walked all around Rome that day—saw the Spanish Steps, the Pantheon, the Coliseum, and the Roman Forum. Can you imagine? All that in one day! We were so exhausted that night we slept about twelve hours, and today we spent most of our time talking about our classes and what we're going to accomplish this summer. I don't think I've ever felt so excited about anything!

I have two roommates, Rob and Charlie. Rob is from Maryland and has a very high opinion of himself. He's going to Princeton next year and seems to think I'm a hick from Cornpone, Iowa. But I get along with Charlie really well. He's from Vermont and he'll be going to Williams College in Massachusetts next year. Charlie also has a girlfriend who was furious when he left, so we have that in common! (Kidding) There are two Italian guys from Milan in the room across from us. They speak English fairly well so I'm hoping we'll get to know them better, too.

I don't know how long it will take for this letter to reach you. I wish you had a computer so we could e-mail each other. Of course, you'll be leaving on your trip soon, so we'd have to rely on good old pen and paper anyway. Will your mother send the letters on to you while you're traveling? I hope your trip is as great as mine.

Sitting down to write you a letter makes me realize just how far away you are. Even though I'm having a terrific time here so far, I do miss you, Robin. I miss you like crazy. I hope you're not so mad at me anymore. I just couldn't give up this chance! You know I love you. I really do.

Ciao bella!

Chris

I read it over about a dozen times, looking for hidden meanings in every word, wishing it was longer, wishing I could hear his voice. He missed me like crazy, or so he said. But how much time could he be thinking about me if he was so busy traipsing all over Rome? Besides which, he sounded awfully darn happy for somebody missing his girlfriend.

I'd heard of the Coliseum and St. Peter's, but what were the Spanish Steps and the Roman Forum? History was never my best subject. Was I going to have to get a Roman guidebook to understand Chris's letters? And those roommates sounded like a stuck-up pair, too, both of them going off to fancy private colleges next year.

And what the heck did he mean, he'd never been so excited in his life? Never? Thank you very much, Mr. Roman Holiday. We may not have any forums or basilicas here in Cornpone, Iowa, but you used to find your hick girlfriend pretty exciting.

What was I supposed to write back about? Shopping with Franny? Eating steak with Michael Evans? No, there was nothing I could say that would compete with the Spanish Steps, whatever they were. I'd just have to wait to write him back until my own trip started—maybe then my life wouldn't sound so utterly boring.

I threw the letter in my desk drawer, but then I took it out again and looked at my name on the envelope in Chris's slanty handwriting. Could this be all I had left of him? I tucked the letter under my pillow and went downstairs to hunt for food.

Chapter Seven

The bedraggled little group that climbed out of Aunt Dory's minivan at two o'clock did not raise my hopes about the quality of the journey I was about to begin. Dory had a frozen grin on her face as Marshall tripped Iris and Iris immediately swung around and kicked him in the rear. If things were this bad after only a few hours, what were the chances of surviving the summer together?

Mom had taken the day off from work and we'd fixed a big salad and some tuna fish sandwiches for lunch because Dory was "certain" they'd be here by noon. It was hard to figure out just why they were two hours late—each of them had a different story.

"Mom got lost the minute we left Chicago," Marshall said. "She got off the highway at the wrong place."

"That was a minor problem," Dory said, then gave her version of events. "If Iris had hung up the phone when I asked her to instead of calling all her friends one last time . . ."

"Don't blame *me,*" Iris chimed in. "Marshall's the one who kept repacking his suitcase so he could bring everything he owns." She ripped her streaked blond hair out of the clip that pinned it high on her head, twirled the hair around her fingers, and then stuck it back in the clip so it looked messier than before.

"*Me*? You have a separate suitcase just for shoes!"

We gave each other some halfway hugs, the kind where you're not really too interested in touching the other person, but you're related to them, so you have to pretend you're glad to see them.

"Well, you're here now, so let's have some lunch," Mom said, leading them into the house. "You'll feel better after that,"

Dory scrunched up her face. "Oh, Karen, you'll kill me. The kids were so crabby I stopped at a McDonald's about an hour ago."

Typical Dory. Anything those kids want, all they have to do is whine.

Mom gave them some iced tea and we took the salad and sandwiches into the dining room so whoever wanted something could have it. Iris picked a few lettuce leaves out of the bowl and half a cherry tomato. I snagged two sandwich halves and loaded my plate with salad. Iris watched in horror as I doused the salad with blue cheese dressing.

"You don't like blue cheese?" I asked.

Dory answered before Iris could. "She's gotten picky about what she eats. You know how girls are—so weight conscious."

I'd noticed Iris had lost weight since her father's funeral. Thirteen years of baby fat had begun to remold itself into a teenage girl's body, and a pretty good one, too. I remembered when my own stomach suddenly became concave and my breasts began to puff up, as if somebody had squeezed my tube in the middle and pushed everything up to the top. I took a quick minute to stare at Iris—she looked older to me, too, and I wondered if her father's death had done that. She'd always had that tight-looking face, as if she was holding back a blast of nastiness for your own good. But now it looked like the misery had infected her whole body, which perched tensely on the edge of the dining room chair.

Marshall, on the other hand, seemed to be in a great mood. He told us a long, silly story about a movie he'd seen while he washed down a sandwich with a glass of tea. Then, with a shy grin he said, "Aunt Karen, do you have any ice cream in your freezer?"

Mom and Dory both laughed. "Do you remember that from the last time you were here?" Mom asked him. "It's been years!"

"Sure, I do! You had three different kinds and I ate all of them!"

"I think it's the only thing he *does* remember about that trip," Dory said. "He still asks me why we can't have ice cream at our house like Aunt Karen has at the farm."

"Yeah, and you never give me a good answer either."

Dory's smile faded slowly as she thought about the question. "Hmmm. Well, you know, Daddy never liked to keep ice cream around. He liked it too much."

"If he liked it, he *should* have kept it around."

Iris looked annoyed. "He didn't want to get fat, you idiot."

Dory gave Iris a look, but didn't say anything to her. "More likely he didn't want *me* to get fat," she said with a little laugh, as if she was telling a joke. But I guess it's hard to joke about somebody you love who recently died when you weren't even expecting it. All three of them got quiet and looked at their plates.

"Marsh, you can go get yourself a dish of ice cream if you want to," Mom said, breaking the tension. "And if you still like cats as much as you used to, there are about eight of 'em out in the barn."

"Thanks," Marshall said. He headed for the kitchen fast, without looking at either his mother or his sister.

Dory played with her paper napkin, shredding it into long strips. "It hasn't gotten any easier yet. People keep telling me it will."

Iris pushed her chair back from the table as if she wanted to be farther away from her mother's problems.

Mom put a hand on Dory's arm. "It will, sweetheart. It just takes time."

"One of the reasons I wanted us to take this trip together was so we could see that it was possible to have good times with just the three of us. To prove we could do it."

"Then why did you want Robin to come?" Iris said.

Dory shot me a look of apology, then shrugged. "What I meant was, to prove we can function without your father. Robin is coming along to up the fun quotient!"

I thought I was coming along to help drive. If my job was to keep everybody laughing, I wasn't sure I was up to the challenge. I wasn't sure Whoopi Goldberg would be up to the challenge.

"Oh, so we're driving across the country to prove to ourselves that we can waste our time just like any other inane tourists, even though we have no father?"

Mom jerked back in surprise at the meanness in Iris's voice. I felt like slapping her to Peoria myself. She was even creepier than I remembered.

"Iris, don't torment me, please. Not today," Dory said, massaging her forehead with her hand.

"Fine. Let me know when I *can* torment you, okay? I'm going outside, too." She got up and slammed her chair into the table so hard the glasses shook.

"To the barn?" Dory asked.

Iris snickered. "Yeah, I think I'll go milk me a couple of cows."

The screen door slammed behind her and Dory groaned. "And she's not even the one I'm worried about."

"Teenage girls," Mom said. "It's not unusual behavior."

And I was sitting right there! "Hey," I said. "I never . . ."

Mom lasered me with her eyes. "I think you should go outside and try to get reacquainted with your cousins. Show them around the farm."

Get out of here and let us talk, is what she meant. It was beginning to dawn on me that this trip might be more than just boring; it might actually be horrendous. I took my time clearing my dishes and those of my disappearing cousins so I could eavesdrop on a little bit of the dining room conversation.

"Marshall seems okay," Mom said. "Why are you worried about him?"

Dory sighed deeply. "When he's at his worst he makes Iris look like a cocker spaniel. There are things going on in him I don't understand. He has all these fears now, and he can't sleep at night, and he was . . . asked to leave the school."

"What? Why?"

"He draws pictures. Violent pictures. People shooting each other and running over each other with cars. Red blood exploding all over. His teacher found one that was obviously a picture of *her,* with her head cut off."

I turned the water off in the sink so I wouldn't miss anything.

"Oh, but surely it wasn't meant seriously," Mom said.

"Schools don't take these things lightly anymore, Karen."

"I know, but he's working it all out, don't you think? You said he's been seeing a therapist. Drawing pictures isn't the worst thing."

"He also hit another boy in the face and broke his glasses."

"Oh, Dory."

Dory shook her head. "He says he hates his therapist—he doesn't want to go back to him. He gets so angry about it, he scares me—he really *scares* me sometimes. That's part of the reason for this trip, too—just to shake us out of our depressing routine. Things have to change, Karen—they have to."

When Dory started to cry, I slipped out the door as silently as I could. What the hell had I gotten myself into? I was going on vacation with a bunch of complete lunatics! Was there any way I could back out now? Maybe Mom would decide it wasn't the best idea for her only child to go sightseeing with Superbitch and the next school shooter.

I wandered slowly toward the barn, in no hurry to see what my fascinating relatives were up to now. As I got closer I heard a shout of fear, and then Marshall, saying, "Get it away, Iris!"

The barn door was open and I could see Iris holding up a squirming Golddigger, our oldest and wildest barn cat, while Marshall hid his face behind his hands.

"Did she scratch you?" I asked. "That cat hates to be held."

"No kidding." Iris dropped the cat to the floor and it took off.

Marshall stood up and took his hands away from his face, trembling and embarrassed, it seemed, in front of me. "Iris *made* the cat scratch me." He pointed to a mark on his chin, then kicked his foot out toward Iris's leg, but missed her.

"I did not!" She glared at him, then stalked off. "You are such a baby! You're afraid of everything!"

Marshall looked up at me, his happy smile now pulled into a tight scowl. "I don't like cats anymore."

I shrugged. "Well, that particular cat scratches when you pick her up, that's all. But some of the others are very friendly." I looked around and spied Hermit, a sweet old guy who's lived with us for years. "Here. You can pet Hermit—he doesn't scratch."

Marshall shook his head and repeated, "I don't like cats anymore." His fingers kept tracing the line on his chin.

"Does it hurt?" I asked. "Do you want a Band-Aid?"

His eyes were big and worried. "Could I get cat-scratch fever? I read about that. You can get sick."

I smiled. "Marsh, I've been scratched by cats about two thousand times and I've never gotten cat-scratch fever. I don't think you have to worry."

He looked only slightly relieved. "Anyway, I don't like this barn. It smells."

"Not a bad smell, though. Just hay."

"Hay? I've got hay fever!" He looked at me furiously as if

I'd *invented* hay, and then stalked off out the door.

Iris had strolled farther into the barn and was swinging around a post, arching her back and letting her head fall back. It reminded me of when I was younger and liked to pretend I was being filmed for a movie. I'd throw my body around very dramatically, thinking I looked beautiful. That was shortly before puberty hit.

Iris looked at me as I came closer. "He doesn't have hay fever. He's just nuts. He thinks he's going to get sick all the time now. Or something awful is going to happen any minute. Ever since Dad got hit by the car."

I nodded.

"Mom took him to a shrink, but Marsh freaked out even more. He's getting really psycho."

"I doubt that," I said. "It's only been, what, seven months?"

"Eight."

"Well, he's still upset about it."

"Duh!"

Oh, this girl was impossible. I decided it was best to just ignore her and turned around to go back inside, but she wasn't finished with me yet.

"My mom says your boyfriend left you. Some guy you're in *love* with."

I bent down and picked up Hermit so I'd have something to do with my hands other than punch out my cousin.

"He didn't 'leave' me. He's on a program in Rome for the summer."

"So, *are* you in love with him?" Iris's mouth was hanging open just a little bit, as if she couldn't wait to eat my answer with a spoon.

"Yes, I am," I said, trying to sound sure of myself. No reason to go into detail for this little punk.

She gave a snort. "I have a boyfriend, too. I'm going with this guy Parker. I'll probably break up with him when I get back, though."

"Why didn't you just break up with him before you left?" I kept my eyes on Hermit.

"So he couldn't date anybody else while I was gone."

"Nice. You're very devious for your age."

"My therapist says I'm mature beyond my years."

"*Something* beyond your years. I don't know if it's mature."

She sighed disgustedly. "Ooh, Farm Girl, you're so funny. What kind of farm is this, anyway—you don't even have any cows!" She swung off the pole and sailed past me out the door.

I gave Hermit a hug and asked him how on earth I was supposed to spend my summer with these aliens, but he didn't have a clue either. I decided to go back inside and sit with Mom and Dory who were, at least, human beings. As I passed Dory's minivan I saw Marshall sitting in the backseat, a big tablet resting on his knees. His back was to the window so I came up behind him to look in at the drawing.

He was obviously a talented kid. The picture was well drawn, like a cartoon in a magazine. You could even tell the cat was Golddigger—he had the markings just right. There was my cat, held to a dartboard by the three arrows sticking out of his chest. When he saw me looking, Marshall frowned, then carefully drew in drops of blood.

Chapter Eight

My sleeping bag and duffle fit neatly into a corner in the back of the van. Dory kept asking me if that was all I was bringing. "We can squeeze more in if you want to bring more," she assured me. But that didn't actually seem very likely. Between the three of them, they had five suitcases crammed into the rear storage space, plus sleeping bags, and the backseat was full of stuff Iris and Marshall obviously couldn't be without for a minute: CD players, earphones, books, magazines, drawing supplies, bags of food, thermal water bottles, head pillows, neck pillows, and polar-fleece blankets. It looked like we were going on an expedition, not a vacation.

There was just enough room to squeeze in four people. Still, the van was comfortable. We each had our own cup holder and our own volume control for our own speaker. The seude-covered seats both reclined and swiveled, and were as padded as easy chairs. Poor Rupert with his cracked upholstery—I hoped he wasn't looking.

I took the front passenger seat and put my shoulder bag at my feet. In it was one novel, a bottle of Poland Spring water, Mom's old camera, two hundred dollars in traveler's checks—which Dory assured Mom was more than I'd need because she'd pay for everything—my driver's license, and a pre-paid phone card. "Just in case you want to call me without telling Dory," Mom said.

She'd come into my room the night before while Dory and the kids were getting ready for bed. Or rather, while Dory was refereeing the fight over who would sleep where. "You think you'll be okay?" Mom asked me. I was hoping she'd come in to say there was no way on earth she was letting me get into a car with such crazy people.

"*I'll* be okay. The question is, will *they*?"

Mom sat down on my bed. "I'm sorry, Robin. Dory didn't give me the whole story over the phone. I didn't realize the kids were in such a state." She tried to smile. "Once you're on the road, seeing the country, I'm sure things will be better."

"They couldn't get much worse."

She leaned in and gave me a quick hug. "I hope this isn't a disaster. I know the kids are annoying, but maybe you can find a way to like them, anyway. All three of them could probably use a friend right now, and you're good at that kind of thing."

"What kind of thing?"

"You know. Helping people who feel kind of lost and alone. Scared."

"I'm good at that?"

"Sure you are. Just ask Franny."

By nine the next morning we'd had our pancakes—all of us but Iris, who selected a nonfat yogurt instead—and were arranging ourselves in the suddenly much too small vehicle we'd be calling home for a ridiculous amount of time. As we pulled out of our driveway with Dory at the wheel, Marshall yelled happily, "Now we're really rolling!"

"Don't forget to send my letters!" I called back. Dory had given Mom a list of addresses where we could get mail; I didn't want to miss a letter from Chris.

She nodded. "I will!"

I watched as my waving mother got smaller and smaller, willing myself not to cry. What was there to *cry* about, for heaven's sake? Sure, it wasn't my dream trip, but at least I was going somewhere. I guess I wished Mom was coming, too. As much as she got on my nerves sometimes, I'd never been away from her for more than a night or two, and never in the company of crazies like these.

"So, where are we going first?" Marshall asked as we turned onto Interstate 80.

"We're going to Minnesota!" Dory announced.

"Minnesota? That's back up north!" Iris said.

"Yes, it is. I'm glad to see you know your geography."

"Jesus Christ. It'll take us a year to get to Los Angeles if we have to stop and see every stupid state in the country!"

"Iris, I told you, this is not a race. The purpose of the trip is the traveling itself, not arriving in California."

"That doesn't even make any sense," Iris said. She pulled one of the big pillows into position against her window and punched it into shape. "Wake me when we get someplace interesting. I've seen enough cornfields to last me the rest of my life."

We weren't quite out of the cornfields when Dory woke Iris up. In fact, we were in Farmer's Paradise: the Iowa State Fair in Des Moines. I could hardly believe it when Dory turned the van into the parking lot. Neither could Marshall.

"What are we stopping here for?" he asked suspiciously.

"We're stopping here so that you and Iris can learn a little something about the culture your cousin and your mother were brought up in," Dory said, smiling at me. "This is one of the biggest state fairs in the country, you know. It's the one the musical is based on!"

"What musical?" Iris said groaning.

"*State Fair*!" Dory said.

"Never heard of it."

It's true that Mom and I used to come to the fair all the time back when Grandma and Grandad were still alive, but then we kind of stopped. Last year Chris and I came one night, but all we did was go on the rides so I could hold on to him and scream. Oh, and he won me a stuffed alligator by throwing tennis balls at plastic frogs. We had a great time, but we didn't bother with the actual farm stuff. I could tell right away, Dory planned to bother with it.

She headed to the vegetable exhibit barn first—it seemed to make her extremely happy. "Oh, you guys, I used to come here *all* the time when I was a kid. Look at the size of those peppers! And that spinach—no wonder that took a first prize. Look down there—have you ever *seen* so many enormous eggplants?"

No one answered, so she kept going. "I always used to enter the pea-shelling contest—the winner was the kid who could finish the bowl first. I came in second once and got a huge red ribbon. It was just thrilling."

"Wow. That *does* sound exciting," Iris said.

Marshall picked up a zucchini and gave it a good bang on the edge of the table.

"Look at those strawberries! They're gorgeous!" Dory was in heaven.

"So, this is, like, a competition for *vegetables*?" Iris said.

Dory ignored her. "Robin, I bet you come here all the time, don't you?"

"I used to, but not much anymore."

"Did you enter things? Did you do 4H Club?"

I shook my head. "We didn't live on the farm back then. I never did 4H."

Dory looked disappointed. "Really? I *loved* 4H!"

I'd never thought of Aunt Dory as somebody who'd loved 4H. I mean, she left Iowa as soon as she could and went to school in Chicago. And never came back. If she loved farm life so much, how come she lived in a city? She didn't even have a vegetable garden in her yard—only a little patio with fancy furniture.

We trudged after Dory until she was finally ready to leave the lettuce and head for the mammals. First the sheep shed, then the cow barns, then the pigs.

Iris had been complaining since the moment her foot hit the the straw of the first animal barn, but the pigs put her over the top. "My God," she said, holding her nose. "I thought the cows were bad, but these animals reek!"

"You would too if you slept in your own shit," Marshall said.

Dory gave him a look. "Marshall, don't say *shit*. Besides, humans have an odor, too—we just don't notice it as much in ourselves."

"I notice it when it's old Mrs. Morrissey," he said. "Phew!"

"This isn't a bad smell," Dory said, but she was going to have a tough time proving it. She took a deep breath to show us how much she enjoyed the scent, but she coughed a bit on the exhale.

"I saw baby pigs born once," I said, just to prove I was not a complete idiot about this farming thing.

"You did? When Grandad was still alive?" Dory asked.

I nodded. "The part I remember best is that he had to clip their teeth right after they were born so they wouldn't rip their mother's belly when they nursed."

"Gross!" Iris said, holding her arm straight out, her hand up like a traffic cop. "That is definitely more information than I ever wanted to know about pigs." She stomped ahead of us and out of the barn.

Lunch was hot dogs and fries for those of us who allowed ourselves to eat, and a salad made with graying lettuce that must have been lying around the vegetable barn all week for Iris. No dressing, of course. Plus, she tossed it in the trash after about three bites. We managed to steer Dory past the crafts barns—there wasn't room in that van for a hand-painted saw or a rag rug—and over to the sheep dog trials.

Marshall got into watching the dogs run side to side, obeying their owner's commands, herding five sheep at a time into a small pen. "That is so cool," he said. "I'd like to have a dog like that."

"Why? So he could herd the bugs in your bedroom?" Iris said.

"I don't have bugs in my bedroom."

"Right."

"Mom, do I have bugs in my bedroom?"

"Iris," Dory said. "Please don't taunt him."

"I'm not! He leaves food on the floor in there. He's probably got bugs."

Marshall's face tightened and his fists clenched. He shoved his face as close to his sister's as he could. "I don't have bugs! I *do not* have bugs!"

Iris pushed him away and before you could say *Australian sheep dog,* they were swinging at each other. Dory had to get between them and grab their arms. People around us were staring so I stared back.

"What is the matter with the two of you?" Dory said.

"I don't know about Slugger, but I'm bored to tears," Iris told her.

Dory thrust the fair booklet at her daughter. "Well then, what do *you* want to do? Or should we just leave?"

Leaving sounded like the best option to me. I liked the fair fine, but I'd been away from home all day already and I hadn't even gotten out of Iowa. If we were going on this trip, let's go, is how I felt.

But suddenly Iris's eyes lit up. "They have horses here. Show horses. Thoroughbreds. We missed that barn." She looked at her mother. "Please?"

"I'm tired of those smelly barns," Marshall said. "I want to go on some rides."

Dory looked sick and tired of both of them, and it occured to me that this was the kind of moment I'd been brought along to deal with. I figured I probably ought to start earning my keep.

"I'll take Marshall on some rides if you two want to go see the horses," I said. Dory gave me a grateful smile and we agreed to meet in half an hour. I liked going on the rides, anyway, even though, in this case, I wouldn't have the pleasure of holding on to my companion.

When we got to the midway, Marshall couldn't decide which ride he wanted to go on first. "I usually like the Ferris wheel the best," he said, looking up at it nervously. I suggested we start with something easier and work up to it.

"Okay," he agreed. "How about the Tilt-A-Whirl?"

So we did that twice, and then bumper cars, and then it was time to either do the Ferris wheel or forget it and go meet Iris and Dory. We got in line and inched our way to the front. I checked my watch, hoping we wouldn't be more than a few minutes later than planned.

"Are we late?" Marshall wanted to know.

I shrugged. "I think we're still okay. We can make it."

But as we got closer I could tell Marsh was having a problem. He was breathing really fast and licking his lips. He couldn't stop himself from looking up to the top of the wheel. When there was only one couple ahead of us, he suddenly exploded. "It's too late!" he yelled at me. "We have to go now! It's too damn late!"

He bolted out of the line and started running back to the place we'd left Dory and Iris.

"Marshall, wait! Wait for me!"

I didn't catch up to him until right before we saw them. He slowed down a little so we could approach together.

"We didn't even get to go on the Ferris wheel," he screamed on the verge of tears. "Robin goofed around so long on the baby rides, we didn't have time! You know I love the Ferris wheel the best!"

I was dumbfounded at his ability to rewrite the truth, but I knew better than to argue with him. He was furious already.

"I'm sorry, Marsh," I said, hoping to calm him down. "I wasn't keeping my eye on the time."

"I hate you, you dumb bitch!" he screamed.

Dory grabbed his arm. "Marshall! Don't you ever say that to anyone! Do you hear me?" Marshall quieted down a bit, sulking and kicking up dirt with the toe of his sneaker. "Apologize to Robin right this minute." It was a rare moment of anger on Dory's part, but she couldn't sustain it. When Marshall didn't respond, she melted and pulled him in to hug, then *she* apologized to me.

"I don't know what came over him, Robin. I'm so sorry."

I shrugged. "It's okay. I'm sorry I messed up about the Ferris wheel."

Marshall curled his lip at me, and I was pretty sure he'd already convinced himself that the whole thing really *was* my fault. He and his mother started back toward the van, arms wrapped around each other, while Iris and I stood for a moment looking after them.

"He was scared to go on it, wasn't he?"

I wasn't sure how to answer her, whether it was okay to betray the little creep who'd just called me a bitch by ratting him out to his obnoxious sister.

"You don't have to tell me. I know. That's how he gets when he's scared. Mean as hell. Mom can't seem to add two and two, though. She can't believe her little angel has turned into the Antichrist, so it's easier to blame everybody else."

I nodded my head, the closest I'd come to agreeing with Iris since she'd showed up in Iowa.

We spent that night at the Moonlight Motel just outside Blue Earth, Minnesota. I kind of liked the place—I mean, it was old and dingy, but one wall of the room was painted dark blue with a big smiling moon in the corner and stars falling down all around it. The people who owned it were old, but very helpful. Dory was going to rent two rooms, one for Marshall and herself, and one for Iris and me, but the old woman suggested that, since we were all family, we could fit in one room and save some money. "There's queen-size beds in 'em. My son's idea—folks seem to like 'em. So there'd be plenty a' room for two a' yas in one bed."

Dory thanked her and rented just one room, though obviously she could have afforded two, then asked the woman for a recommendation on where we might get some dinner. The diner down the street seemed to be the only thing still open, so we piled our suitcases in the room and walked there. Iris, of course, started complaining the moment the old woman was out of earshot—at least she had that much sense.

"Why are we all stuffed into one room, Mother? Just because that old lady thought we should be?"

"We'll be fine," Dory said.

"Couldn't you have just told her we wanted two rooms? Why

do you always do whatever people want you to do?"

Dory forced a smile. "It'll be like a slumber party, Iris. What's the problem?"

"The problem is we have to share *beds.* A queen size isn't that big."

I felt so exhausted from listening to her all day, I wanted to say, *You spoiled brat! You're the one who's always telling your mother what to do. She's driving you all over the country and you're bitching about having to share a queen-size bed for one lousy night!* But I managed to stuff my anger back down. I was along to help Dory, and me getting mad at Iris was just going to make us all more miserable.

Marshall and I were both silent except when we ordered the very same meal from the waitress: cheese omelets and hot cocoa. I tried not to look at him, and he did the same for me. Iris managed to keep up the argument with her mother so Dory didn't notice that Iris's turkey sandwich was being picked into tiny pieces but not actually eaten. By the time we got back to the Moonlight Motel, I was so tired I could have fallen asleep in the bathtub. The queen bed looked great to me, even if I did have to share it with the Queen herself.

Chapter Nine

That was a night to remember. It must have been about two o'clock in the morning when Marshall woke up screaming. At first I couldn't remember where I was, and then, when I did, I figured the motel must be on fire or something. But no, he was just having a bad dream, which I guess is not that unusual for Marshall these days. Of course, he's not usually sleeping in a small room with three other people when this happens.

Dory knew right away what was going on. She shook him awake gently and then cooed to him, "It's okay, Marsh, honey. You're just dreaming."

Iris popped up in bed, her hair a messy golden nest. "God, Marshall, you scared the crap out of me!"

I sat up, too, since everybody else was up. "Is he okay?"

Now that he was awake, Marshall was angry. Nothing like having a big audience around to witness your nightmare. He shrugged off his mother's hug. "I'm fine. Let me go."

"Yeah, *you're* fine, but the rest of us are in cardiac arrest," Iris said.

"Iris, go back to sleep," Dory told her.

"That's *so* likely. My heart's pounding like mad."

"Shut up, you idiot!" Marshall yelled at her.

A few more heated exchanges occurred before we all laid our heads back on our pillows. But the mattress, which had seemed comfortable and plenty large enough a few hours before, had suddenly turned into a thin, lumpy pad that sagged in the middle and threw Iris and me together elbow to elbow.

"I'm never sharing a bed with you again," she crabbed. "You're hogging the whole thing."

"I can't help it." I said. "It sags in the middle."

"Yeah, so do *you*."

I was pretty sure Dory had heard that comment, but she was pretending to have slipped magically back into sleep in record time.

I tried to ignore Iris, too, but her groans and grumbles kept erupting just as I was about to nod off. We infuriated each other for another hour or so, and then, finally, I got up, located my notebook in the dark, and retreated to the bathroom. As long as I couldn't sleep anyway, I figured I might as well sit on the toilet lid and write Chris a letter. At least now I had things to say.

Dear Chris,

It's four A.M. *and I'm sitting in a bathroom at the Moonlight Motel in Blue Earth, Minnesota. The trip from hell has begun. Whatever I might have said before about my cousins from Chicago, I was wrong. They are MUCH crazier than I ever knew—possibly even psychotic.*

Iris and Marshall insult me constantly, but I guess I'm lucky because they actually slug it out with each other. Meanwhile, my aunt Dory ignores it all and pretends we're having a lovely vacation together. And this was only the first day! We went to the Iowa State Fair this afternoon, or I guess it was yesterday, and spent about an hour looking at large vegetables. Dory is all nostalgic about her Iowa roots or something. The kids thought the whole fair stank.

Remember last year when we went on the Ferris wheel about seven times? That was so much fun. Remember how from the top you can see all over the countryside and how pretty that is? Just thinking about last summer reminds me how much I miss you. I promised myself I wouldn't go on and on about missing you, but since you said you missed me, I think I should be able to say it, too. I miss your arms around me. I miss your voice. I miss your smell. I miss that great thing that is YOU. Especially now, at four o'clock in the morning, when I'm hiding out in the bathroom so I don't wake up my lunatic relatives—I MISS YOU!

Your letter sounds like you're having a great time. How are your roommates by now? Is that Rob guy still so stuck up? If they think you're a hick, what would they think of me? Have you gone back to St. Peter's yet, or the Coliseum? And what the heck are Spanish Steps? Have your classes started?

For some reason I feel like I'm asking you the same questions your mother's asking you. Sorry if I'm boring. I'm mostly not mad at you anymore, although once in a while I think about how great our last summer together would have been and then I get sad. I AM still mad at your parents.

Franny is going out with Des Sanders. And my mother's still dating the giant. Are there any girls on your program? I don't know why I didn't think of that before. Do you all live in the same dorm? Are there gorgeous Italian girls everywhere? Don't tell me I shouldn't be jealous because how can I not be?

I'm so tired I have to stop writing—my eyes keep closing. Tomorrow I'll mail this off to the Via della Vittorio, which sounds so romantic and beautiful. Is it? Do you still miss me, or are you too busy having a great Italian life?

Love, love, love,

Robin

To tell you the truth, I wasn't that tired. It was just too frustrating trying to say what I meant in a letter. When I read over what I'd written I couldn't even tell if it sounded like me or not, but I decided I'd better mail it anyway, so Chris didn't think I'd forgotten him or something.

By the time I got back into bed, Iris was asleep. I finally fell asleep too just about the time it was getting light around the edges of the window shade. Dory turned the alarm off at eight A.M. but nobody got up. Around nine thirty she gave us all a shake.

"Get in and out of the bathroom quickly, guys. I'm going to go pick up some coffee and muffins at that place down the road so we can get going. Lots of driving to do today."

Iris groaned but managed to get up fast enough to be first into the bathroom. Marshall stood in the motel room doorway and screamed at his mother's back.

"Chocolate milk! Get me a big carton of chocolate milk!"

"Okay!"

The kid is barely awake and he's barking at Dory already. "Do you order everybody else around the way you do your mother?" I asked him.

He looked surprised. "What do you mean?"

Some of my leftover anger from yesterday crept out. "I mean, you don't ask for things—you demand them."

Marshall scowled at me. "I *asked* her."

"No you didn't. You said, '*Get me chocolate milk*!' That's not asking."

"What do you care? Mom doesn't care."

"Well, I'm sure she's used to it, but that doesn't mean she likes it. Nobody would like it."

Marshall wrinkled his nose at me. "You're crazy," he said, then marched to the bathroom door and started pounding. "Hurry up,

Virus, it's my turn!" Iris, of course, screamed back at him. I should have brought earmuffs.

We were ready to roll by the time Dory got back with the caffeine and pastry. And chocolate milk, of course. After a quick stop at the post office so I could get stamps and mail my letter, she announced she wanted to get across the rest of Minnesota and into South Dakota before stopping for lunch. She told me to rest in the morning while she drove, so I could take over in the afternoon. The car was quiet for a change—both Iris and Marshall fell asleep the minute they'd finished eating. I didn't really feel like sleeping, even though it was only Minnesota we were driving through and not *Italy,* it was still my first vacation and I was sort of excited. Minnesota didn't look that different from Iowa, mostly farmland stretching out on all sides, but just the idea that I was in a different state made me look at everything more closely.

I started wondering what the other states would look like. Would the mountains in Colorado look the same as the mountains in New Mexico? Were there mountains in Arizona, too, or only desert? What did it look like where Dad lived? Just the thought that we were actually headed there, that I'd actually be staying in his house with his family made me feel dizzy. I'd never visited my dad at his own place, even when he lived in Iowa. It was such a normal thing to do, but it felt weird to me. I mean, I hardly even knew the guy.

Dory was sipping her enormous cup of coffee as she drove. She had gray circles around her eyes and I wondered if that had happened overnight, or if I just hadn't noticed them before.

"Dory, can I ask you something?"

"Sure, honey. What is it?" She smiled at me in a sad sort of way, which seemed like it was probably her real smile. A twenty-watt smile, conserving energy.

"I was just wondering about my mom and dad. When they first

got married. Mom doesn't talk about it much. Did you know Dad very well?"

She shook her head. "Not that well. They were juniors at the university and I'd just started college in Chicago so we didn't see each other very often. I did spend a week with them the summer after you were born. That was kind of strange."

"How come?"

"I don't know. They seemed so *old* to me. Here they were married, with a baby, living in a dumpy apartment—I couldn't understand it. I'd just gotten away from all that down-home farm life for the first time. I was going to clubs and art openings and trying hard to put my small town past behind me, and here was my sister settling in to middle age when she was only twenty."

I brought my bare feet up onto the seat and hugged my knees. "Well, I don't think it was her first choice. If she hadn't gotten pregnant . . ."

"Oh, sure, honey, I understand it now. But at the time it was just the last thing I could imagine."

"But you got married and had kids as soon as you graduated."

Her little smile picked up again and then sagged. "Well, you never know when love's gonna hit you. I thought I'd go on to graduate school and get my Ph.D. in English. Until I met Allen the first day of my senior year. He just bowled me over. All my other plans got put on hold."

"But then you got your teaching certificate."

She nodded. "I probably wouldn't even have gotten that, but Allen thought I should have something to fall back on, just in case . . . as if he knew."

I thought about Allen. He'd never had much to say to me, but I remembered he had a formal way of talking that made me kind of uncomfortable. As if he were *highly* educated and wanted everybody to know it. One time he took us down to the lakefront and we rented a sailboat for the afternoon—I remember thinking he looked better when he wasn't wearing a suit. Still, it was hard to imagine him bowling anybody over.

I figured I should get off the topic of Allen. "Do you think Mom was bowled over by Dad?"

"By Jerry?" Dory gave a laugh. "I'm sorry, I don't mean that the way it sounds. Jerry was a nice guy, a very sweet guy, but he was too confused in those days to do much bowling over. I don't think he knew what he wanted—your mother made all the decisions. And I think, once she got pregnant all she wanted was that baby—*you*—but she thought she'd better get Jerry into the picture, too, or Grandad would really throw a hissy fit.

"Jerry was the one who was bowled over. He didn't know what hit him. He was crazy about your mom, but the poor guy was just a kid himself—he was in no position to be *raising* a kid. Nobody was too surprised when he left, including your mother."

"So she didn't love him?"

Dory thought about that. "She probably did, but maybe not as much as she thought at first. She was young. They both were. Sometimes it's hard to tell about love until afterward. When you look back." She swallowed hard.

"You loved Uncle Allen, didn't you?"

She nodded and gulped more coffee.

I probably shouldn't have asked her that. I wondered if she'd known it while Allen was alive, or if that's what she meant by *sometimes it's hard to know until afterward*. "How come Mom never dated anybody else? Until now, I mean."

"Maybe you should ask her these questions," Dory said. She looked tired, so I decided I'd better shut up. But then she answered me, anyway. "Karen never thought any guy was good enough to be your dad, that's what I always thought."

I looked out the window while I let that sink in. The thing is, you don't think about your mother like that—she's just your *mother*, the person who tells you to hang up your clothes and eat your broccoli. But now I was imagining her at twenty—a few years older than me—getting married, having a baby, getting divorced, becoming this Supermom who wouldn't even go out on a date with somebody unless they were daddy material. Was Dory right about that? And if she was, what was so special all of a sudden about Michael Evans? Or was I grown up enough now not to need a father?

Of course, I already *had* a father. Jerry Daley, a nice guy, as Dory said. A nice guy I never really got to know, who eventually married a nice woman and moved to Arizona.

What would it be like to see him again? What if he'd said I could visit them because he felt guilty about me, but now they were all dreading it? Allison was probably already complaining about having some kid she hardly knew sleeping on her couch. What if she was one of those neatniks who make you take your shoes off outside? Or what if she was a terrible cook and I couldn't stand eating what she served? Or what if she didn't want David to know he had a half sister? There could be all kinds of problems. Maybe stopping in Phoenix wasn't such a great idea after all. I leaned against the window and stared at Minnesota farmland until I conked out, too.

When I woke up, Marshall was reading aloud from one of the guidebooks in the backseat. "The Corn Palace in Mitchell, South Dakota, has been standing for over seventy-five years. It is built out of reinforced concrete, but every spring the outside of the building is completely covered in murals and other decorations made from bushels of corn, grain, and grass. Mitchell is called the Corn Capital of the World and the Corn Palace is sometimes referred to as the World's Largest Bird Feeder."

I sat up and rubbed my stiff neck. "Are we in South Dakota?"

"Yup," Dory said. "Headed for the Corn Capital of the World."

"And *lunch*," Marshall added.

The landscape looked drier than it had in Minnesota, kind of parched for so early in the summer. But the Corn Palace itself, when we pulled up in Mitchell, was spectacular enough to keep even Iris quiet for a few minutes.

"It really is made out of corn," Marsh said.

"No false advertising," Dory agreed.

"It doesn't look like it belongs here," Iris said, trying her best to be negative.

"The onion domes and minarets make it look Russian, don't they?" Dory said.

I could figure out that the onion domes must be the big round ornaments on the roof, but I wasn't sure what a minaret was. Probably the swirly roof decorations that reminded me of a soft-serve cone from Tastee-Freez.

"They redo the outside every year?" I asked. The golden murals were quite intricate, portraying farmers on tractors and birds swooping low over cornfields.

"That's what the book says." Marshall actually seemed to be excited. "They even named their high school teams the Kernels."

"That's corny," Iris said, then blushed and gagged at her unintended joke. "I'm *starving*," she said. "Can we please eat?"

There was a restaurant up the street that looked fine and we all ordered big lunches—those muffins hadn't lasted us long. I'd never seen Iris eat so greedily. Normally she could have pecked at the biggest bird feeder in the world and been satisfied, but today she was stealing French fries off her mother's plate while simultaneously stuffing a bacon cheeseburger down her throat. Dory didn't seem to notice any difference.

Personally, I'd been pigging out since Chris left. My shorts had even gotten a little tight, so I decided to go easy on the grease for a while. Iris's comment about my saggy middle was a little too close to home these days, so I let her pick through my potato chips while I ate a turkey sandwich.

"Are we staying here tonight?" Marshall wanted to know.

"Nope, we've still got a long drive ahead of us."

Marshall groaned.

"Where *are* we staying tonight?" Iris asked. "Not in another one of those crummy hotels, I hope. And not all in one room either."

Dory swirled a fry around in her ketchup pool. "Well, we will be in one room, but not in a hotel." All three of us looked at her—it didn't sound good. "I made a reservation for us to camp in the Badlands National Park tonight. Isn't that great?"

I tried to rally a smile, but the idea of being within earshot of Marshall for a second night in a row was less than thrilling. Plus, in a tent we'd really be on top of one another. But I was definitely not the person most annoyed by the idea of camping out.

"You're kidding! You expect us to sleep in that *tent*?" Iris glared at her mother.

"Of course! Why do you think we brought it?"

"I thought it was just for an emergency—like if we got stuck someplace where there weren't any hotels!"

"I don't want to sleep outside all night," Marsh said, chewing his bottom lip.

"Don't worry. We'll be in a National Park," Dory said.

"The *Badlands* . . . that sounds inviting," Iris said. "Why are they *bad*? Because the wildlife eats the tourists?"

"There aren't any bears, are there?" Marshall asked. "I'm not sleeping outside if there are bears!"

Dory closed her eyes. "There won't be bears. We'll be in a campground area, with many other people. It'll be fun."

Iris slumped down in the booth. "This sounds so stupid, Mom!

Sleeping in a tent surrounding by a lot of other people sleeping in tents—how is that fun?"

"It just *is,* isn't it, Robin?" Dory looked at me for reinforcement, but I knew Iris and Marshall didn't care what I thought, and, anyway, I wasn't nuts about the idea either. Still, I was supposed to be Dory's *helper.*

"It can be, yeah," I said. "I like camping at Thunder Lake."

Dory grinned. "Oh, I used to go there, too. Grandad would take us all and he'd build a big fire and we'd roast hot dogs . . ."

"You don't even know how to build a fire," Marshall said. He was rhythmically kicking his sneaker into my shin as he glared at his mother, arms folded protectively across his chest.

"Well, we'll eat in town before we get to the campground. It's a warm night—we won't need a fire."

"This is a very bad idea, Mom," Iris said, shaking her head.

"No, it isn't," Dory said sternly. The kids weren't used to Dory saying *this is just how it is,* so they argued a while longer, but what choice did they have? What choice did I have, for that matter? It was Dory's car and the rest of us were along for the ride, wherever the ride might take us.

We stopped for dinner at Wall Drug Store because Marshall demanded it. There had been signs for hundreds of miles advertising the place, which turned out to be not only a drug store, but a restaurant, a playground, and a huge gift shop selling all kinds of cornball stuff: cowboy hats, little painted drums, Indian dolls, leather coin purses, ugly belts. Marshall wanted a T-shirt with a jackalope on it and Iris got a silver bracelet and two dozen silly postcards to send to her friends. Dory kept asking me if I wanted anything, but what would I do with any of that junk?

By the time we got to the campground it was almost dark. We found our reserved spot without too much trouble. Our little plot was between two other groups, both of whom had brought along everything from toddlers and puppies to CD players and cell phones. Why not just stay home?

Getting the tent up wasn't hard—Dory had gotten one of those new pop-up kinds so it was almost foolproof, but apparently she hadn't tried it out since she bought it. The screen flap wouldn't zip closed—when Dory forced it, it jumped the track altogether.

"Dammit! They have a nerve charging so much for something that breaks this easily!" she said.

I tried to get it back on track, too, but it was impossible. We were all still so tired from the night before, we just rolled out our sleeping bags and flopped down on them.

"Oh, well, we don't need it zipped—the fresh air is nice," Dory said.

"God, this ground is all rocky!" Iris said, shifting from side to side. "I hope there aren't any snakes."

"Snakes?" Marshall said in a weak voice. But he was already half asleep and way too exhausted to fight it.

I heard Iris swat at a mosquito, but her swear was barely audible either. It gave me hope that we might all be able to sleep through the night.

Chapter Ten

We must have slept like we were in hibernation. I was pleased to wake up and see that no bears had made us their midnight snack. But I'd hardly had time to appreciate this when I realized a much smaller creature had found its way through the unzipped screen and feasted on our slumbering bodies: the lowly mosquito—and a few thousand of his friends.

I brushed my fingers lightly across my stinging ear and neck, which made them itch more than ever. My right arm, which had been lying outside the sleeping bag, was also full of hot red lumps. No sooner had I sat up to survey the damage than Iris woke too and began screaming.

"I can't see anything! I can't open my eyes! Mom!"

Dory was out of her bag instantly and crouched at Iris's side. "Oh, my God. Your eyelids are swollen shut! How . . . what . . . ?"

"It's mosquitoes," I said, holding out my arm. "I've got a million bites, too."

"Mosquitoes? They bit my *eyes*?" Iris started to cry, which looked really pathetic, the tears squeezing out beneath her puffy lids.

Now Marsh was awake, too, taking it all in and checking himself over. "I only have a few. Just on my jaw," he said. "Wait, here's one on my forehead."

Dory had some on her face, too, but Iris must have tasted better than the rest of us. "It looks like you and Robin got the worst of it," Dory told her daughter. "Robin's arm is swollen, too."

Like Iris would care. "*Do* something about my eyes!" she commanded through her tears. Typical.

"I'll go to the snack bar and get some ice, sweetie. That'll take down the swelling some." Dory pulled on her shoes and a sweatshirt and crawled through the open door. "Don't cry! It's over now."

Iris was feeling the lumps and bumps on her face. "It's *not* over. I look like a freak!"

"That's for sure," Marshall said.

I couldn't decide which of them annoyed me more. "Do you two always have to make a bad situation worse by picking on each other?" I said. "It makes me glad I don't have siblings."

"She *does* look awful!" Marshall said.

She did look pretty bad, but I actually felt a little sorry for her, bawling through her battered eyes. "It's not that bad," I said. "And besides, you should be thinking about how to *help* her, not how to make her feel worse!"

"Why? If my eyes were swollen shut, she wouldn't be thinking about how to help me."

True. I gave up and crawled outside to wait for Dory. She was running back across the campground with several zippered plastic bags filled with crushed ice. "The guy at the snack bar was really great. Apparently this happens all the time."

Marshall came outside to take his bag of ice from Dory, but Iris was staying hidden. Everything but her voice.

"How could you *do* this to me?" she yelled. "First you make me go on this stupid trip with you and then we have to sleep in all these horrible places—even *outside*—and now my face is totally ruined! Do you hate me? Is that why you're doing this to me?"

"Iris, calm down now," Dory said.

"She's not just doing this to *you*, you know," Marshall put in from his post outside the door.

"Keep the bag on the bites," Dory said, but her voice sounded . . . oh no, like she was ready to cry, too.

"Marsh, put the ice bag on your bites," I said, running mine up and down my burning arm.

"Mine aren't that bad."

"Well then, *shut up*," I said. He glared at my face, and then, remarkably, said nothing else. I took the bag from him and handed it inside the tent to Dory so Iris could have one for each eye. "Marsh doesn't need his."

Quiet tears were cascading from Dory's eyes, too. "Thank you, Robin. I'm sorry about this. I'm so sorry. I shouldn't have made you sleep outside when you didn't want to. And then with the broken zipper . . ."

"Don't worry about me," I said. "I'm fine."

"I have to pee," Iris whined. "Do they have bathrooms out here in Sherwood Forest?"

Dory sighed and struggled to her knees. "There's a public rest room just a little way up the path."

"I'll take her," I said. "I need to go, too."

"Oh, good," Dory said, wiping away the tears and trying to sound normal as she and Iris came out into the sunlight. "Marsh can help me take the tent down, and then we'll go back to Wall Drug and get some calamine lotion. And breakfast."

I could tell Marshall was about to start complaining about having to help his mother, but I gave him a look I hoped was terrifying and he only frowned. I took Iris's arm to lead her to the bathroom.

"You don't have to *grab* me," she said.

I waited until we were out of earshot of Dory and then I said, "You don't have to be a bitch either. Ever thought of that?"

She pulled her arm away from me. "I can see the ground well enough to walk by myself. Just make sure I'm going in the right direction."

Yes, your Exalted Crabbiness. I let her stumble a little on the step up to the bathroom, then grabbed her arm tightly. "Whoops!" I said, and maneuvered her in the door. She felt her way into the stall and banged the door behind her. I used the stall next to her, then waited for her by the row of sinks.

"Your right eye is opening a little bit," I said when she emerged. "If you keep the ice on them, they'll both open up soon. My friend Franny got badly bitten once when we camped at Thunder Lake, and we . . ."

Iris banged out of the stall and felt her way over to the sinks. "You know everything, don't you? You win the Good Camper Award."

A young woman with two small boys came out of another stall and washed her hands and theirs at the sink next to us. She glanced up at Iris who was looking into the mirror out of the thin slits of her eyes, trying to get some idea what she looked like.

"Wow! I guess you forgot the bug spray!" the woman said.

"My *mother* forgot the bug spray. *And* broke the tent zipper."

"Well, those things happen," the woman said, shrugging. "It's all part of camping. Don't let it ruin your day." She chased her little boys outside.

"Is she kidding? Where do all these perky people come from? Is that a farmer trait, or something? *Don't let it gitcha down, yuk, yuk!* I wouldn't live in these backward boondocks if you paid me. Just because she grew up here, Mom thinks she has to *expose* us to it. I'd rather be exposed to pneumonia."

Suddenly I'd just had it with all her insults and nastiness. "You are such a brat, Iris! Just because your mother treats you like royalty doesn't mean you *are.* This is a *vacation,* even though you and your brother are doing your best to turn it into a death march."

She put her head back and tried to look at me from underneath her lids. "What do you know . . . ?"

But I didn't let her talk. "For God's sake, you've got some mosquito bites, and you're acting like it's malaria! Get over yourself! If you and Marshall intend to spend the whole summer bitching and moaning about every single thing, I swear I'm going to find a bus station and go back home. Because being around the two of you really sucks!"

She continued to squint at me for another minute and then turned back to the mirror. "The right eye *is* going down a little, isn't it?"

I didn't answer her.

"I'm ready to go back," she said finally, offering me her arm as if I was her escort to the ball. I wondered if she'd even heard me.

The clerk at Wall Drug advised us to use the old-fashioned bug bite cure of baking soda and water. "Stops the itching better than calamine lotion, I think," she said. She got us a box and showed Dory how to mix up a paste with water. We got calamine lotion too because Iris didn't want to put baking soda on her eyelids. By the time we'd slathered ourselves up with white paste and pink goo, Iris could actually get her right eye almost all the way open and the left one was better, too.

We were all starving after our morning of high adventure and ordered big breakfasts. All except Iris. I couldn't figure out her eating habits; she either ate everything in sight or nothing at all.

Marshall looked at her delicately spooning up a small yogurt. "That's all you're eating? Your eyes are swollen shut, not your mouth."

Iris looked at him, but, for a change, said nothing. Maybe my little speech had had an effect after all.

Dory gave Iris a worried look, but I didn't know if it was about the yogurt or the mosquito bites. When Marsh and Iris went back for one more tour of the gift shop, I decided I'd ask her.

"Dory, do you think Iris eats strangely? I mean, sometimes she eats almost nothing, and other times she eats like a horse."

Dory's head bobbed up from the map she was looking at. "Oh, well . . . I don't think there's anything wrong with that. I mean, she's a teenager. A *young* teenager. Don't you remember being worried about your weight sometimes?"

"Sure. I just don't remember being so extreme about it."

Dory sighed and circled her neck on her shoulders. "Well, don't worry about it, Robin. I'm sure she's fine." She turned her attention to my arm. "How's that doing? I feel so bad about you girls getting bitten to pieces."

I sighed. "It's not a big deal. When you go camping, you get mosquito bites."

She smiled and ran her hand over my hair, a thing adults do that I hate. "You're a great kid, you know that? I hope your mother appreciates you."

I didn't know about that, but I was certainly beginning to appreciate *her* after a few days with the Tewksburys.

By late morning Iris's eyes were open far enough for us to take a hike in the Badlands. Dory filled a thermos with lemonade and I carried a backpack with our lunch in it: a loaf of bread, cheese, apples, and cookies. Marshall's backpack held several liters of water and the rest of the sun lotion that we'd applied heavily over the top of the baking soda paste scabs. Iris, of course, had only herself to think about as we headed out from the visitor's center looking like a band of badly glued action figures.

As soon as we started on the trail, though, I felt more like an extraterrestrial than a toy. The landscape became suddenly stark and bizarre and it was hard to believe we hadn't left earth. That this was South Dakota, no less. Rows of sharp pinnacles rose up and dropped away in ridges up and down a valley. The colors fascinated me: Shades of red, white, black, and brown ran in bands from pinnacle to pinnacle and across the ravines. It reminded me of the glass bottles of colored sand Franny and I used to make when we were little, the green layer over the blue over the red.

Marshall read from the guidebook. "The landforms known as badlands are sculptures made by wind and water. The accumulation of sediment began 75 million years ago when the Rocky Mountains rose up in the West, and sand, silt, clay, and volcanic ash were stacked layer upon layer, thousands of feet deep."

He looked up from the book. "Seventy-five million years. *God.*"

"Exactly," Dory said.

"It says that many mammals died here in floods 40 to 25 million years ago. And there are still many fossils found here all the time, but if you find one you can't pick it up—you have to remember where it was and report it to one of the park rangers. Wouldn't that be neat? I want to find a fossil!"

"I'm sure ten-year-olds find them all the time," Iris said as she tied a straw hat on her head and covered her poor eyes with sunglasses.

"It's possible!" Marshall said. "You never think I can do anything!"

I got my baseball cap out of my backpack, and then placed

myself in the line of fire between my cousins so that when Iris turned to level her brother again, she found me staring at her instead.

Her grin was like a dog baring its teeth before it bites. "That's probably your boyfriend's hat, right? That he hit home runs in or something."

"It's *my* hat, that *I* hit home runs in," I said, running my hand over the carefully curved brim and wishing my home runs had been more numerous. Diamond dust had dulled the bright yellow, but the hat fit me like it was born for the job.

"You play baseball?" Marshall asked.

"Softball. I'm a shortstop."

"Hmm. Good hat," he said. "If you don't mind looking like Big Bird."

Dory led the way up a series of stairs built into a hillside and then we walked along a high ledge. The hike felt good after sitting in the car the past two days. Even my cousins seemed to be enjoying themselves—at least they'd stopped bickering for a while. Everybody was quiet for a change, thinking their own thoughts, I guess. Personally, I was thinking about the letter I'd written to Chris—was it too needy? Was I nice enough? Would he be happy to get it, or would it just remind him of what a drag it was to have this clingy girlfriend back home?

But then, I suddenly realized where I was—on vacation and, apparently, on the moon—and I just decided to stop thinking about my problems for a while. Maybe there would be something to worry about when Chris got back from Italy and I got back from California, but right now I was in an amazing place and I just wanted to *be* here.

We stopped for lunch at a beautiful spot with views out over the whole valley. Dory and I each got out our Swiss Army knives and started cutting off chunks of cheese and bread and passing them around. Amazingly, Iris poured glasses of lemonade for all of us, not just herself. Marshall immediately pulled out a small drawing pad and some colored pencils and got to work. I didn't blame him for thinking art was more important than lunch; being here made me wish I could draw, too. I took some pictures, but I had a feeling Marshall's drawings would capture the place better, his crumbly pencils so similar to the crumbling stone. Unless, of course, he was drawing the three of us with arrows buried in our chests.

Dory seemed sad again, looking at the gorgeous landscape around her. She watched Iris grab a handful of cookies and said, "I wish Daddy could be here to see this." Neither of her children responded. Instead they looked away as though the feeling embarrassed them. Iris stuck the cookies back in the bag.

I didn't think we should all ignore Dory when she seemed to want to talk. "Did Uncle Allen like to take trips like this?" I asked.

"I don't really know," Dory said. "He was always so busy—the only vacations we took coincided with his work. We went to London once when he had to give a speech at a conference there. And last year we spent a week in Paris while Allen went to all sorts of meetings. That was fun, wasn't it?" She looked eagerly at Iris and Marshall.

Iris shrugged. "Shopping was fun."

But Marshall was enthusiastic. "I liked going to the museums. Paris has the *best* museums."

"Yes, it does," Dory agreed.

"It's too hard when you can't talk to people," Iris said.

"So learn French," Marshall said. "That's what I'm going to do."

Iris sniffed. "Not if they don't let you back into school." One step forward—two steps back.

Marshall looked away, then folded up his drawing pad and stuffed it back into his backpack. Dory gave the dirty look to Iris this time, but she didn't say anything. We packed up our garbage and got back on the trail.

This time Marsh took the lead, running ahead and even detouring off the path to walk around some of the big rocks. Suddenly he disappeared from sight altogether.

"Marsh," Dory called. "Don't get too far ahead. I don't want to lose you."

There was no answer.

"Marshall! Where did he go? Did you see which direction?" Dory asked.

"He's okay," Iris said. "He's over there someplace."

"*Marsh*!" Dory shouted again, this time with panic in her voice. "Where are you?"

Then he shouted back. "I *found* something! Come here!"

Sure enough. When we wound our way through the rock maze, we found Marsh crouched over a small boulder. "It's a fish," he said, pointing to a fossilized skeleton imbedded in the side of the stone.

Dory knelt down and gave him a hug. "I was worried when I couldn't see you."

He shrugged. "Why? There wasn't anything dangerous going on."

"You could have gotten lost or . . ."

I interrupted her. "Dory, look at this . . . what Marsh found."

Reluctantly, she looked away from her son. Her eyes widened. "Marsh, oh, my God!"

"You *did* find a fossil!" I said.

"Told ya." He glared at his sister who was silent.

He got out his drawing pad again and did a quick sketch of the fish caught in the rock, the scales, the eye, the fins . . . an entire fish. Dory and I did our best to help him memorize the exact location of the fossil find: off the trail to the left as you come down from the ridge, below a pinkish pinnacle, an oblong rock about two feet across. Marshall just about flew back to the visitor's center. By the time we arrived he was already busy drawing a map for the ranger while the man looked at his sketch.

"Do you think it's a new find?" Dory asked.

"It could well be," the ranger told her. "We had a heavy rain here last week that stirred up a lot of new rocks. This place is constantly changing."

"Will you let me know if it really is a new find?" Marshall asked him.

"I sure will. Write your name and address on the bottom of the map and I'll let you know. If it's really a whole fish fossil, that's a great find, young man. Maybe you've got a future in paleontology!"

By the time we left Marsh was glowing. Dory and I kept complimenting him, too, on the way back to the car, but Iris was conspicuously quiet. As we stood next to the open doors of the van, waiting for the inside to cool down a little, Dory and I both turned our eyes on Iris.

"What?" she said. I shook my head and Dory looked away.

But when they crawled into the backseat together, Iris gave her brother a light slap on the knee. "Not bad, Marshmallow. Not bad."

"You're telling me," Marsh said, grinning like mad.

"So now you're gonna be a paleontologist, I guess."

"Maybe," he said, but then added, "if I knew what it was."

It was the first time we all laughed together without meaning to hurt anybody's feelings.

Chapter Eleven

"Really, Mom, the bites are mostly gone already."

"I can't believe Dory didn't bring any bug spray along if she intended to camp outside. Did she forget *everything* she learned growing up?"

It was great to hear Mom's voice. I'd only been gone four days, but it seemed like ages since I'd spoken to anyone who wasn't on the verge of either hysteria, rage, or depression.

"Are they right there?" she asked. "Can you talk? How's it really going?"

"They're outside packing the car. I think Dory wanted to give me some privacy." It had been Dory who'd suggested I call Mom before we left the hotel. She'd even wanted me to use her phone card to do it, but I used the one Mom had given me. I guess Dory thinks we're poverty-stricken or something.

"So, tell me."

"Well, it's okay, I guess. I mean, Dory kind of goes up and down. Last night she was crying in the bathroom with the shower running. I wouldn't have known about it—Iris and I were in the room next door—but Marsh got scared and came running into our room."

"Oh, gosh. Maybe this trip is too much for Dory."

"Most of the time she seems all right—too all right, considering how weird her kids are."

"Are they driving you crazy?"

"Sometimes they're okay—like when they're asleep. But, take last night for instance. Marsh was all upset because Dory was crying, and all Iris would say to him was, '*Grow up, Marshall. The woman's husband is dead.*' And she said it in this terrible voice—you had to hear it—like the *woman* wasn't her own mother, and the *husband* wasn't her dead father. Then, Marshall got furious and started hitting her . . . then she hit him *back* . . . they're almost as dysfunctional as Franny's family."

For a moment there was silence on the other end of the line, then Mom breathed a sigh. "This whole thing was a big mistake. I shouldn't have talked you into going. They should be spending the summer in therapy, not on the highway. If you want to come home, I'll put the bus ticket on my credit card."

It's not as if I hadn't thought about it myself, getting the hell away from these nutcases. But that wasn't all there was to this trip—I'd loved walking through the Badlands, and yesterday's drive to Mount Rushmore and then the Crazy Horse Memorial was amazing, too. Just the fact that people had figured out how to carve those giant heads into a mountain made you feel like you might want to do something more interesting with your own life than the puny ideas you'd imagined.

We could actually see people working on the Crazy Horse monument—it's going to be enormous—the chief and his horse will look like they're riding out of the mountain. It was amazing to think that people had goals so huge they knew they'd never accomplish them in their own lifetime—that their children and grandchildren would have to finish what they started.

It had never even occurred to me that all these wonderful,

strange places existed. And now I was in *Wyoming,* a state I never gave a thought to before this trip, and here I was looking at maps and helping to plan our route through it. We were going to see the Big Horn Mountains and the Rockies, too, at least from a distance.

"I'm not really having that bad a time," I said. "I mean, I like traveling. We're driving through Wyoming today, which Dory says is beautiful. And she has some kind of surprise planned for us tonight. The place we're staying, I think."

"Right. She told me about it."

"She told you? She planned it before?"

"You need advance reservations for this place. Besides, I had to know where to send your mail, didn't I?"

How could I have forgotten to ask her! "Did I . . . ?"

"Yes, you did. I sent it on—you should get it in a day or two."

"He probably didn't even get mine yet. I should have written him sooner, but I'm not that good in letters."

"I'm sure you're good enough to please Chris, honey. He's in love with you. He won't be critical of your writing ability."

I could see from the window that the van was ready to go. The doors were all open, Dory had her driving sunglasses on, and the kids were leaning against the tailgate as though their spines wouldn't support their weight. I swear, those two were always tired.

"I think they're waiting for me, Mom. I better go."

"Okay. Don't let them get you down. And, remember, if it gets really bad, you can ditch 'em and come on home."

"Thanks, Mom. Oh, I forgot to ask you, are you still going out with Michael Evans?"

She laughed. "I guess I am. Nobody else is vying for my attention."

"But you still like him?"

"Sure I do. But I'm not making too much out of this, Robin, so you don't need to either. Get going now, so Dory doesn't get antsy."

"Bye, Mom! I'll call you again soon." I was happier than I thought I'd be to know that she wasn't taking this Michael Evans thing too seriously. Not that I had anything against him personally. It was just strange to think of my mother loving somebody I hardly knew. For as long as I could remember, the only person she'd really loved had been me. And, right now, I didn't feel like splitting that pie into smaller pieces.

Dory let me drive the morning shift. The first couple of times I'd driven the minivan I'd been nervous, and, of course, Iris howled every time I braked too hard or parked crooked or anything. But by now I was getting used to it—I could relax a little and enjoy it. I kept thinking about how the world is supposed to be overpopulated, but out here you can drive for an hour and never even pass another car. Wyoming makes Iowa look crowded.

Something about looking into the distance like that makes you think about your own future. I mean, there are so many possibilities out in front of you, so many roads you could take. I decided Dory was right to zigzag across the country instead of making a beeline for Los Angeles. I'd seen pictures of L.A.; I knew what to expect. But all this stuff in between was constantly surprising.

Iris read a book and Marshall listened to his headphones all the way to the Big Horn Mountains where we had a picnic lunch in a field. Marsh was a little bit nervous that one of the sheep we could see in the distance might suddenly lower his big curly-horned head and charge us, but the sheep couldn't be bothered with tourists.

"I'm finished," he said, stuffing the last quarter of his sandwich into his cheeks. "Let's get going."

"What's the big hurry?" Iris said. "It's nice out here. Besides, I'm sick of being stuffed into that backseat."

"You shouldn't have brought so much junk. Mom wouldn't have had to take the third seat out." The two of them never stopped arguing about who brought more luggage.

"It's beautiful here," Dory said, spreading her arms and taking a deep breath, "but I guess we should get going. We've got a fairly long stretch still to drive."

"Great. Why can't you just *tell* us where we're going?" Iris said.

"No, don't tell!" Marshall said. "I want to be surprised!"

"I'm not telling," Dory said.

Marshall was jumping around, kicking sandy dirt into my lemonade. "I bet I know! I looked at the map. I bet we're going to Yellowstone Park, aren't we, Mom? I figured it out!"

"I thought you didn't want to know?" Dory said.

"I'm right though, aren't I? It's Yellowstone."

Dory shook her head. "No, actually we're not going to Yellowstone. We're heading south—I told you that. Yellowstone is west."

Marshall's chin dropped. "What? Yellowstone is, like, the only famous place out here. Why can't we go there?"

"Because it's overcrowded with tourists. I don't feel like driving through a park in bumper-to-bumper traffic."

Iris grunted. "Figures. The one place we *want* to go and you won't let us."

"Since when did *you* want to go?" I said.

"Was I talking to you?"

"Girls!" Dory said. She hated hearing Iris and me squabble, even though we did it much less than Iris and Marshall, whose fighting she seemed able to ignore.

Since Dory was driving next, I offered Iris the front seat, which was a little roomier than the back. But instead of being grateful, she just tossed my purse over the backseat and announced, "I'm not sitting with all your junk under my feet!" The backseat, of course, was strewn with piles of her crap.

It was hard to read in the backseat—too bouncy—and besides, Dory had let Iris put on a CD of some awful prepubescent boy group, and I couldn't concentrate. Marsh had just finished drawing something in his book, so I asked him if I could take a look at his pictures.

"What for?" He eyed me suspiciously.

"Because I want to see them."

"How come?"

"Because I haven't got anything better to do!"

He shrugged and tossed the book onto my lap. "Okay."

He must have started this drawing pad at the beginning of the trip because the bulls-eye drawing of Golddigger was one of the first ones. There were lots of cartoon-inspired figures drawn in black pen, many of them toting guns and knives. Also a certain number of monsters holding other monsters' heads in their hands—he seemed to like that theme. Even the picture he'd drawn of the Badlands had a large Cyclops crawling up over a hill. And, as Dory had warned, a good deal of blood was inked in with a red pen.

But there was another theme emerging in some of the more recent pictures: Fish. Even though Marsh had left his fossil drawing with the ranger, he'd obviously stored it in his memory because he'd redrawn it several times, changing the original with odd details. One fish, as you might guess, had a bloody eye with droplets falling down the page. But another one had little wings where its gills should be, and a third had leaves where it ought to have scales—you had to look closely to notice. And all the drawings, even the monster ones, were very well done. I don't know why I was surprised; it makes sense that if you draw all the time, you'd probably get pretty good at it.

"These are good, Marshall. I really like this one!" I said, pointing to the leaf-scaled fish.

Marsh leaned over to see what I was looking at. "No blood."

"True. You like the bloody ones better?"

"Sometimes. They make me feel sort of . . . good."

Jesus, this kid. "What do you mean, they make you feel *good*?"

He shrugged again and looked out the window. "I don't know. When I'm nervous or something. It makes me stop feeling so jumpy. When I draw something ugly and bloody it makes me feel better."

I thought about that. "So, you mean, if you draw something awful, it stops you from worrying so much about real things?"

He looked at me seriously. "Sort of. Yeah, I guess so. It calms me down."

"Hmmm. That makes sense." I smiled at him and his chin quivered.

"Does it?" he asked quietly.

"I think so. Maybe you should tell your therapist about it."

"Yeah, maybe I will. So he won't keep talking about my *violent tendencies.*"

"From what I can see you're mostly violent toward your sister. And she wouldn't win the Nobel Peace Prize either."

"Are you talking about me?" Iris shouted, never one to miss a reference to herself.

"NO!" Marshall and I said in unison, and then laughed.

"God," Iris said, craning her neck around the seat in order to give us a disgusted look. "You two deserve each other."

It was almost six o'clock before Dory pulled the car off the main road and onto a dirt one. Iris and Marsh had been complaining of hunger for fifty miles. I just wanted to get out of the backseat and move my legs.

"Where are we *going?*" Iris said. "We're in the middle of nowhere and I'm starving!"

Dory was driving slowly and consulting a hand-drawn map. "This is the right way. We're almost there."

"Do they even *have* any restaurants out here?" Marshall said, leaning over the seat.

"We won't need a restaurant. We'll be just in time for the barbecue," Dory told him.

"What barbecue?"

"There!" Dory pointed to a big wooden archway over a road that went off to the right. "The Lazy River Ranch! That's the place!"

The name was burned into the wood of the arch. Dory turned into the road and stopped in front of a big wire gate. "Hop out and open it, please, Iris."

"Why's there a gate, anyway?" Iris could never just obey a command.

"So the cows don't get out onto the road."

"What cows?"

I opened my door. "I'll do it. I have to straighten my legs before they break off." I limped over to the wood and wire gate and unhitched a fancy latch, walked the gate to the side so Dory could drive in, then latched it up again. Before I climbed back in the car I noticed a string of horses coming across a field up ahead, their riders looking a little droopy in the afternoon sun.

"Dory, is this a dude ranch?" I asked.

"That's what it is!" She was grinning widely.

"A *dude* ranch," Marshall said. "A ranch for dudes? I don't get it."

Iris groaned. "It's a vacation place for wusses who want to pretend they're living on a real ranch, except they aren't. This is our big surprise?"

"It *is* a real ranch," Dory said. "A working ranch. They have five hundred head of beef cattle besides the tourist business. We can go on trail rides, and learn how to rope cows, or we can go fishing or hiking or swimming or whatever we want. There's lots to do here."

"Cool!" Marsh was hanging out the window now. "How long are we staying?"

"Three nights," Dory said. "Long enough to take it all in and relax a little."

"This might even be *better* than Yellowstone!"

I was glad for Dory's sake that Marshall was enthusiastic about the place. Even from the road, the views were amazing; you could see all the way to the Rocky Mountains.

Dory pulled up in front of the office and turned to Iris. "I thought you'd be pleased. You love horses."

Iris was nibbling on a cuticle. "I *love* them, but I can't ride them," she said quietly. "Don't you remember?"

Dory put a hand on Iris's arm and Iris shook it off like it hurt her. "You'll be able to ride these horses. They ride western saddle out here. That silly place you took riding lessons—I don't think they knew what they were doing."

"Neither did Iris," Marshall put in. "She fell off and broke her wrist!" He laughed loudly, looking to me for appreciation, but when I frowned, he settled down again. Seemed like he wasn't so angry with me now that I liked his drawings.

"You dipwad! You better not tell anybody!" Iris looked more upset than angry.

"I never really learned to ride either," I said, hoping to keep them from beating on each other again.

"You didn't?" Dory said. "Living out in the country your whole life?"

"We didn't have horses like you and Mom did growing up. None of my friends did either. I rode a few times, but I never really got how to do it without bouncing up and down."

"You probably never fell off, though," Marsh said, quietly.

"We'll all take some refresher lessons in the corral before we hit the trail." Dory bustled into the office with more energy than she'd had for days.

Our "bunkhouse" was number 12—two bedrooms, two bathrooms, and a sitting area in between with a small refrigerator stocked with soft drinks. I had a feeling real bunkhouses never looked like this. The walls were knotty pine and the single beds all had pretty quilts on them. The floors were covered with rag rugs and cactus plants decorated the bureau tops. From the windows you could see across to the stables and behind them the snow-capped mountains. I could get used to this place.

This cowboy guy, Mel, who ran the office, told us to hurry over to the "grub barn" where the barbecue was getting started. You could smell the meat and something like corn bread all the way across the courtyard. There were long tables set up both inside and outside, and a huge grill ran the length of the barn just outside the open door with about three cows already sizzling on it. There were pots of baked beans on a side table and buckets of corn and baked potatoes, and, sure enough, corn bread. Suddenly I was starving, too.

We all heaped our plates with more than we could really eat—it seemed like the right thing to do on a ranch—and found seats at one of the long indoor tables next to a family with two young boys who looked like twins.

"Hello," Dory said cheerfully as Iris rolled her eyes.

"Hi," the woman answered. "You just get here?"

Dory introduced herself and all of us and the other woman did the same. Her husband was too busy chowing down on steak to do more than nod, but the little boys, Howie and Bobby, were interested in us. At least, in Marshall.

"We're eight," Howie announced. "How old are you?"

"Ten," Marshall said proudly. "I'll be eleven soon."

"You don't look that old," Bobby said.

Fortunately, before Marshall could get mad, Howie interrupted. "There's a lot of dogs and cats here. Do you like dogs and cats? We could go play with some after dinner."

Marshall considered this. "I like dogs okay, as long as they don't bite. I used to like cats, but some of them are mean."

"These ones aren't," Howie assured him. "They're little ones. I'll show you!"

"*I'll* show him!" Bobby said.

Their mother made them finish their dinners first and then wait for Marshall to finish his, and then they pulled Marsh off the bench and led him away, giggling happily. I hoped the kittens really would be sweet and the dogs not biters *or* barkers—you never knew what might throw Marshall into a panic.

Dory had gotten into a conversation with the twins' mother, so I dumped my trash and decided to take a look around. I was surprised that Iris followed me, and even more surprised when I saw her plate, which had almost as much food left on it as she'd originally taken.

"I thought you were starving," I said.

She chucked her plate of perfectly good food into the garbage and said, "I'm a vegetarian."

This was the first I'd heard of it, besides which, if she was a vegetarian, why did she take a big hunk of steak to begin with? "You could have eaten the beans and potatoes and bread, couldn't you?"

She shrugged. "None of it looked good to me."

This I was not buying. I waited until we'd gotten clear of the barn and were heading toward the stables.

"Iris, are you trying to lose weight or something?"

She glared at me. "Are you saying I'm fat? You're the one who could stand to lose a few pounds."

"I'm not *saying* you're fat. You've lost weight since . . . your dad's funeral, and I'm kind of worried about the way you're eating. Some days you pig out and some days you hardly eat anything."

"You're not my baby-sitter, you know."

"I know that. It's just . . . well . . . you aren't anorexic or bulimic or anything, are you?"

Her face turned red. "I'm not *anything,* Robin. Why don't you mind your own business?"

"Look, Iris, I don't really care, to tell you the truth. I just feel bad for your mother—she's got enough problems right now without you doing something dumb, like starving yourself to death."

The smack came so fast I didn't even see it. She'd slapped me in the face! For a second I just stared at her and then I grabbed her by both of her skinny wrists as hard as I could.

"Don't hit me, Iris! You can't just hit people!"

Her eyes got big and dark. "I wish you'd go back to stupid Iowa! We don't need you following us around!"

She twisted out of my grip, turned abruptly, and stopped following *me* around. It certainly was going to be fun getting to know my relatives a little better, especially the insane one with the eating disorder.

Chapter Twelve

Dory had booked us for an afternoon trail ride, so we spent the morning trying to learn how *not* to fall off a horse. Iris was nervous at breakfast and Marshall was anxious to get going, but once we got to the corral, they switched moods. When the horses were trotted out, Iris was paired with a pretty white-speckled horse, and she took the reins lovingly, whispering into the animal's nostrils and playing with his mane. I'd never seen her look so good-natured.

Joe, the cowboy in charge, told Iris, "This here's Silverfoot. She's an Appaloosa pony."

"I love Appaloosas—they're beautiful!" She was gazing at Silverfoot rapturously.

Dory seemed surprised, but pleased.

Joe pointed to Marshall. "And for you, little wrangler, I think Oklahoma here is the perfect mount." He led a pretty dark brown horse up to the fence where Marsh was perched. Oklahoma wasn't as big as some of the other horses, but I guess she still looked pretty large to a ten-year-old. He leaned back from her inquiring nose.

Joe slipped Marsh an apple. "Put this in your hand and hold it out real straight—she'll tickle ya' gettin' it." Marsh took the apple, but you could tell he was worried about losing a finger to Oklahoma's teeth.

"Go ahead, honey," Dory urged. "He won't hurt you."

Marsh's face clouded up. "How do *you* know?"

I climbed up onto the fence so I was sitting next to him and reached out to scratch under Oklahoma's chin. Even though I'm not much of a rider, horses don't scare me. I like all kinds of animals—they're more predictable than human beings.

"Nothin' Okie likes better than a good chin scratch," the cowboy said. "Except maybe that apple."

Okie stuck his nose under my armpit, the better to have me pet him. This horse was a sweetheart—Marsh would be perfectly safe, if only he'd get on the thing. I pulled the roll out of my pocket I'd brought from the breakfast buffet to make friends with *my* horse and laid it on my open palm. Oklahoma sniffed it gently and nibbled at it a little, but he'd seen that apple; bread must have seemed like a poor substitute. "He wants what you've got," I whispered to Marsh.

There was fear in his eyes when he looked at me, but he nodded and carefully placed the apple on his outstretched hand. Okie waited until the hand was held out and the apple offered, then he curled back his big lips and snuffled the thing up in two seconds.

Marsh pulled back his empty hand. "It *did* tickle. Can I give him another one?"

Joe laughed. "Let's wait until the lesson's over. The poor guy'll be so full he won't be able to waddle around the corral."

After that Marsh let Joe help him mount Okie. I could tell he was still nervous being so high off the ground, but he kept up a running conversation with old Oklahoma so that, by the time the rest of us got seated on our horses, I think they were pals. Dory had a bay mare named Elsie and I had an enormous palomino called Charlie.

Our lesson consisted of trotting around the corral one after the other. Joe gave us instructions on how to turn the horses left or right, how to get them to stop, how to change their gaits—that stuff I kind of knew, anyway. Then he told us "the secret of how to keep your rear ends from slapping up and down in the saddle," a secret that is safe with me. It had something to do with getting into the same rhythm as the horse, but I guess Charlie and I weren't listening to the same music. Marshall was banging up and down, too, but after the first few circles of the corral, he didn't seem to care—he was obviously having a great time.

Dory knew how to ride, even though she pretended she'd forgotten. I guess it's like riding a bicycle—I'm a lot better at that fortunately. The big surprise, though, was Iris. At first she was as clumsy as Marsh and me, but she listened to Joe like he was handing down the tablets from the mountaintop, and before long she'd gotten it. She was sailing around the corral without a bit of air space between her and that saddle. How in the heck was she doing that?

When the lesson was over, Joe praised us all—it's his job, after all. But he saved the major flattery for Iris.

"You're a regular little cowgirl up there! I thought you said you never rode before?"

"Once or twice," she said, blushing, "but that was English saddle."

"Yeah, and she . . . ," Marsh started. Iris and I both shot him instant looks. "She . . . wasn't very good that time."

"Well, obviously, that's because she's a western type a' girl!" Joe said. "Why, if you were here a few more days, I'd have you barrel racing."

Iris's blush lasted halfway through lunch. She couldn't stop talking about riding. "That was *so much* fun! It wasn't anything like how they teach you in Chicago!"

"You just had a bad experience at that place," Dory said. "You took to it right away here."

"I wish we were staying a week—then I could really learn a lot. Why can't we stay longer?" she said, in a rather accusing tone of voice.

"Iris, yesterday you didn't even want to go to a dude ranch," Dory said. "Today you want to move in for the summer."

Joe had told us we'd need hats for three hours on the trail unless we wanted to get headaches and heatstroke, so after lunch we headed for the shop in the main building. I was glad I had my baseball hat with me because everything in the shop was really expensive. Of course, Iris and Marshall both wanted the prettiest, most expensive cowboy hats in the place. Dory acted like the prices were scandalously high and then ended up buying them just what they wanted, anyway, and getting herself one, too. She wanted to buy me one as well, but I felt funny about it. It seemed wasteful to buy something that cost so much money for only a couple weeks' use—I wasn't going to wear a cowboy hat once I got back to Iowa. I told her thanks, but I liked my own hat.

We were all pretty hyped up after our morning lesson and arrived back at the stable promptly at one for the trail ride. Other people were gathering, too, and Joe and a couple of other ranch hands were getting them saddled up.

As soon as he saw us, Joe said, "I told old Silverfoot and Okie you guys were coming back. They're waiting for ya'." Marsh got a little quiet and shaky, but as soon as Oklahoma came clopping over, he straightened up and took the reins.

"Hi, Okie. Remember me? I'm gonna ride you again!" Okie seemed fine with that idea.

It turned out Joe didn't lead the trail rides. There were two other guys going with us, Glen and Jackson. They didn't look much older than me, but they were pretty cocky, trotting around and showing off their abilities for the dudes. While we were saddling up, they rode their horses in nervous little circles around us, and then suddenly turned and raced each other up a nearby hill.

"Chrissakes," Joe called out. "Give those poor ponies a rest." He shook his head. "Couple a' hotshots, those two."

We started off slowly with Jackson in the lead and Glen bringing up the rear, as if they were herding cattle, which I guess they kind of were. There were fifteen of us altogether: a bunch of older women who were very nervous and kept giving little shrieks every time a horse tossed its head, two guys who looked like schoolteachers to me and talked to each other through the whole ride, and a family with three grade-school-aged kids who plodded along like they were hypnotized and hardly said a word to anybody.

The countryside we rode through was gorgeous—first we went over some low sage-covered hills, and then through a large stand of white birch trees, always with the Rocky Mountains for a backdrop. We forded several little streams—it felt good to have the water splash up on you on such a hot day.

We all had water bottles along, and every now and then Glen would ride up alongside the column of horses and remind us to keep drinking so we wouldn't get dehydrated. Then he'd race his horse back past us to the end of the line again. It seemed like more of an exhibition than was necessary, but I had to admit he was sort of cute.

Meanwhile, Jackson had let his horse fall back a little so he could ride alongside Iris. I couldn't get a real good look at his face, but from the way Iris was giggling at him, I presumed he was good-looking, too. About halfway through the ride, Glen rode up to the front of the line again and there was some kind of talk among the three of them. It must have been Jackson's turn to ride in the rear because, after a few minutes, he turned his horse and trotted in that direction, with guess who following along beside him, beaming happily. I wasn't surprised. Iris looked older than she was; a couple of times on the trip I'd noticed guys turning around to stare at her when she tossed her blond hair in their direction. I tried to imagine what it must feel like to know you're that attractive, but I couldn't.

Nobody fell off or anything, so I guess it was a successful ride. I'd enjoyed it quite a bit until I saw Iris cantering around with her cowboy. I told myself it was ridiculous to be jealous of a thirteen-year-old flirting with somebody she'd never see again, but it made me remember how it felt to be with Chris, how it felt to have somebody look at you that way, like you were special. And I couldn't help wondering if Chris was looking at somebody else that way these days.

I was glad Marsh had had a good ride. It was nice to see him relaxing and smiling easily. Since the day he'd shown me his drawings, I'd started liking the kid more. After all, he was a ten-year-old whose father had just died—he hadn't been catching many breaks lately. Who wouldn't be mad?

Once we dismounted and led our horses into the barn, we started to feel which muscles were going to be sore by the next day. People were walking stiffly, like they still had a horse between their legs.

"I know most of you are headed for the hot tub or the swimming pool," Joe said, "but if anybody wants to hang around I'll show 'em how to curry and cool down their horse."

Most people groaned at the idea, but Iris piped up, "I want to! Can I stay?"

Joe grinned. "See? I knew we had a cowgirl on our hands with you!"

"Really?" Dory asked her. "I'm heading for the hot tub."

Dory's idea sounded good to me, and Marshall was anxious to go to the pool. But the cowgirl and her male admirers stayed behind to "cool down" the horses. I imagined nothing else was going to cool down much.

I think Dory and I would have fallen asleep in the hot tub and hard-boiled ourselves if Marshall hadn't come to get us to change for dinner. We were all as hungry as if we'd been mending fences or branding cattle all day instead of just roaming around on gentle horses' backs.

Even Iris gnawed her baby back ribs down to the bone marrow and took seconds on potato salad. Both kids had had great days and were interrupting each other to talk.

"Those twins Howie and Bobby said that you can learn how to rope a calf if you go to the far barn in the morning," Marshall said. "There's this guy Pete who shows you how to hold the . . ."

Iris was paying no attention to him. "I *love* being in that stable. Everybody really *understands* the horses. You should hear how the guys talk to them, it's . . ."

Marshall leaned forward so Dory's attention was diverted back to him. "*Or,* you can go tubing in the river or even fishing. They have all the equipment in a little house right there . . ."

Iris spoke louder. "Tomorrow I'm going to take the all-day trail ride. Jackson and Glen lead the one that leaves at nine A.M. They pack a lunch for you and everything, and Jackson says . . ."

She had Dory's attention now. "An all-day ride? Are you sure you're ready for that? I know you had a good ride today, but . . ."

"Jackson says I'm a natural on a horse."

Marshall glowered. "I don't think a *natural* would fall off . . ."

Iris whirled around. "Will you stop talking about that? It wasn't my fault!"

I put a hand on Marshall's knee and he managed not to snap back at her.

"It's just that a full day on horseback, if you aren't used to it, can be pretty hard on you," Dory said.

"Well, I'm going. We only have two whole days here and I'm not going to waste one *fishing* or something when I could be riding a horse."

Just then Mel got up on a little stage at one end of the barn with a microphone. "Ladies and gentlemen! Or should I say Cowgirls and Horse Thieves? Anyway, today's Saturday and you all know what that means. It's Square Dance Night at the Lazy River Ranch! While you're all prettyin' up for the festivities, we'll be folding up these tables and chairs and the world-famous Lazy Holler Ramblers'll be tunin' up their fiddles. So go put your cowboy boots on and meet me back here at eight o'clock ready to do-si-do!"

Some people hooted and yelled like a square dance was just what they'd been looking forward to all week. Our table was more subdued.

"I'm not going to any dance," Marshall said.

"Well, it's not exactly my cup of tea either," Dory said, "but it might be fun to watch the other people dance."

Iris chewed a nail. "Do you think they teach you how to do it?"

"I'm sure they do. Most people won't know how."

Iris looked at me. "Are you going to do it?"

Why was that suddenly important? It's not as if we did anything else as a pair. She must have been self-conscious about showing up alone for something she'd never done before. I was a halfway decent dancer, so I said, "I guess. I'll go with you."

She actually smiled. Iris Tewksbury *smiled*. She ran ahead of us back to the bunkhouse and was ripping through her suitcase by the time we got there.

"Of course I didn't bring anything to *wear* to a dance," she said, then glared at Dory. "Why didn't you tell me I'd need a skirt!"

"Well, first of all, I didn't know there would be a dance, and secondly, you don't need a skirt for a square dance. Wear jeans and a fancy shirt."

"I don't even have cowboy boots," she wailed.

"Iris, don't be silly," Dory said.

"Can I go buy some at the ranch store?" she asked, pleading with her eyes.

After some arguing they agreed on a new cowboy-style shirt from the store, but not the incredibly expensive boots. "You kids have to get used to the idea that we don't have unlimited amounts of money anymore. We have to tighten our belts a little bit now." She sounded so apologetic, as if not having five-hundred-dollar cowboy boots was such a terrible thing.

"I don't want any boots," Marsh reminded her.

I had to admit, Iris looked pretty amazing even without cowboy boots. She'd picked a bright blue shirt with stud buttons and LRR (for Lazy River Ranch) embroidered in yellow on the pocket flap. Her hair was tied back, but there were a few loose strands outside the scrunchy for that slightly disheveled look actresses always have. She pulled her soft brown cowboy hat down low on her brow and tucked her shirt into very tight jeans.

"God, I shouldn't have eaten all that potato salad," she said. "I can hardly breathe."

"Wear another pair of pants—you've got others," I said.

"I want to wear *these,*" she said in her usual good humor.

I'd put on the only pair of jeans I'd brought along and my favorite shirt, which was a lime green check, and was sitting on my bed reading while I waited for Iris. I saw her go into the bathroom, but I wasn't paying much attention until I heard the gagging noise. She'd turned on the water faucet, but it wasn't quite loud enough to cover the sound.

Dory was in the other bedroom on the far side of the living

room and Marshall was running around outside with the twins, so neither of them heard it. I knew if I knocked on the door Iris would just deny everything, so I walked right in. She was on her knees in front of the toilet with a finger down her throat.

"Iris! What the hell is going on?"

She gagged again and then coughed, but it didn't look like she was having much luck getting that potato salad back. She got to her feet, looking furious. "None of your damn business. Get out of here!"

"No, I won't. You're trying to puke up your dinner so you can fit into a pair of pants. It's ridiculous."

There were tears squirting from her eyes as she pushed past me out of the bathroom. "You don't know anything about it, so just shut up!"

I followed her, trying to keep my voice low so Dory wouldn't hear. "I know it's a terrible thing to do to your body. And I know you can end up killing yourself with this stupid behavior. Don't you think your mother has enough to worry about right now without a bulimic daughter, too?"

"I'm not bulimic!" she said. "I wish I was, but I'm not. Most of the time I can't even make myself do it. I can't even do *that* right." She flopped down on her bed and picked up a corner of the quilt to dry her face.

"Then don't *try*! You're thin enough already. Most girls would love to have a body like yours."

"You don't understand anything, Robin."

"Well, I'm trying to, if you'd . . ."

"How can I explain it to you when I don't understand it myself?" she said, brushing away the remaining tears. "You can't help me—I'm just messed up, all right?"

Suddenly I felt like it was six years ago and Franny was dissolving in front of me. Except that I'd always loved Franny, even when she was driving other people crazy with her silence and her dark-lidded stares. I forgave Franny for everything because I knew she was in pain. I remembered thinking that if other people saw her heart the way I did, they'd love her, too. Did that mean Iris might possibly have a functional organ beating beneath her designer clothes, too? It occurred to me I ought to feel some sympathy for her, but it wasn't going to be easy.

She stared up at me. "You're not going to tell Mom, are you?"

"Iris . . ."

"Please don't tell her. She'll freak out."

I thought about it. "If you promise to stop doing it, I won't tell her, but you've got to *stop*."

She nodded. "I will. I promise. Okay?" She stood up and tucked her shirt in a little tighter. "*Okay*?"

I sighed. "Okay."

"So, let's get going. I don't want to miss the lessons." She adjusted her hat, rebuckled her big silver belt buckle, and checked her lipstick in the mirror. If I'd been barfing and crying my face would look like sausage, but Iris looked like Dude Ranch Barbie with flat feet. She'd metamorphosed from pitiful weeper to poised fashionista in thirty seconds flat.

The minute we walked into the barn we saw Jackson and Glen leaning against the wall up near the front. They saw us, too, or at least, they saw Iris. Both pairs of bowlegs came striding over immediately.

"Hey, Iris!" Jackson got there first. "Can you dance as well as you ride?"

She blushed. "I don't know how to square dance."

"It's easy," Glen said, trying to get a little face-time with her, too. "The caller tells you what to do and you just follow along."

Hello, there's another person standing here.

You could tell Jackson was used to getting what he wanted. He tipped his hat back on his head and gave Iris a big grin. "I'm the best square-dance teacher there is, ya know." He reached out and took her arm and led her away just as more squares were forming for the next dance.

As we watched them go, Glen looked at me uncomfortably. "Did you want to . . . ?"

"Don't worry about it," I told him. I didn't feel like being anybody's sloppy seconds, so I headed over to the row of chairs that surrounded the dance floor. I remembered the feeling that was starting to rise up in my gut, and I didn't like it at all; I'd felt it so often before meeting Chris—that awful, lonely feeling that nobody would ever appreciate me the way I was.

But just then Jackson called, "Hey, Glen, come on! We need two more to fill up a square. Get her!"

I decided not to turn around—Glen probably wouldn't remember my name either. But he clopped over behind me. "You want to? They need two more."

How could I refuse such a lovely offer? "My name is Robin, by the way," I told him.

"Cool," he said. "Like the bird."

Fortunately, you didn't need to be an original thinker to square dance.

We proceeded to swing our partners, and do-si-do our corners, and honor everybody in sight, all in slow motion until we got it down. Then the band kicked in with some hee-haw music and we were off. Glen wasn't much of a dancer, but you don't have to be good to square dance—you mostly just have to not get in anybody else's way and screw them up, and he was capable of that. Jackson, of course, was a great dancer and seemed to love doing it. Iris did fine, although she was self-conscious and got flustered and mixed-up once or twice.

I decided, the hell with it, I don't know these people, I've got nothing to lose—I can just have fun. And I did. I danced with Glen a few times and then he disappeared into the crowd, but there were lots of ranch hands to go around. I figured they probably got paid to dance with the customers, so I might as well take advantage of it. Dory came in about nine thirty and sat and watched. She looked kind of sad, and I wondered if she was thinking about dancing with Allen before he died.

I'd been do-si-do-ing with a tall, skinny guy who was having a ball, kicking his long legs all over the place and whooping up a storm. So when we finished a song I took him aside and explained the situation with Dory and asked if he'd dance with her a few times. Before she knew what hit her, Tall and Skinny had whipped Dory out of her seat—despite her protests—and was swinging her around the circle.

As the evening wound down, I ran into Glen again and we actually danced one of the few slow dances of the evening together. He was staring over my shoulder most of the time, out into the dark.

"So, do you guys *have* to come and dance with the guests?" I asked.

He gave me a quick grin. "It's part of the job. I don't mind."

Thanks so much. "I don't mind it too much either," I said.

He ducked his head. "Am I being rude? I'm sorry. You're a good dancer."

"Ah-huh. How many people have you said that to tonight?"

"No, really." He smiled again. "A few."

"Some job."

"Yeah. I like it. Not as much as Jackson does, though. Looks like he and your friend ran off somewhere."

"They did?" I looked around the barn and realized I hadn't seen Iris in at least half an hour.

"He's a player," Glen said. "I guess your friend can take care of herself, though."

I stared at him. "She's my cousin, and she's only thirteen years old."

"She is? God, I thought she was sixteen."

"When you say he's a player . . ."

He laughed. "Don't worry. Jackson won't do anything she doesn't want him to—he'd get canned if he messed with a guest. Wait'll I tell him she's only thirteen, though! He sure can pick 'em."

"Maybe I should go check on her," I said. "I don't think she has much experience with guys like that."

He nodded and we broke apart. Then, as I turned to leave, he said, "Hey, Robin, you're not thirteen, too, are you?"

"Not in four years," I said.

He grinned. "Good. Maybe I'll see you tomorrow."

Chapter Thirteen

I checked around the tennis courts and the swimming pool and then down behind the stable, but I wasn't going to wander out into total darkness looking for them—Iris wasn't nearly likable enough for me to risk death by snakebite. Then, as I was walking back to our bunkhouse, there was Jackson himself, suddenly heading right toward me, his long legs covering ground fast. He didn't look happy.

"Hey, do you know where Iris . . . ?"

"In your bunkhouse. Safe and sound," he said through gritted teeth. He barely glanced at me, then strode on past, down to the ranch hands' quarters.

When I came into our living room the only sound I could hear was Marshall's deep breathing from the other bedroom. Dory must still be at the square dance. The only light was from the bathroom I shared with Iris. *Oh, please,* I thought, *don't let her be puking again.*

But when I looked in Iris was just standing in front of the mirror, staring at herself, her blond hair loose and falling in her face.

"Are you okay?" I asked.

She nodded. "What kind of a person do I look like?"

"What?"

She tipped her face up and looked down at herself. "You know. Do I look dumb or something? Or do I look like a baby? I just don't know what I look like."

"Well, you don't look dumb and you don't look like a baby. But apparently you look older than thirteen. What happened with Jackson tonight?"

"He kissed me," she said, staring deeply into her own eyes. "He kissed me a lot."

I took her by the arm and led her out of the bathroom so she'd stop looking at herself like that—it was creeping me out. We sat on her bed in the dark. "Did you want him to kiss you?"

She shrugged. "At first I did. He's cute."

"Yeah, I know, but that doesn't mean he can kiss people whenever he wants to."

"Well, I wanted to kiss him. But then . . ."

"Then what?"

"It's not a big deal . . . I know girls my age who do this stuff. I should have let him." She bent over to untie her shoes and slip them off.

"Let him *what*?"

She sighed and flopped backward on the bed. "Touch me. Under my shirt and stuff. You know."

"Iris! You just met this guy today! *And* he's about eighteen years old!"

"So?"

"*So*, you're only thirteen! God, you can't just let guys do whatever the hell they want!"

"I *didn't* let him. Which is why he hates me now." I heard the catch in her throat and was pretty sure there were tears running down the sides of her face onto the patchwork quilt.

"Iris, you were right not to let him do that. You'll never even see him again once we leave here. And, anyway, you're much too young for him. He and Glen thought you were sixteen."

"They did? Did you tell them I wasn't?"

"Of course I did!"

"Why?" Now I could actually hear her crying.

"Because . . . because a sixteen-year-old flirting like that probably *does* want a boy to try stuff with her. I don't think you know what messages you were giving out."

"What do you know about it? You live out in the sticks."

I almost laughed at that one. "Believe me, Iris, even in the outback of Iowa teenagers are interested in sex. Do you think Jackson is a city boy?"

"Whatever. I *did* want to kiss him—he's cute, and I never got kissed before."

"Your boyfriend, Parker, never kissed you?"

The snuffling calmed down a little. "Parker's thirteen, too—he barely had the nerve to hold my hand."

"Oh." At thirteen I would have been too nervous to touch the opposite sex, too, so my sympathies were definitely with Parker.

Iris bounced her fists on the bed. "This is so embarrassing—I never want to see Jackson again. Which means I can't even go on the trail ride tomorrow." That realization brought on another burst of tears, but at least she was crying about horses now, which seemed more appropriate.

"Aren't there two trail rides every morning? Couldn't you do the other one?"

She gave a deep, shaky sigh. "Yeah, there's a ten o'clock ride, too. Maybe they'll let me switch."

"Sure they will. That Joe guy loves you."

The living room door squeaked open and then clicked closed: Dory was back. Iris sat up, the tears immediately dry.

"Go into the bathroom," I whispered. "I'll talk to her."

"Don't tell her *anything*!" Iris pleaded. "She'll freak!"

"I won't," I said. Iris shut the door behind her and I switched on a light, then walked out to see my aunt. She was getting herself a ginger ale from the fridge.

"Is everybody back? You want a drink?" she asked.

"No, thanks. We're all back. Iris is getting ready for bed."

"Did you two have fun? I saw you dancing with that Glen guy, but I didn't see much of Iris."

"We had fun," I said. "She danced a lot, too, but she came back before I did. You stayed the latest," I said, cleverly shifting the focus to her.

"It's funny. I almost didn't go over at all, and at first I felt so stupid just sitting there all alone. I haven't spent much time alone over the years, I guess. But then one of the cowboys asked me to dance, and then another one did, and pretty soon I didn't have time to catch my breath between dances. Square dancing is so much fun!"

"That's great!" She looked so happy that, without really thinking about it, I gave her a hug.

"I'm so glad you came along on this trip, Robin. I think the three of us were starting to go a little crazy—we needed somebody to get in between us."

Well, that certainly seemed to be where I found myself most of the time—caught in the middle. But I had to admit I didn't mind it as much as I had at the beginning. I said good night to Dory and went back to the other bedroom.

The dance *had* been fun, but it made me wonder what Chris had been doing while I was do-si-do-ing cowboys. After all, he was living with a bunch of kids our age. What were the chances he wouldn't look for another partner?

Iris cracked open the bathroom door. "Is she gone?"

"Yeah, she's going to bed. She had a good time at the dance."

"Did she *dance* with people? Men, I mean?"

"Several, apparently."

Iris seemed a little stunned by the news. She staggered over to her bed and fell onto it like a broken toy. By the time I was done in the bathroom she was under the covers. As soon as I turned out the light, she started to talk.

"I wonder if she wants to get married again? That would be way too weird."

"She might eventually. She's not that old."

"I don't want her to," she said, a touch of anger in her voice. When I didn't respond she said, "But I guess that doesn't really matter, does it?"

"I don't know."

Neither of us said anything for several minutes, and I was dropping off to sleep when Iris said, "Are you in love with your boyfriend? What's his name again?"

I groaned. "I'm half asleep, Iris."

"Just *tell* me."

"Yes! Okay? Yes, I love Chris."

Dammit. Now Chris's ghost was here in the room with me, which was going to make getting to sleep that much harder. I squeezed my eyes shut.

"Do you sleep with him?" Iris sounded wide awake.

"Iris, I'm not talking about this stuff with you. I'm tired!"

"You do, don't you?" She made a gagging noise. "Gross."

"Go to sleep!" I pulled the pillow over my head, knowing I'd have to run through at least half a dozen memories now before I could be happily unconscious.

* * *

Marshall was the first one up, of course, and he had a million ideas about what he wanted to do with the day. He went off to breakfast with Howie and Bobby and their parents so they could get to the roping lesson on time.

"Well, I'm glad I picked this place for an extended stay!" Dory said. "It seems to appeal to everyone."

Iris smiled, but she was quieter than usual at breakfast. She did, however, eat a normal amount of food, which I was glad to see. She'd already checked with Joe and he'd booked her for the later morning trail ride.

Dory and I decided we'd try our hand at fishing this morning, or at least sitting on the riverbank with a pole in our hands, and then in the afternoon, when Marsh joined us, we'd go tubing.

It was funny how different Dory was from Mom, even though they were sisters. I guess living in the city changes you, or maybe Dory wanted to live in the city because she was different to begin with. I don't know. But she always had a nice outfit to put on, with things that matched, like her socks and her blouse, or her earrings and her belt. And every morning she got up early enough to wash her hair and dry it with the hair dryer so it looked perfect, but always the same. She even wore lipstick to go fishing!

I knew exactly what Mom would wear for a trip to a river—her old tennis shoes with the holes in the toes, her jeans, a T-shirt (probably gray), and no jewelry. She'd shower and wash her hair, too, but it would be hanging wet or maybe pulled back with an elastic or stuffed under a hat. And definitely no lipstick.

I wondered if things would change now that Michael Evans was around. After all, she'd worn a white blouse to grill steaks that night he came for dinner. I guess I felt the same way Iris did about the possibility of my mother getting remarried: I didn't want her to. I knew it was selfish, and that I'd probably get used to it if she did, but if you asked me right out I'd have to say, no, the idea gave me gooseflesh.

Dory and I settled down near some cottonwood trees at the edge of the river. The ranch provided nightcrawlers for bait, which was what I'd used the times I'd gone fishing in Iowa, too. I baited my hook, threw it in, and looked over at Dory. She was making an awful face trying to stick the worm on her hook.

"Need help?" I asked.

She sighed. "I used to fish all the time back home. I can do this." But after a minute or two she'd mangled her worm to death and had thrown it in the river in disgust. "God, I've turned into a wimp. Can't even bait a hook anymore."

I took her pole and stuck the bait on the hook. It's not that hard.

Dory smiled. "Thanks. What would I do without you?" She dropped her hook into the water with a little splash. "I know I keep saying that, but I'm so relieved at how well the kids have taken to you, Robin."

I must have laughed.

"They *have*!" Dory said. "They can be monsters when they don't like somebody."

Yeah, I'd sure hate to see *that*.

Dory swished her line around in the river absentmindedly. "I'm afraid there may be some fireworks ahead, though."

"What do you mean?"

She grimaced. "I have to tell them about school in the fall. They won't be happy. I needed to find a different school for Marshall, anyway, so I made a big decision: I'm putting them both in public school."

"You are?"

She nodded. "There's a good one not far from our apartment, which is a combination middle and high school. I wanted to send them to public school to begin with, but Allen always felt . . . well, we could afford private schools and he wanted the best for them. But now, I have to be more careful with my money if I'm going to be able to afford college for them both. I've got a teaching job for the fall at a high school across town. Obviously, we're not poor, but we can't have everything we want anymore either—choices have to be made."

"Will the kids be upset?"

"Marsh knows he'll be at a new school—he may not care too much which one it is. But Iris! She loves Forest Hill. All her friends are there. I know it will be tough, but I always had a few issues with the attitudes they picked up there, anyway."

So Dory did notice her kids were snobs!

"When are you going to tell them?"

"Soon. I'm not sure. I was hoping once they started having fun on this trip it would be easier to hand out the news. They're having fun now, but I'm not sure it's enough to soften the blow. Anyway, I thought you should be prepared—there may be some rough water ahead."

"I can swim," I said.

"I know you can," she said. "Better than the rest of us."

We didn't catch anything, but that was okay. Fishing isn't really about catching fish anyway. Grandma always used to say, "*Fishin' is just gettin' off your feet and watchin' the river flow by.*" When I reminded Dory of that, she smiled, but tears came to her eyes. Even though you couldn't always see her sadness on the outside, I had the feeling her inside was so filled up with it, it didn't take much to spring a leak.

While we were eating lunch, Mel got up on the little stage and read out the names of the people who'd gotten mail. "Robin Daley," he called out.

I jumped up from the bench so fast I kicked Marshall in the shoulder. "Ow, be careful, would ya'?"

"Sorry, Marsh," I said, giving his shoulder a quick rub before I headed down the aisle to claim my letter. As I was walking toward him, Mel said, "And another one for the lovely Robin. You're mighty popular, sweetheart!" He handed me a postcard and a letter in a thin blue envelope. The letter, of course, was from Chris, but I didn't want to rip it open in front of an audience, so I walked back to my seat, trying to look at the postcard instead. The words kept blurring.

"Two pieces of mail!" Dory said.

"Yeah. The postcard is from . . ." I concentrated on the signature. "Oh, Franny!" I flipped it over to the picture side and laughed—it was a picture of our strip mall. "This is where she works—in the video store."

I tried to make my heart stop booming so I could read the card from Franny, but it was hard to forget there were words from Chris, words that might say anything at all, sitting in a sealed envelope in my lap.

My hand was shaky as I held up Franny's card and read it out loud.

"Dear Runaway,

It's your fault I'm forced to spend so much time with Des Sanders. He said to tell you thanks. Liz says you might decide to stay in New Mexico with your dad, but I told her she's nuts. If you don't come back, you're dead meat. Say hi to Ben Affleck for me when you get to L. A., and bring me back a cowboy!

Yours in Purgatory,

Franny."

"What's purgadory?" Marshall said.

"An uncomfortable place," Dory told him, then said to me, "I like your friend. She's funny."

"Yeah. We're like sisters."

"Oh, wait! *Franny.* She's the one with the crazy parents. She practically lived with you for a while, right?"

I nodded. "Things have calmed down more now. Her parents don't fight over her anymore. As a matter of fact, they sort of ignore her."

"Is she okay?"

"More or less. She still gets mad at her parents, but she's kind of outgrown them. She writes poems about the whole thing."

"Well, that gives me hope."

"What do you mean?"

"She means maybe me and Iris won't grow up to be ax murderers either," Marsh said.

"Iris and *I*," Dory said. She glanced at the blue envelope balanced on my clenched knees. "That from Chris?"

I nodded.

"Who's Chris?" Marshall asked.

"Another of Robin's friends," Dory said, rising and pulling Marsh with her. "We'll go back to the bunkhouse and put on our suits. Take your time with your letter."

"Thanks," I said. I waited until I saw them walk all the way back to the bunkhouse before I even moved. Finally, I picked up the letter and walked out of the barn—I wasn't going to read it surrounded by busboys tossing silverware into aluminum basins. Behind the barn were some wooden chairs from which there was a pretty view over to the mountains. Nobody was in any of them at the moment, so I sat down and looked at my envelope. It was all I had of Chris anymore. In a way, I hated to read it because once I'd read it the anticipation of what might be inside would be over. All I'd have of Chris, again, would be old news. I looked out at the mountains for a few minutes, then slid my finger under the flap of the envelope and ripped it open.

Dear Robin,

I've been here almost a week and I still haven't heard from you. I guess the mail is slow between America and Italy, but still, I'm feeling kind of lonely. I thought you'd write me as soon as I left. I hope this doesn't mean you're still mad at me.

I'm learning a lot here, but the program is hard. We have Italian classes for two hours every morning, then an hour of Roman history before lunch and an International Relations class after lunch. It's so hot here nobody feels like studying in the afternoon—in fact, the Italians mostly take siestas then (or whatever they call them here) and we do, too! I study in the late afternoon when it cools off a little bit, and then around seven o'clock I usually go to dinner with my roommate Charlie and my two friends from Milan, Giacomo and Dante. We usually eat at school and then go out to walk around the city, but sometimes we decide to eat in a restaurant instead.

The food here is so wonderful. You'd love it, Robin. Pasta—your favorite thing—with every meal! And everybody drinks wine here, even the little kids—there's no such thing as being underage. Even the school serves wine with dinner! It's great having Giacomo and Dante show us the city. They've been to Rome many times before so they know where everything is. They make fun of our Italian, which is quite lousy, but I think they enjoy showing us their country. I've started drinking espresso coffee in those little cups. It always seemed stupid to me in Iowa, but here everybody does it. It gives you a great buzz, especially after a carafe or two of red wine!

My other roommate, Rob, doesn't hang around with Charlie and me much. He's the one I told you about who's kind of a snob. He found this group of kids who are going to the Ivies next year—you know, Harvard, Yale, Princeton, etc.—and he hangs with them. Suits me fine—I don't need somebody looking down his nose at me just because I'm from the Midwest. It does make me worry a little bit, though, whether there will be kids at Georgetown who'll feel that way, too.

Robin, please write to me. I couldn't stand to go the whole summer without hearing from you. I miss you so much, even more than I thought I would. I wish you were in Rome, too, so you could be seeing these wonderful things with me. Someday we'll come here together!

All my love,

Chris

Chapter Fourteen

I started composing a letter to Chris in my head even before I'd finished reading his. He'd sent such a great letter, I felt awful that I hadn't written to him immediately, the minute his plane left Cedar Rapids. It hadn't occurred to me that he'd be lonely, too—I thought he'd be having such a great time in Italy he wouldn't even think of me. At first I felt sort of smug reading the part about how he missed me more than he thought he would, but then I also felt guilty. The truth was, I'd actually missed Chris *less* than I thought I would.

Since I'd come on this trip I'd been so busy dealing with my crazy relatives, and wondering if each new stage of our journey would be a triumph or a tragedy, that Chris hadn't actually been on my mind all that much. If I *thought* about him, I missed him, but—and I was stunned to realize it—I just hadn't thought about him all that much. At least, not since I left Iowa.

By the time I got back to the bunkhouse, Marsh and Dory were ready to go down to the lake.

"Would you mind if I came down a little later?" I asked. "I want to answer Chris's letter right away."

Marsh looked disappointed. "You mean, I have to go tubing with just *Mom*?"

Dory sighed. "You poor thing. There'll probably be some other kids down there, too."

"I'll come as soon as I'm finished," I promised.

"I'm taking my drawing tablet along, just in case I get bored," he said.

After they'd flip-flopped down the path, I sat at the desk in the living room and took a piece of thick ivory stationary out of the top drawer. It said Lazy River Ranch across the top in swirling red letters. I sat and stared at the paper for a while.

A month ago I'd imagined this summer much like the one before it—Chris and I trying to get our work schedules to match up so we could spend afternoons at the lake or evenings at the Fish Shack, and this year, if we were lucky, up in my bedroom. It would have been a great couple of months. But back then, I would never have imagined a summer like this one: me sending letters from the Lazy River Ranch in Wyoming to Chris at the Via della Vittorio in Rome, Italy. For some reason, sitting there looking at those red letters, I began to understand that we were both having adventures.

Dear Chris,

Your second letter arrived today. I'm so sorry I didn't write to you the minute you left—I was so upset I did nothing but eat junk food for about four days. But I did write to you from a motel in Minnesota, and now I'm writing you from a ranch in Wyoming.

Before I tell you about my trip though, I want to make sure you know that I do miss you, and I'm not *mad at you, and I love you as much as ever. I wish I was in Rome with you or you were here in Wyoming with me, but we can do all those things together later, like you said. I'm lonely for you, too, Chris, but it won't be long before we're together again, at least for a while.*

I can't believe how much studying you have to do! I hope Italian comes more easily to you than French did—as I recall it wasn't your favorite subject. I wish I could meet Charlie and Giacomo and Dante, and go out for a big pasta dinner with you all! I'd have some of that wine, too, but I don't think I could get into espresso—isn't it sort of like drinking coffee grounds?

I think the last time I wrote to you it was mostly about how horrible my cousins were. I might have to take a little of that back. They are pretty annoying sometimes and crazy all the time, but now that I've gotten to know them a little better I don't hate them anymore. Iris and Marshall have both got some problems to work out, partly from that fancy shmancy school they went to, but mostly from their father's death. And my aunt Dory is sad a lot of the time, too. I feel bad for them, up to a point, and then suddenly I just want to scream at them, "You're only making things worse!" (Which, now that I think about it, is probably what you were thinking about me before you left for Italy.)

Anyway, I think this trip might be helping the kids a little bit. Iris seems to be rediscovering a love for horses, and Marshall has begun to draw a few things that aren't covered in blood. He's an amazing artist for a ten-year-old.

So far we've driven through Minnesota and South Dakota and most of eastern Wyoming. The Badlands are fabulous—maybe we could go there together some time, too! And Wyoming is amazingly beautiful. We're staying at a dude ranch for a few days—riding horses, fishing, swimming, even square dancing. It's nice because we all like it here—nobody's complaining for a change. Next we're going to Denver, and then, I think, south to Texas. This is the s-l-o-w route to California. Sometimes home seems terribly far away. It must really seem that way to you. But it's nice to know we can leave Thunder Lake and it doesn't go anywhere—it's still there waiting for us to return. You know what I mean?

Mom is forwarding your mail on to me at addresses Dory gave her before we left, so please keep writing. There's nothing better than getting a letter from you. When you go to dinner tonight, think of me with every forkful of pasta you put in your mouth, and don't ever forget how much I love you.

Love, love, love,
Robin

I sealed the letter in an envelope and slipped it inside my shirt for just a minute, next to my heart. As soon as I'd started writing the letter my longing for Chris had come back with a vengeance. Writing my feelings down was frustrating—sheets of paper and stamps and all the time zones between us made it so complicated. I was used to looking into his eyes when I said I loved him—but writing a letter I had to wonder where he'd be, who he'd be with, what kind of mood he'd be in when he read it a week from now. We'd been apart two weeks already. He'd made new friends I'd never meet. Would he be different when we met again? Would he still be my Chris?

I ran right over to the ranch store to get stamps and mail the letter, my ambassador to Rome. I bought a few postcards, too, one for Mom (a trail ride at sunset) and one for Franny (a cowboy clown riding a horse backward). I told Mom about the square dance the night before, but not all the extraneous details, of course. Just about how much fun we'd had dancing with ranch hands. To Franny, I wrote:

Dear Gwyneth,

I am only slightly stupider looking on horseback than this guy, but you should see me do-si-do a cowboy! The trip is sort of fun, even though my aunt and cousins are bizarro. Don't listen to a word your mother says, and tell Des Sanders he owes me big. Ben says take a number.

Love,
Winona

Writing to Franny made me miss her too. I had the feeling if I could just talk to her about Iris and Marshall, she'd be able to help me understand them better. She'd make me *want* to understand them.

By the time I got down to the river, Dory was drifting sleepily in her tube, but Marsh had gotten out, dried off, and was sitting under a tree, drawing.

"*Finally,*" he said when he saw me coming.

"Sorry." I dropped down beside him. "You got tired of floating?"

He shrugged. "It was fine—I just feel like drawing a lot these days. There's lots to draw here."

"Can I see?"

He handed the pad over to me without me having to beg. The picture he'd been working on was a close-up of the grasses and wildflowers that surrounded his shady nook—and then off in the distance, in the background, was Dory in an inner tube on the river, her legs dangling loosely over the side. I expected the drawing itself to be good after seeing the earlier stuff he'd done, but the great thing about this one was the perspective he'd gotten on the scene. It was so original.

"I love this one, Marsh. It's great!"

"I've drawn other stuff at the ranch, too, while you guys were eating or dancing or something," he said.

I flipped back through the book. There was a picture of two kids who looked alike—must be Howie and Bobby—playing with cats. "Those cats are nice," Marshall said. "They don't scratch. We call them Pinkie and Marmalade."

"They look like good cats." I flipped back again, and there was a drawing of a horse in its stable, nostrils open and sniffing. "Is this Okie?"

"Yeah. I didn't want to forget him."

"Marsh, you'll never need a camera—your pictures are better

than photographs because they have the feeling of the place in them." I wasn't just giving him some bull either—I meant it.

"This is the first one I did here." He turned back one more page to a drawing of Iris sitting at a table in the barn with a heaping plate of food in front of her, staring off into the distance. He must have drawn it the night we arrived. He'd captured the look on her face perfectly—deliberate disdain almost covering up any vulnerability, except for the eyes. When you looked at the eyes, you could see Iris in there, hiding.

"This is wonderful, Marsh. I mean it."

"Yeah? I'm not showing it to Iris. She'd hate it."

"Hmm. You might be right. It gets down inside her—she might not appreciate it. Did you show these to your mom, though?"

Marshall sighed. "Maybe I will one of these days. She'll get all *happy* about it, you know? Because I'm not drawing bloody stuff. She'll think it's a *big thing*."

I nodded. "She might."

"It's not like I'm never gonna draw anything bloody again. I like drawing cartoons. But after I drew that fish fossil at the Badlands I started to think it might be fun to try drawing some other stuff, too. I'm just experimenting."

"No harm in that. I won't tell anybody," I said, realizing I now knew secrets from each of my cousins that I couldn't report to their mother. This probably wasn't what Dory expected when she asked me along to help her with her children. But, hey, helping didn't mean I had to be her spy.

Marsh mumbled something I couldn't hear.

"What?"

"I'm sorry about that time at the fair." He looked at me guiltily, but I wasn't catching on. "You know, about the Ferris wheel. I said it was your fault I didn't go on it."

"Oh, right. No big deal."

He stared at his tablet. "I get scared sometimes. I don't know why. I never used to."

I knew it was important not to say the wrong thing, but I didn't know what the right thing was. So I said what I thought. "Everybody gets scared, Marsh. I think the older you are, the more scared you get."

He looked at me, surprised. "I thought grown-ups *didn't* get scared."

I shook my head. "I think grown-ups are scared of lots of things because they know bad stuff can happen to people. You know that now, too."

"Yeah. But grown-ups can get on a stupid Ferris wheel."

I thought about that one. "Well, I guess they know that bad things *can* happen, but they usually *don't*. You're taking a chance when you ride a Ferris wheel, but it's not a very big chance. You can't give up doing everything that's a little bit risky, or life wouldn't be much fun."

He kicked his heel into the dirt. "My dad got killed just crossing the street."

"I know. It was a terrible accident, but you haven't stopped crossing streets, have you?"

He shook his head. "I'm really careful now, though."

"Well, that's okay. You should be." I wanted to put my arm around him, but I was afraid that might be stepping over the line. He was staring at his drawing pad again, trying, I thought, not to cry.

"I'm going to swim a little, okay?" I said.

He nodded without looking at me. But when I stood up and patted him on the shoulder, he didn't flinch. For just a second I had an urge to ruffle his hair, but I stopped myself. God, I must be turning into a grown-up.

I swam a little while and then sat in Marsh's tube. What a

luxury to have nothing to do on such a beautiful afternoon—not only did I not have to scoop ice cream for sweaty kids, but somebody else was probably getting the coals ready to roast *my* dinner. I could get into this vacation thing. Marsh went back to the bunkhouse before Dory and I got out of the water; I hoped I hadn't said anything to upset him. By the time we returned the tubes to the shed and climbed back up from the river, we saw Iris heading into bunkhouse number 12, too.

"How was the ride?" Dory asked Iris as soon as we came inside. "Are you exhausted?"

I was a little nervous to hear Iris's answer—I wasn't sure how much of the glory of yesterday's ride had to do with Jackson paying so much attention to her. But I needn't have worried. She was dusty but radiant—it was horses she loved.

"I adore this place!" she said. "And I adore Silverfoot! When we get back to Chicago, do you think we could find someplace for me to take riding lessons? Maybe there's a place where they do western saddle, and I could learn barrel racing and stuff. Could we try to find one?"

"We can try," Dory said. "Who were the leaders on your ride?"

Iris's smile dimmed a bit. "Two older guys—I forget their names. They were nice, though."

"Too bad you missed the early ride with Jackson and Glen." Dory thought she was teasing her daughter, but Iris grimaced.

"The older guys know better what they're doing," she said. "They aren't such *hotshots.*" She glanced at me when she said this and I had to lower my eyes so as not to give anything away.

After another huge dinner, Mel announced that tonight was the weekly rodeo at the corral. Not a real rodeo, with bulls and everything, but one where the kids could try their hands at roping calves, and whoever wanted to could do some barrel racing, and then a few of the cowboys, the hotshots, I figured, would do some rope tricks and ride a bronc or two. Marsh wasn't going to do anything, but when Bobby and Howie ran forward to sign up for calf roping, Marsh followed along. "I was better at it than them," he told Dory.

Iris asked Joe if he thought she could do some barrel racing and he said, "Sure!" like he always did, so she signed up for that. Dory about had a heart attack.

"Iris, you've never even done it before! Don't be ridiculous . . ."

"I'm not trying to win or anything. I just want to do it."

"There are some risks that are just foolhardy, Iris . . ."

"Joe said it was okay, and I can ride Silverfoot. Don't worry, I won't fall off him."

Iris was stubborn, and Dory finally gave up, although I could tell she was really scared about letting Iris ride. It reminded me of the talk I'd had with Marsh this afternoon. I think once somebody in your family dies, you must get very worried about the rest of them.

We sat on the top rail of the fence to watch. Just as the kids' roping contest got started somebody swung up onto the fence next to me: Glen.

"Hey," he said.

I said hi back, figuring that would be all he'd expect from me. I was surprised to find he was in a talkative mood tonight.

"So, I hear you guys are leaving tomorrow."

This was big news in the cowboy bunkhouse? I wondered if the story of Iris and Jackson had made the rounds there.

"Yeah. On to Denver next."

He nodded. "Where you headed after that?"

"Los Angeles is the final destination, but we're not in a hurry. It's the trip that's important." Out of the corner of my eye, I thought I noticed Dory smiling.

"I've never been out to the coast," he said. "Never seen an ocean."

"I haven't either. This'll be my first time."

"I guess it's real nice to look out over all that water."

I had to stop talking to him then to cheer for Marshall who'd managed to get the rope over the head of a hay bale with a plastic cow head on one end. Three other boys had achieved the same goal, including Howie. Bobby was standing next to his father, hands shoved in his pockets, looking sullen. I felt bad for him; one of the hardest things about growing up is figuring out there are some things you just aren't going to be very good at.

With the four winners still in the corral, Mel shooed half a dozen calves out of the barn. They were still pretty young and kind of spooked by all the noise and people, but Mel chased them out into the middle. "Okay, wranglers, see if you can catch ya a real live calf!"

"Oh, my Lord," Dory said. "I didn't know they'd let them do that! They'll get trampled!"

Glen leaned over. "Nah, the most that happens is they get a few scrapes or a rope burn or something. No big deal."

I patted Dory's arm. "It's okay. Look, Marsh isn't scared."

She looked up at her son. "You're right. He's not." She managed a small smile, then clenched her jaw. "Okay, I can be calm, too."

Sure enough Marsh managed to swing the rope high enough and wide enough to get it over the head of a calf. I thought Dory would fall off the fence. "Pull it tight!" she screamed, as if she was at the Little League championship. Pulling it tight proved harder for Marsh to accomplish. The calf stepped through the large loop of the rope with one foot and tripped itself. Marsh ran up to it, I guess to take the rope off—he was probably afraid the cow would get hurt—but the calf jumped up suddenly as he approached and knocked him over. The rope tightened then and Marsh got dragged a few feet behind the scared animal until he let go of the rope.

"Yay, Marshall!" I screamed, hoping he would not stand up with a bloody, tear-streaked face.

Mel hauled him to his feet almost immediately and announced, "The winner of the calf-roping contest! Let's give this cowboy a hand!"

Everybody whooped and hollered so loudly that Marsh's stunned look soon turned into a huge smile. There was no facial blood evident, but when he came running back to us, a blue ribbon pinned to his shirt, he held out his palms, scratched up, rope burned, and filthy. "I *won*!"

"You were great out there," Glen told him, then reached in his shirt pocket and pulled out a tube of salve. "Go wash your hands real good and then put this on 'em—by tomorrow they'll be almost like new."

Dory took the salve and shakily climbed down the fence to help Marsh clean himself up.

"You always carry that stuff around with you?" I asked Glen.

"For the rodeos. Makes the kids feel like real cowboys if I tell 'em what to do. If their mothers gave it to 'em, they'd feel like sissies."

"Aren't you the psychologist?"

He shrugged. "By tomorrow his hands'll feel like hell, but he won't bitch about it too much because he used the magic cowboy potion. You wait and see."

I smiled. "Do you do this all year round?"

"No. I just finished my first year at the University of Arizona. I grew up about an hour from here, which in Wyoming is right in the neighborhood. This is my third summer working for Mel."

I liked talking to Glen—the conversation was easy and natural. By the time Dory and Marsh got back we'd covered topics such as his major (animal husbandry), why he chose Arizona (his girlfriend was going there, but they broke up two weeks into the first semester), and why I was traveling all over the country with my cousins (I gave him Dory's story, not mine).

We hadn't even noticed that the barrel racing had started until Dory and Marshall got back and she said, "Iris didn't race yet, did she? I didn't miss her?"

I said she hadn't, but I was embarrassed that I didn't really know for sure. How could I have gotten so involved talking with Glen that I wasn't even watching? Thank goodness, a few minutes later we saw Iris come trotting out of the barn on Silverfoot, her brown hat tilted back, her chin held high.

Each horse did the circuit alone so there was no chance of running into anybody else—the contest was just about who was the fastest. Mel started everybody off and held the stopwatch. Most of the kids weren't very good, although two of the girls were obviously veterans. Iris didn't go very fast—you could tell she was sort of nervous leaning so far over to the side when Silverfoot rounded the barrels—but she didn't fall off and she finished the race. Joe ran up and took Silverfoot's reins when she finished and you could tell he was praising her performance. I sort of wished we could stay here longer, for Iris's sake.

She was so happy when she came to join us on the fence—positively glowing. Glen said hello to her and told her she'd done a great job, and she thanked him, but she didn't look at his face.

As I'd imagined, Jackson was among the cowboys demonstrating their roping and riding skills.

"Aren't you going to show off, too?" I asked Glen.

He grinned. "Not tonight. Sometimes I sit one out so Jackson can look good."

"Oh, what a good sport," I said, teasing him. Who'd have guessed he'd be so easy to talk to?

When the rodeo was over we all headed back to the bunkhouse and Glen walked part of the way with us. When the others pulled ahead he stopped walking and I did too.

"Well, I guess I'll say good-bye since you're leaving in the morning."

"Yeah. Nice to talk to you."

He nodded. "I wish you were staying longer. That's the problem with this job—you just get to know somebody and then they leave."

I knew right then that Glen wanted to kiss me and I was shocked. Chris was the only boy I'd ever kissed—since I met him I'd never even thought about kissing anybody else. What was even worse was, I sort of wanted Glen to kiss me. Not that I had a big crush on him or anything, but I liked him, and it would have been very nice to kiss him, a sweet memory to take away from the Lazy River Ranch.

Of course, I *couldn't* kiss him. No way. I'd really feel like a totally horrible person then. The only thing I could think to do was to stick out my hand. I felt very dorky, but Glen got the message. We shook hands, and said good-bye, and I ran on into the living room of our bunkhouse. I closed the door and my eyes simultaneously, thankful to have escaped a close call. But when I opened my eyes, Iris was standing in front of me, waiting, fuming, her hands on her hips.

"What is going *on*, Robin? I thought you had a *boyfriend*?"

Chapter Fifteen

Apparently Iris was hoping to stay up late into the night debating whether it was right or wrong for me to enjoy Glen's company for a few hours if I was in love with someone else. I assured her all we'd done was talk.

"You were walking awfully close to him," she said accusingly. "And laughing, too!"

"There's a law against laughing?"

"You know what I mean!"

I did, but I wasn't going to admit it to a thirteen-year-old. "Calm down, Iris," I said, and walked into the bathroom to get ready for bed. She followed me.

"You said you were in love with Chris!"

"I *am*. I didn't *do* anything!"

"You better not."

"What are you—the Romance Police?"

She watched me in the mirror as I brushed my teeth, which gave me time to remember her indiscretions of the night before. I spit, then said, "What about you? You kissed Jackson last night and you have a boyfriend at home."

She scowled. "First of all, I'm not in love with Parker, and second of all . . . he's not my boyfriend anymore."

"I thought you said you were hanging on to him until you got home?"

She shook her head and flopped down on the toilet seat.

"You already broke up with him?"

I could barely hear her say, "He broke up with me before we left."

"Oh." I soaped up my face and tried to think of the right response. After all, it wasn't like this was a tragedy—most thirteen-year-olds' relationships didn't last more than a few weeks.

"You can't tell Mom, though."

I sighed. Every day there were more things I couldn't tell *Mom*. "Why not? I don't think she was expecting you to marry the guy."

"Just *don't*. I don't want her to think there's something wrong with me."

"Don't be ridiculous—she wouldn't think that. People break up with each other all the time." Iris gave me a nasty look, grabbed her nightgown off the back of the door, and went into the bedroom.

I waited until we were both in bed and the light was out. "The only thing wrong with you is your barfing habit." It wasn't actually the *only* thing wrong, but I was in a generous mood.

She sprang back up. "It's not a habit. I only do it once in a while."

"Yeah, only after the meals where you've actually eaten something."

"So, are you, like, *watching* me all the time now?"

"Should I be?"

"No!"

"Okay. Then you don't need to watch me either."

She threw herself down on the bed and burrowed beneath the

quilt. I don't know about Iris, but I fell asleep right away. Although not before wondering if I'd see Glen in the morning.

Of course I didn't. Glen was out on an early morning trail ride by the time we packed up the car and checked out. Just as well—what would have been the point? Even if I was ever going to see him again, it would be silly to lead him on when I already had a boyfriend. Although, now that I thought about it, I didn't much like the idea that I'd never be able to get to know any other boys ever again, unless I broke up with Chris. Which would be terrible, of course. But at least I wouldn't feel guilty for even thinking about somebody else!

I drove first. Everybody was quiet as we left the Lazy River Ranch—I think we all would have been happy to spend another few days there. As soon as I pulled back out onto the highway I got a little thrill, like *here we go again!* There's something so exciting about starting out on a trip, wondering what you'll see and do—and this trip started new every day. I think I could get addicted to life on the road.

When we crossed into Colorado, the mountains got bigger. Dory asked if I was nervous driving in them, but I loved driving those roads. They were like roads on postcards, with big pine trees growing close on both sides so you felt like you were in a green tunnel. Then, when you came around a corner, the view was suddenly opened wide and you could see the Rocky Mountains with their snowy peaks.

We were headed for Denver, but Marshall had been reading the guidebook and wanted to stop in a town called Golden first, to see the grave of Buffalo Bill. We weren't in any hurry so we did. Actually his first choice was to go to Water World water park, but

Dory said that was the kind of thing you could do anywhere, so they compromised on Buffalo Bill.

Marsh was telling us all about a book he'd read on Buffalo Bill and Annie Oakley and their Wild West shows. He was all excited about seeing where the guy was buried, but when we got out of the car and actually walked up to the big white stone, he got very quiet. After a minute I realized we were *all* very quiet, and it hit me why that would be. I was the only person there not suddenly remembering the last time I was at a grave site, or at least, the only person not remembering it sadly.

All four of us stood staring mournfully at Buffalo Bill's grave as if he'd just passed on yesterday. The silence was starting to give me a headache, but then Dory suggested we go through the museum as long as we were there—probably just to get us away from the grave. For some reason, looking at a bunch of old guns didn't do much to perk us up either, so we went for lunch. Eating usually cheered people up, I'd noticed, even those who might not be planning to actually *digest* that cheeseburger.

I was keeping my eye on Iris now, although I hoped she wouldn't notice. She went into the bathroom first, but I followed soon enough after that I figured I'd be able to tell what had gone on. She passed me on her way out and smiled. "Don't worry, Scooby Doo, you won't find any clues in there." So much for subtlety.

Dory had found the Denver Botanic Gardens on her map and was determined to locate the real thing. When Iris and Marsh heard this, they dug in their heels.

"A *garden*?" Marshall said. "Talk about something you can see anywhere."

"No, you can't," Dory explained. "Each region of the country grows different kinds of plants. I love botanical gardens."

As soon as we pulled into the place, Iris said, "I'm going to sit under that big tree and read. It's too hot to tramp all over the place. I'll look at your pictures later."

"Yeah!" Marsh agreed. "I'll stay here and draw. I like *drawing* plants."

I could see Dory wasn't crazy about the idea of leaving them alone. I wouldn't have minded walking through the place just for the exercise, but then I remembered Dory with the squash and watermelons at the state fair. She was probably a fanatic about peonies or something, too.

"I'll stay here with them. I have my book along."

"Are you sure? It's such a beautiful place."

"It's beautiful right here, too," I said. "We'll enjoy one small part in depth while you take the grand tour."

Rather than being disappointed not to have company, Dory seemed sort of excited. I guess she didn't get many chances to be by herself. She traded her sandals for hiking boots, dug a flower book out of the back of the car, and headed off, stopping every three feet to squat down and look a daisy in the eye. This wasn't going to be a walk, it was going to be a meander. Just like this whole trip—the Zigzag Plan.

The three of us grabbed our books and other gear and waved good-bye to her, for about five minutes. Finally she was out of sight and we sprawled on the grass under a huge beech tree.

"That was brilliant!" Marshall said, looking at me with huge eyes. "That thing about how we'll see one part *in depth* while she tramps all over the place—she really bought it."

"Oh, right. Like she thinks we're going to be studying nature while she's gone," said Iris. "She's not *that* stupid."

I had to agree. "I think she just wanted to be alone, to tell you the truth."

"I know how she feels. I wouldn't mind being alone for a change either," Iris said.

"Me neither," Marsh agreed. "I'm sick of always being with *girls.*"

I laughed. "Well, I'm fairly sick of you guys, too, but we're stuck with one another for a few more weeks, anyway."

After a moment's silence, Iris shrugged. "I guess it could be worse."

"Yeah," Marshall said. "We could be here without Robin."

Denver was okay. We did some city stuff. Ate in fancy restaurants, stayed in a big hotel, went to the zoo, went to an art museum. Marsh really enjoyed the museum; it was fun to watch him soak up the paintings he really liked.

I kept waiting for Dory to bring up the subject of the new school, but she didn't. Maybe because we'd somehow managed the delicate balance of goodwill among cousins and she was afraid to rock the boat. Then, the morning we were leaving Denver, Dory said, "Oh, heck, let's go to Water World after all!" It smacked of bribery; I figured she'd spring the news on them before nightfall.

We parked in the sprawling lot and opened the back of the van to search through the luggage for our swimming suits. I pulled out my old Speedo, which had once been red and white, but was now more like gray and pink from many hours in the sun and Thunder Lake. Iris had unpacked two tiny strips of vivid blue cloth from her bag and let them dangle from her fingers while she inspected my suit.

"You're wearing *that*?" From the look on her face you'd have thought the Speedo was made from small dead animals.

"What's wrong with it?"

Marshall glanced over. "Looks sort of dirty," he said.

"It isn't *dirty,*" I said. "It's just faded."

"And about thirty years old," Iris continued. She picked at the seat gingerly. "The elastic's all out of it."

I snatched it back from her. "So? I've had it for a while. I like it." Even as I was defending it, I was remembering the way the material crawled up in the crack of my butt so I had to keep pulling at it all the time. But who even cared? Just because these two were used to having everything brand new all the time. . . .

"I'll tell you what," Dory said. "They have a shop right here. Let me buy you a new suit."

Dory was on their side. Embarrassed to hang around in a stupid water park with somebody in an old swimming suit. I glared at her.

"Robin, you haven't let me buy you *anything* on this trip," she said. "These two want everything they see, but you don't ask for anything. Let me get you this. Please? You can't really say you don't *need* a new suit." She smiled kindly.

Of course I needed a new suit. Why hadn't I realized that before I left Iowa? Mom would have given me the money for it. Letting Dory replace my ragged old suit was too humiliating. I shook my head.

"*Why not?*" Iris was incredulous.

Dory turned to her daughter with an irritated look. "Because your cousin was raised, as I was myself, to get full use out of an item before you throw it away and buy yourself a new one. I fully approve of that and I wish I'd been able to pass a little bit of midwestern frugality on to the two of you." Then she turned back to me. "But really, Robin, that suit has outlived its usefulness."

When she put it that way, I had to laugh. "I guess you're right."

All four of us walked around the swim shop looking at the overpriced tubes of rubbery material. Marshall's contribution was primarily to point out the particularly ugly suits or the ones with flippy skirts to cover problem thighs.

"Get this one!" he said, holding up a tiger-print suit with a tiger head snarling toothily in the crotch vicinity.

Iris thought I needed a bikini. "You're not *that* old and fat," she told me. I thanked her heartily.

I tried on a few as quickly as possible and settled for another Speedo with a racer back—black and orange this time.

Dory approved, Iris said it was okay if I wanted to look like an athlete, and Marshall, by then, had lost all interest in me and was trying on goggles.

I actually thought I looked pretty good in the new suit—the extra pounds I'd put on after Chris left must have gotten worked off by all the exercise I'd been getting. Still, I was glad I'd stuck my old red-and-white suit back in my bag instead of pitching it as Iris suggested. I might want it again when I got back to Iowa. It was hard to know what I'd want, what I'd be like, after a trip like this.

An odd thing happened when we got back to the parking lot after a few hours of sun and water. I offered to drive because Dory seemed a little bit tired—I thought she might have a headache because she kept squinting her eyes into the distance. But she said she was fine; she wanted to drive. So we climbed into the car and she turned on the ignition, then sat there staring out the windshield like she was at a drive-in movie.

"Dory, are you okay?" I asked.

She nodded. "Just thinking about things."

"Let's get rolling!" Marshall commanded.

Dory put the car in reverse and without even looking in the mirror or anything, started to back out of the space.

"Mom! Stop!" Iris screamed. "There's a car . . ."

The rear bumpers of the two minivans banged each other and then bounced free.

"Oh, my God!" Dory pulled the car back into the space and

jumped out. "Are you all right? Is anybody hurt?" she yelled, running to see.

A woman got out of the matching van. "We're okay. I'm sorry—I thought you saw me backing out. It seemed like you were waiting . . ."

"Oh, I was. I mean, I don't know how this happened . . ."

The woman inspected both their bumpers. "Well, no harm done, anyway. Could have been worse."

At that Dory burst into tears. "Oh, God, I'm so sorry! I'm *so* sorry! It's my fault!"

Surprised, the woman took Dory's arm. "Really it's fine. No one was hurt, the cars are okay . . ."

"Somebody could have been *walking* . . ." She sobbed even louder.

I got out then, too, and convinced Dory to get in on the passenger side and let me drive. Once she was in the car she stopped crying, but her eyes looked out of focus, like she was seeing ghosts. The other woman backed carefully out of her space and disappeared.

Neither of Dory's normally outspoken children said a word to her about the accident. The car was abnormally quiet. I guess all of us were thinking about Allen Tewksbury and how quickly everything in your life can change.

By late afternoon Dory seemed more like herself again, reading from the guidebook, determined to provide a good time for all. I'd driven south to the Garden of the Gods, a gorgeous park with huge red sandstone rock formations rising out of the earth. It was another of those places you couldn't quite believe really existed. Some of the formations looked like a huge hand had balanced one rock on the other.

We took a guided walking trail through the park and I brought my camera along. I could have just bought postcards, but something about this scenery made me want to capture it myself. Iris and Dory walked ahead, listening to the guide, while I took photos and Marsh made a few quick sketches.

As we joined the tail end of the tour group, Marshall said, matter-of-factly, "What's it like to be poor?"

I was so surprised, I gave a sharp laugh. "Why are you asking me? I'm not poor." But I knew what he was thinking of—the dingy swimming suit.

"You're not? You don't have much stuff, though."

"Well, I'm not rich, like you guys. I don't go to private school." As soon as I said it, I realized that was a tactical error, since the Tewksbury siblings weren't long for the private school world either. But Marsh didn't know that yet.

"You go to a regular school? Do you like it?"

"Yeah, my school's fine. There's nothing wrong with public schools. I guess some of them aren't that great, but mine is good."

"But you don't get lots of clothes and toys and stuff, do you?" He gave me a look of such heartfelt pity I felt like strangling him.

"I have plenty of *stuff,* Marshall. You don't even know what *poor* means. Poor is when people don't have jobs or can't pay for a decent place to live or buy enough food. It's not when your *swimming suit* is old."

He was offended that I wasn't receiving his sympathy more generously. "You don't have to get all mad at me. I'm just saying, it's too bad you're not as rich as we are."

I knew by his tone of voice he wasn't trying to be mean or offensive—he thought he was being kind, wishing me the wealth that hadn't done all that much good for his own family. It reminded me of the Melvilles in their big house with all the empty bedrooms. They never seemed all that happy either. If they weren't working, they were busy buying things you weren't supposed to get dirty. It seemed to me money must sometimes get in the way of happiness.

I rested a hand on Marshall's shoulder. "Sorry. I'm not mad at you. It's just that being rich really isn't all that important. It seems important to you because that's how you've always lived. But, take my word for it, it's not."

He looked up at me, confusion clouding his face. "I think it's the *most* important thing. Well, not counting religion and stuff like that."

I looked around once more at the amazing scene. "How much did it cost us to walk through here?" I asked.

He shrugged. "It was free, I think."

"There you go," I told him. "A lot of good stuff is free."

He wasn't sold. "What about Lazy River Ranch. That wasn't free."

"No, it wasn't," I admitted.

"So, it's still a good thing to have money," he concluded.

I sighed. "But money isn't the *only* good thing. And you don't need *piles* of it to be happy. That's all I'm saying."

Marshall shrugged. "Well, sure, I knew *that*."

Chapter Sixteen

I kept waiting for Dory to tell her kids about their new school; I was pretty sure she intended to do it over dinner that night, because she got me on to the subject of my school, and what I especially liked about it. Of course, my favorite thing about my high school is Chris, but I came up with a few ideas I thought were more suited to Dory's purposes. I told them about how our basketball team went to the state championships this year, and about how the kids who took TV production ran the local cable channel right from the school building, and about how I'd had great English teachers the last three years. I didn't mention that the yearbook usually didn't get finished by the end of the school year because the staff hated the advising teacher so much they tended to quit. Or that the swim team and the drama club were both cut along with last year's budget. Or that I hadn't had a decent math teacher in years.

I think Dory was just about to launch into her news when Iris, in a remarkably good mood, started telling us about *her* favorite teacher, Mr. Dobbins, who she'd had for biology this year and would have again next year for some other science course. He was so fabulous, there was no better teacher alive, etc. Dory's smile froze, then cracked apart like an ice cube in warm water.

She grabbed the bill and stood up. "Okay, let's find a motel," she said. "Another long drive tomorrow."

Groans.

"I'm sick of cars and motels," Marsh said.

"Tomorrow night we're staying someplace nice again. For two nights," Dory promised.

"Where?"

"In Texas."

"*Texas*? We're going to *Texas*?" Iris said.

Dory put her hands on her hips. "How can you see the West if you skip over Texas? At least a corner of it anyway. Don't worry. After Texas, we're headed for New Mexico, Arizona, and then California."

"California!" Marshall said.

"The trip that never ends," Iris said.

"It would be nice if it didn't, if we could just keep zigzagging across the country, planning life day by day," Dory said wistfully.

Iris tossed her hair. "Well, that's *my* nightmare."

I knew Dory wouldn't appreciate my agreeing with Iris on this particular subject, so I kept my mouth shut.

I guess Dory didn't sleep too well that night. The next morning she looked groggy and annoyed as she herded us into a half-empty coffee shop. She'd barely had her first sip of caffeine before she launched into the announcement. I guess she didn't want to get sidetracked again.

"I have something to tell you. I've made a decision, and you may not like it, but that's the way it's going to be." She took a deep breath, readying herself for the explosion.

"We're going home!" Iris screamed. "Yes!"

"No. It has nothing to do with the trip," Dory said. "Besides, I thought you were enjoying yourself now?"

Iris shrugged. "Sometimes."

"I'm enjoying myself. Mostly," Marshall said. "But maybe I won't be after you tell us about the thing we aren't going to like."

"Yeah, tell us," Iris said.

The waitress brought our eggs and corn muffins and slowly refilled Dory's coffee cup as we all watched and waited. The minute she turned around, Dory said, "I'm taking you both out of the Forest Hill School."

"What?" Iris was so incredulous she was almost laughing.

"I thought I was *already* out?" Marsh said.

"Well, that's just it. I had to find another school for you, anyway, and when I went to visit the Russell School it seemed like a wonderful place, and it's so near our building you can *walk* there . . ."

"Russell? That's not a private school," Iris said.

"No, it isn't, but it's a fine school in spite of that."

"Do they have art classes?" Marshall said. "I'm not going if I can't take art."

Dory leaned eagerly across the table. "They have a wonderful art program. That was one of the things I really liked about it."

Marsh shrugged. "Well, I don't care then. I mean, I have to go someplace new anyway. Besides, Robin goes to public school." He grinned at me as if he was happy we'd have something in common.

"You don't really mean that *I'm* going to the Russell School, too, do you?" Iris asked, a look of near hysteria forming on her face.

Dory looked her daughter right in the eyes. "Yes, Iris, that's exactly what I mean. Marsh will be in the Middle School and you'll start Russell High. They're right next to each other, so you can walk to school together."

Iris's eyes grew enormous. "Well, I'm *not*. No way! You can't make me go there. I won't!"

"Sweetheart, I'm not paying tuition at Forest Hill, so you can't go *there.* I need you to try to be sensible about this. You know I'm starting back to work in the fall and I can't drive you out to the suburbs every day for school."

"I'll find another way to get there then. I'm not going to Russell!" Iris insisted through clenched teeth.

"The truth is, Iris, we can't afford the tuition for private school anymore. Not if I'm going to pay for your colleges, too."

"Let Marsh go, if he wants to. He's the one who screwed up last year! I'm doing great at Forest Hill! That's where all my friends are!" Her face was so red she looked like she was going to burst into flames.

"I realize that, honey. But this is your first year of high school; a lot of other kids will be new, too. It won't be hard to make new friends. I know you don't want to leave Forest Hill, but we have to make some mature decisions now." Dory put her hand on Iris's arm, but Iris shrugged it off and jumped up.

"Well, this is the dumbest decision I ever heard of, and I'm not doing it!" She stormed out of the restaurant and stood outside kicking the tires and belting the bumpers on the minivan while the rest of us picked at our breakfast.

Marshall smeared jelly on his muffin and licked the knife. "I liked Forest Hill, too. It was a good school."

"I know," Dory said.

"Except for Mrs. Marvin. She was an asshole."

Dory was so shocked she choked on her coffee. Marsh smiled, and then Dory and I started to laugh and couldn't stop.

"Oh, God, she really *was,* wasn't she?" Dory said.

That cheered us up a little bit, but we all knew the ride down to Texas was going to be pretty joyless with Iris so angry. I guess she couldn't believe the rest of us stayed in the air-conditioning, ate our breakfast, and came out smiling, when she'd been standing there starving in the hot sun for fifteen minutes in order to make her point. She slammed into the backseat and jammed on her headphones. When Marshall accidentally bumped her getting his pencils from a bag on the floor, she elbowed him in the side. Even Marsh knew better than to escalate *that* war—he curled into his own corner and we drove on.

The landscape became a lot flatter, and a lot dustier, too. We had to drive back eastward a little bit into Lamar, Colorado, and then through a corner of the Oklahoma panhandle (the skinny part of the state that looks like a ruler) to get down to Amarillo, where we were headed. It was a little depressing to think we were going east again. I really wanted to be going west, getting closer to . . . what? My dad? California? The end of the trip? All of those things, I guess. And, of course, the end of the summer, too, which meant seeing Chris again.

The thing that was starting to seem the strangest, though, was the idea that I'd be seeing Dad again in a week or so. That had been more my goal than California from the beginning. But what would it be like to step into his house? To sit at his dinner table with his wife? To meet my baby brother who didn't even know me?

When I thought about Dad opening the door, what I'd say to him, what he'd say to me, it made my knees weak. I almost wished we could skip Arizona so I could relax and stop worrying about it, but I also knew if Dory told me we *weren't* stopping, I'd be disappointed and unhappy. In other words, I was as confused about my dad as ever.

By mid-afternoon we pulled into the Big Steer Resort just outside Amarillo. It was an enormous place, a lot fancier than the Lazy River Ranch, but hokier, too. For instance, when you checked in, they handed everybody a "yellow rose of Texas." The swimming pool was shaped like a big cow, and the restaurant had rattlesnake on the menu. That kind of thing.

But they did have stables, and Iris disappeared into them as soon as possible while the rest of us enjoyed the cow-pool. By the next morning she was still speaking only when absolutely necessary, so Dory let her take a morning trail ride while the rest of us drove into Amarillo and wandered around the livestock auction and a snake museum.

We were all in agreement on one thing: we wanted to see the Cadillac Ranch that afternoon. It's not really a ranch—it's just a place out in the middle of some wheat fields where, back in the seventies, a group of artists stuck ten old Cadillacs in the dirt, nose first, tail fins in the air. I'd seen pictures of it before and it seemed like such a weird thing to do, I wanted to see it for real. The desk clerk at Big Steer told us to buy some spray paint before we went because part of the idea is to put your own "art" on the cars, or at least your name. We stopped at a hardware store and got ourselves some primary colors and black, which Marshall insisted on, for outlining.

Cadillac Ranch looks best from a distance, I think. Like a bunch of cars just flew in all together and made crash landings. If I'd done it, though, I would have buried the backs of the cars so it looked like they were all growing up from underground, like alien plants, or steel trees or something. For a while we just walked around the cars, reading all the graffiti messages and looking at the pictures people had painted. It was hard to know where to put your own message because you felt bad covering up somebody else's. I finally just put my name on a back fender, low down. Dory wasn't interested in painting; she just took pictures, but Iris and Marshall went a little nuts.

Iris took the red paint first and sprayed *Iris Tewksbury: goddess* all across the roof of a car, then took the blue and yellow cans and decorated the words with shadows and curlicues.

Dory took her picture standing next to it, and (in an obvious attempt to butter her up) said, "I had no idea you were so artistic,

Iris." The silent treatment must have been starting to get to Dory.

"There's lots you don't know about me," Iris spit back.

Please. Whenever I started to think there might actually be a human being under all that hair, Iris turned back into a pod person. I walked down the row to see the car Marsh was decorating. Uh-oh. Dory wasn't going to like this one. Along a tail fin he'd painted two cars crashing head-on, the occupants either falling out of windows or flying through the air. The color red had been lavishly applied.

"What do you think?" he asked me.

"I think you draw as well with a spray can as you do with a pencil."

"Mom won't like it."

"Probably not."

"It's just a drawing. It's not like I want it to happen."

"I know."

"You can't draw a dog or some *flowers* or something on a car!"

I laughed. "You're right."

Dory was approaching, camera at the ready. "What are you two laughing about?" she asked, obviously hoping to join in. She stopped and stared at Marshall's drawing.

"Well . . ." she said, smiling weakly. "I guess you just like drawing blood, don't you?"

"Yeah!" Marsh said, happy that at last his mother got it. "Especially when I have red paint like this. I wish I could spray paint *our* car."

Dory put a hand on his shoulder and smiled. "Dream on, my dear. Dream on."

"Let's go!" Iris called. "I want to have some time at the mall."

Dory rolled her eyes. "Sorry, guys. I promised Iris we'd stop at that mall we saw on the way back to the Big Steer."

"A mall? Do they only have clothes stores?" Marshall made a face.

"I think there was a toy store, too."

"All right! Let's go!" He and Iris raced back to the minivan.

I was not a big fan of malls. I never had much money to spend, anyway, so why waste my time walking up and down inside a stuffy mall? But I could tell right away what this was all about. Dory was trying to buy back Iris's good humor for the cost of a couple of new outfits. Of course she was perfectly willing to buy stuff for me, too, but I wouldn't let her. The swimming suit was bad enough. It made me uncomfortable the way Dory just flashed credit cards around. It was so easy. Did these people really even want the things they bought, or was shopping just something they did to pass the time?

Even Chris used to do it. He had closets full of clothes already, but he'd wander around some ridiculously overpriced mall store buying sweaters and shirts he didn't need, just because he *could*. I never really understood that.

I volunteered to go with Marshall to the toy store so I wouldn't have to watch Iris take advantage of her mother. Marsh was disappointed that Dory gave him only twenty dollars, but he didn't argue. The toy store had a model train set up and we played with it for half an hour instead of looking at the other toys. I don't think Marsh really wanted anything, anyway, but then, when I said it was time to go meet Dory and Iris, he looked around quickly and grabbed a small telescope from a shelf.

"Do you really want a telescope?" I asked.

"Sure, why not? Look, it costs nineteen dollars so it's just right."

"Will you even use it?"

He gave me a funny look. "I don't know. I might."

"I just think it's silly to buy things you don't really want."

"I have to buy *something*," he said, shaking his head at me as though I didn't understand his role in keeping the economy afloat.

On the way back to the Big Steer, Dory asked Iris to show me what she'd bought. Iris sighed and reached down into the large bag she'd lugged to the car. She hauled out a lacy tank top, two pairs of pants and a tiny flowered dress.

"And we got shoes, too!" Dory said proudly, as though there had been some difficulty involved in the getting of these things, as if they'd *fished* for them or something.

"Just regular sandals," Iris said, unwilling to unfurl another bag for show-and-tell.

"They're beautiful!" Dory raved. "Red sling backs."

"I wish they'd had them in black. *You're* the one who likes red so much," Iris said scornfully, making clear to Dory that the battle had not quite been won. Money could buy shoes, and shoes might cheer you up a little, but it was obviously going to take more than a new wardrobe to make it up to Iris for Dory's betrayal.

What I thought was, *Maybe if they stopped spending money on junk they didn't need, they could* afford *the private school.*

"Hi, Dad. It's me. I thought I ought to check in and let you know where we are." I was calling from a pay phone in the lobby of the Big Steer so Iris wouldn't be able to critique the call later on.

"Good to hear from you, Robin." There seemed to be a lot of noise in the background.

"Did I interrupt something?"

"No, not at all. David is just complaining about eating his vegetables. Nothing new about that." He laughed fondly, a laugh I didn't remember ever hearing before. A laugh that had never been directed at me.

"If you're, uh, eating, I can call back . . ."

"Nonsense. Dinner hour is not a sacred ritual in this house.

Where are you by now?"

"Texas."

"Texas! You guys really are going around your thumb to get to your finger." I thought I heard Allison laughing in the background. Laughing at me?

"Yeah, you know, Dory wants to see everything. So, anyway, tomorrow we're finally heading west. Dory wants to spend four or five days in New Mexico so we can see some Indian pueblos. I guess there's lots to do around Santa Fe."

"I guess so. I've never been there."

"You haven't?"

"I've never been much of a traveler. Kind of a homebody, I guess. So we should expect you in about a week, then? At Dory's pace?"

"Um, yeah." I was still puzzling over the fact that my father considered himself a *homebody*. "I'll call you again the day before we arrive. Okay?"

"Sure. We're all ready for you. Whenever."

"Thanks, Dad. I'm looking forward to seeing your house and everything." How lame. I sounded about seven years old. To tell you the truth, I *felt* about seven years old.

"Don't get your hopes up. We don't live in a palace or anything." He laughed good-naturedly.

"I know. I just meant . . ."

"Plain old suburban ranch house."

"I *know*. I just want to *see* it." I sounded desperate, even to myself.

Neither of us knew what to say then. Fortunately, his other child intervened and got us off the hook. I could hear the clatter and crying behind him.

"Oh, my, David just knocked Allison's plate off the table. I think I'll have to get off here and help get things under control."

"Sure. Okay. I'll talk to you soon, Dad."

"Bye, Robin."

I sat in the phone booth for a few minutes after I hung up, imagining what was going on in that ranch-house kitchen in suburban Phoenix, Arizona. The life that was my brother's childhood.

Chapter Seventeen

The letter had been slipped under the door of the room I was sharing with Iris. She'd gone in first and tromped right on top of it, but when I came in and picked it up, she said, "God, is that another letter for *you*?" She'd probably have opened it and read it if she'd realized what it was.

"Why don't you go try on your new shoes?" I said, then disappeared into the bathroom with the blue airmail envelope.

"Hey, I need to use the bathroom!" she hollered.

"Use your mother's," I said, closing the toilet lid and plopping down. I deserved a *little* privacy, didn't I? Three pages fell out of the ripped open envelope into my lap. *Three whole pages of Chris.*

Dear Robin,

Hey! I just got your letter today! I'm glad you're not mad at me anymore because that means my life is now totally perfect. I LOVE being here. Rome is not only amazing to see and to learn about—it's also FUN!

Last night a whole bunch of us went to a bar together. Bars in Italy aren't like bars in Iowa, full of pool tables and old guys guzzling beer. For one thing, there's no drinking age here, but also there are lots of bars where kids our age hang out and dance. For some reason teenagers seem older and more sophisticated over here. Maybe that's because I am from Hicksville, Iowa, but I don't think so. Most of the American kids are a little bit shocked, although, of course, the kids from New York and Washington, D.C. (like my roommate Rob), pretend not to be.

Anyway, about eight kids from my dorm all went barhopping together last night. Charlie and Giacomo and Dante—I told you about them—and some girls, too. Yes, there are girls in my dorm, but you don't have to worry about them or be jealous. Not that they aren't pretty and fun to hang out with. Gabriella is an Italian girl from Verona, which is where Romeo and Juliet lived, supposedly. She's really smart and she's helping me with my Italian. Then there are three American girls we like, too: Julie, Kate, and Delphine (whose mother is actually French, hence the name). So we all went to this bar called Caffe Enrico, which is right near Piazza Navona. It was a great place, but then Gabriella (who's been to Rome before) remembered this other little place that was down closer to the Corso Vittorio Emanuele, by the river, and that place was great, too.

The wine over here is so good you can just keep drinking it and drinking it. We didn't have to drive anywhere so we let ourselves get sort of blotto. The DJ was spinning amazing tunes and we danced so much we were soaked with sweat. I guess that sounds gross, but it was so much fun. It was like we all <u>bonded</u> or something. We walked back to the dorm with our arms around each other, singing and laughing. It's hard to explain on paper what it meant to me. Am I making any sense? I wish you were here to be part of this with me.

What else? The work is hard, but I'm learning so much. I'm really looking forward to the last four weeks when we get to travel around—we're all going together so it will really be great. We'll be going through Verona so Gabriella can show us around there.

I just reread your letter. Wow, the Moonlight Motel in Blue Earth,

Minnesota, really does sound like hell. I'm sorry your trip isn't going to be that much fun. Your cousins sound awful. And your aunt is kind of a kook, too, huh? Too bad. At least you'll get to visit your dad.

I do remember our trip to the state fair last year. It seems like ages ago, doesn't it? Next year we'll take a real *trip together.*

Franny is going out with Des Sanders? Wow. I didn't know she even knew him. Does he still have that goofy haircut? Of course, Franny would probably like that about him. When I think about it, they're probably a pretty good couple—both a little crazy.

The Spanish Steps are these huge outdoor stairs near the Villa Borghese (a big park). They're always full of people lounging around, talking, or eating ice cream or something. They're called the Spanish Steps because they end up in the Piazza di Spagna, where the Spanish Embassy is—even though the money to build them came from the French! Apparently in the eighteenth century all the most beautiful men and women would gather on the steps hoping to be chosen as an artist's model. There's a fountain by Bernini, the sculptor, in the middle of the piazza, and Keats, the poet, died in a house right at the bottom of the steps.

Ciao! Miss you a lot!
Love, Chris

By the time I got to the end of the letter I was holding the sheets by the tips of my fingers, as if they were filthy or rotten or something. I let go of the third sheet and it floated to the floor. *Well,* I thought, *I guess it's a good thing I'm* not *in Rome. If I was, Chris, the world traveler, might die at the bottom of those stupid steps, too. After I pushed him down them.*

What kind of horrible letter was that to write to your girlfriend? *My life is perfect. Gabriella, a beautiful, smart, sophisticated Italian girl, shows me around and sweats all over me. We have bonded like Romeo and Juliet. I am visiting all sorts of Villas and*

Piazzas you've never even heard of and I know all about them. Too bad you're having a crappy time. Bye!

He sounded like some bratty show-off who didn't care about anybody but himself. He certainly wasn't thinking about my feelings. If I'd had my notebook in the bathroom with me I'd have immediately written a scathing letter right back to him.

Dear Asshole,

Here I am in Hicksville, Texas. We've been doing nothing but playing pool and guzzling beer for days. (The beer here is so good you can just keep drinking it and drinking it.) Sure hope you and Juliet have had more chances to get blotto down by the river—that sounds so educational. Yes, I understand exactly what you mean—I bonded to a cowboy in Wyoming, and Iris bonded to a horse—they both had great perspiration. We're staying at the Big Steer Resort in Texas. Apparently in the eighteenth century all the most beautiful cows hung out here hoping to get chosen by the Big Steer. Today we saw Cadillac Ranch where in the twentieth century cars came to be buried by famous artists. Am I making any sense? Hope not!

However, I knew Iris was right outside the door, and I didn't want her to know there was anything wrong with the letter. If she was still in her lousy mood, she'd smirk and laugh and get a big kick out of my anger. And if she was in a talkative mood, she'd want me to tell her all about it so we could have a big discussion. Which was not going to happen.

The more I thought about it, I decided I wouldn't answer this letter at all. I'd pretend I hadn't gotten it yet and write him a letter about what a great time *I'd* been having out here in the great American West. Which wasn't even a lie. As crazy as my relatives were, I was glad to be here with them, discovering things I never knew about my own country. Maybe even about myself.

Dinner at the Big Steer was just that: a side of underdone cow that had probably turned more than one diner into a vegetarian. I know I was considering it strongly. Iris hardly touched her meat, but I couldn't really fault her for it—she ate the baked potato and green beans.

Dory wanted to go to some kind of corny Wild West show, that advertised "audience participation" as if that was a good thing. The show featured saloon girls and gunslingers, but I wasn't up for watching stereotypes tonight—I wanted to stay in and write my letter. Marsh was willing to go along. Iris, of course, didn't want to go, but then decided she would, anyway.

"It's too boring just sitting around a hotel room with Robin," she said, but it occurred to me she might be vacating the premises so I could be alone to answer my letter. It was unusual for Iris to consider anybody else's feelings, but, on the other hand, watching the locally staged shoot-out didn't seem like her kind of evening either. I decided to give her thoughtful impulse the benefit of the doubt.

I was glad to see them poke their cowboy hats on their heads and head off, Dory promising ice cream (or anything else their hearts desired) after the performance. The Big Steer Resort had great stationery, too, tan paper with a big bull head at the top.

Dear Chris,

Things have certainly gotten better on this trip! I wish you were here with us to see the amazing scenery: the sky that goes on forever, the Rocky Mountains in the distance, and the Garden of the Gods. What a place that is! It's just south of Denver (which is a great city—remind me to tell you about the museum and the Botanic Gardens sometime)! Anyway, when you walk through the Garden of the Gods you start to feel like nature is the only truly great artist. It's awe inspiring.

Speaking of artists, my young cousin Marshall (who's only ten) is so talented! I've sort of taken him under my wing and we've become buddies—he shows me his drawings even though he won't show anyone else. And the drawings are amazing—I really think he'll be famous someday. I'm getting along so well with my aunt and cousins now. They're troubled, of course, by their husband/father's death, but they're such interesting people once you get to know them. Iris and I have long girl talks before bed each night, and Dory has begun to confide in me, too. Maybe I should be a social worker or something!

I guess the best days we've had so far were on the dude ranch. There were lots of young cowboys there for Iris and me to hang out with. (Don't be jealous—they're very good-looking, but we're all just friends.) They took us on trail rides and danced with us at the square dance and walked us home after the rodeo. It's great to meet new people, isn't it? You've probably met some kids you like in Italy, too.

Anyway, this trip has been eye-opening for me. There's a big world out there and I want to be part of it! We leave Texas tomorrow and head west for New Mexico. Dory says we'll see an Indian pueblo where people have lived for a thousand years. I can't wait—this trip is a real adventure!

I'm sorry you have so much homework to do—doesn't seem fair in the summer, does it? Does your snotty roommate speak Italian well? I'm sure yours will improve over the summer since you know so many Italian kids.

Iris wants me to take a late night walk with her under the starry skies of Texas, so I'll have to wrap this up now. She probably wants to ask my advice about boys or something—it's like finally having a little sister—so much fun!

Miss you! Buenas noches.

Love,

Robin

It's not like I was really lying to him. Most of what I said was the truth. Okay, maybe not the part about taking a walk with Iris and thinking of her as a sister. And maybe I exaggerated the cowboy friendships a little bit, but when I read the letter over I was surprised at how much of it was actually true. I *did* love watching the western landscape change from state to state, I was getting along better with Dory and the kids, I *did* think Marshall was a terrific artist for a ten-year-old, and—most surprising to me—I *did* want to be part of the "big world out there." I was starting to love the traveling for itself.

After I reread the letter and sealed it up to mail, I was feeling so many emotions I didn't know what to do with them. So I called my mother.

"Robin!" Mom said when she heard my voice. "I didn't expect you to call this evening."

"I know. I just wanted to talk to you."

"Is there something wrong?" I could hear her pull out the stool in the kitchen to sit down.

"No, not really. I just got a letter from Chris and he's having a great time in Italy, and . . . it just made me feel kind of rotten."

"Oh, Robin. You don't want him to have a bad time, do you?"

"No, but . . . he's making all these friends. Girls, too. I'll never even meet them."

She sighed. "Well, this is the beginning of the hard part, honey. When he goes away to school he'll make new friends, too. And when *you* go, *you'll* make new friends. That's the way it works."

"I know, but . . ." Tears started to roll down my cheeks, even though I tried to sniff them back. "I don't want to lose him!"

At first Mom didn't say anything. I know she could tell I was crying. "If I were you," she said finally, "I would try not to look too far into the future. Enjoy what you have right now. Everything changes, Robin, and I'm afraid crying about it doesn't help."

It was her usual good sense advice, which sometimes made me crazy, but tonight it seemed just right. I reached for a tissue and blew my nose.

"How's everything else going?" she asked. "Are you still in Texas?"

"Yeah. We leave tomorrow for New Mexico. Dory is really looking forward to Santa Fe."

"Oh, I'd love to see Sante Fe. Take lots of pictures to show me."

"I will. I really love seeing all this country, Mom. I'm glad I came."

"Good. How are the kids?"

"Some days fine, some days crazy. I like them, though—I mean, not all the time, but basically, they're okay. I think all three of them mostly need somebody to talk to. Sometimes I feel like their therapist or something."

"Oh, dear."

"I don't mind it. I feel like I'm helping them. It's good."

I could almost feel her smiling. "Robin, you'll be fine, you know that? No matter what happens to you, you're a survivor."

I laughed. "I guess I get that from you, huh?"

She laughed, too, but I could hear some noise behind her, like somebody else talking.

"Is somebody there?" And then I figured it out. "Is Michael Evans there?"

"Yes, Michael's here. We were just watching an old Cary Grant movie." She said something to Michael I couldn't hear, which made me feel really weird. Now *both* my parents had lives I wasn't part of.

"I'm sorry. I didn't mean to interrupt you."

"You didn't, sweetie. Well, you did, but a phone call from you is always more important than a silly movie."

"Thanks."

"Michael says it certainly *is* a silly movie. And he also says to tell you hi."

"Okay, tell him hi, too." Now I just wanted to hang up. Talking to Michael Evans with my mother as the intermediary was ridiculous. "I should probably go anyway—Dory and the kids will be back soon."

"Okay. Have a wonderful time in New Mexico, and call me whenever you want to. I love you!"

"I know. I love you, too."

"Michael says good-bye."

Jesus. "Tell him good-bye."

She smooched me an air kiss and then we hung up. It sounded like Michael Evans had become a regular part of her life. Which meant he was part of mine, too, whether I liked it or not. Another change I wouldn't be able to do anything about.

Don't look too far ahead. Tomorrow . . . that looked good.

Iris banged the door against the wall as she entered in her usual belligerent manner. "My mother drank a beer, and then went up on stage and sat on an actor's lap! I was never so embarrassed in my life!"

I smiled. Things change.

Chapter Eighteen

We pulled out of the Big Steer early, bringing muffins and juice with us instead of stopping for breakfast. Dory said it was a long, hot drive and she'd just as soon get underway. I drove first so she could drink her coffee and wake up, and so I could pull over at the post office and get rid of my letter to Chris before I had second thoughts about sending it.

We took Route 40 out of Texas and into New Mexico, a long straight highway with little to see but dust and sagebrush along the way. Dory told us that the "famous" Route 66 had run through all the little towns down here before Route 40 was built. Route 66 had started in Chicago and run south to St. Louis and then west to Los Angeles. I wondered if it was more fun to drive than Route 40, which was just one big trailer truck after another, breezing past fast enough to knock you off the road.

"This is the dullest part of the trip yet," Iris said. "I thought you said New Mexico was beautiful?"

"Just wait. It's a big state."

"Looks just like Texas to me."

"Where are we going again?" Marshall asked.

"Now? We're heading for the Acoma Pueblo," Dory said. "It's

called Sky City because it's up on a high mesa. Acoma people have lived there since 1075, which means it's the oldest—"

Iris interrupted. "*Oldest continually inhabited city in the country.* You've said that about twelve times already."

"Marshall was asking me."

"Okay, I got it now," Marsh said. "It's special because it's old."

"Not just that. There's no water source on top of the mesa so in order to live up there the people have to haul their water up. There's no electricity either, and until recent years there wasn't even a road. For centuries the Native American people climbed up and down the side of the cliff. In a climate this hot and dry—can you imagine?"

"Why did they live up there then?" Marsh said.

"It was very safe. They could see their enemies coming from far away. They could never be surprised."

What a life. Not only did you have to carry water up the side of the mountain, but you never got any surprise visitors either. I wondered if my dad and Allison had given any thought lately to moving to a place like that.

"Great," Iris said. "You die of thirst, but at least you don't get an arrow in your back."

Dory sighed. "Iris, I think we're all getting a little tired of your sarcasm, aren't we, guys?"

Marshall and I were silent as stones. Iris's smart mouth wasn't at the top of my list of problems. I'd spent the morning trying to rid my brain of the image of Chris and Gabriella bonded with sweat.

Iris shrugged. "Nobody else cares but you."

"Well then, for me. Please cut it out."

"No," Iris said. "I don't think I will."

Which was about the last thing any of us said until we ordered lunch outside of Albuquerque. I'd stopped paying close attention to Iris's eating habits because she seemed to be more normal now. Of course, the news of the school change had put her back in a seriously lousy mood, and I wondered if that would affect things. But she ordered a tuna sub and ate three quarters of it, so I decided she'd turned a corner on the eating disorder thing.

We piled back into the van after lunch and were just about nodding off when Dory pulled the car over. "Look," she said. "There it is."

We were stopped at the top of a mesa from which we looked across a wide, open plain toward another very flat mesa, which seemed to be made of bleached pink stone. Perched on top, we could just make out some whitish structures—the pueblo of Acoma. The four of us got out to look.

"People still live up there?" Marshall asked.

"That's what the guidebook says," Dory said.

"Cool."

Iris obviously couldn't think of anything snotty to say so she kept her mouth shut.

"How do we get up there?" I asked. "Drive?"

"No, we park at the bottom and take a shuttle bus up."

"Let's go!" Marsh shouted, jumping back in the car. "Come on!"

The long straight road up to the base of the mesa passed by big pink rock formations that seemed almost like man-made sculptures. We pulled into a parking lot next to a squat white building that said TICKETS FOR BUS on a sign out front, but it was hard not to be distracted by the line of vendors who surrounded the lot, all of them selling pottery. Dark-skinned men and women, young and old, sat on folding chairs with trucks and station wagons backed up behind them and card tables in front of them displaying their work. A few were talking, but most sat quietly. Two children, four or five years old, sat in the dust and played a slapping hands game. A man in a baseball cap, the only person wearing a hat in the blazing sun, carved a figure from a chunk of wood.

"That's tacky." Iris had found her voice.

"Shh! Iris, they'll hear you!" Dory said.

Iris shrugged but lowered her voice. "They sit right here by the parking lot? We're not even in the pueblo yet. It's like they can't wait to sell you something."

"Well, they probably *can't*," Dory said. "This is how they make a living."

We trooped inside to buy bus tickets and found we could also purchase postcards, hot dogs, Lay's potato chips, or Coke.

Marshall whispered to me, "I'm not being mean, but it doesn't seem like it's *real* if you can buy Coke here."

"I think this is what real is here now. Some things are the way they were hundreds of years ago, but I guess everybody in the world has junk food now."

He thought about it for a minute, and then said, "That's sort of cool—how some things change and some things don't."

"Yeah, it is," I agreed, restraining myself once again from a fond, yet condescending, hair ruffling.

We boarded a shuttle bus and in a few minutes were headed to the top of Acoma Pueblo. A young man in a Nike T-shirt, his long black hair pulled back with a piece of leather, introduced himself as our guide, James. He was a good-looking guy, and I could tell Iris thought so too. But James never smiled at anyone—he didn't even seem to look at any of us—and his speech was so rehearsed you felt sorry for him having to say it all again.

"Here ahead of us is the San Estevan mission church. It was built in 1629 when the first priest arrived at Acoma. In order to build the church and convent, our people had to move twenty thousand tons of earth and stone from the canyon up to the top of the mesa. There was no road to the mesa top in those days—all supplies were carried on burros or on the heads and backs of our people."

It was pleasantly cool inside the white adobe church and a few people sat down in chairs. The four of us backed up against the chilly walls. There was something about the way James kept saying "our people" that made me feel like I didn't belong there, that even looking at the places he described was somehow stealing something from them.

"You will notice the vigas, or large beams, overhead. You will also notice when you look across the valley from the mesa top, that there are no trees within sight. These forty-foot-long logs had to be carried for over twenty miles, up and down mountains, to reach this place." James's mouth clamped shut in a hard line as though he wouldn't let out one extra word for us—he would give us only what we had paid for, nothing more. He waited for us to react to the amazing abilities of his people before he continued.

We followed James out of the church, then wandered up and down the narrow dirt roads where a station wagon and a rusty convertible were parked beside ancient houses in which wooden ladders were still used to reach the upper floors. We saw the round adobe brick ovens that the community used for baking, and the steep "stairs" that they climbed up and down before the road was built. But mostly we saw people sitting beside tables full of pottery, hoping to make a sale.

"You may stop to buy pottery quickly, or you may return to a particular vendor afterward if you see something you like. However, you may not leave the tour to buy," James warned. "An Acoma guide must always be with you."

Why? So we wouldn't steal things? So we wouldn't decide to stay?

We huddled around the display tables, looking at clay animals and bowls, vases and plates. In some booths the pottery was beautiful, carefully painted with tiny details, while in others the work seemed poorly done, hurried, in the hope of making a little money. At one table where the work was especially nice, Dory bought a beautiful white bowl with small black arrows painted all around it. I could tell James was ready to move us along, but Dory was talking to the woman artist, and I decided I wanted something, too . . . something to help me remember this haunting place where I could never belong. A young girl, maybe the daughter of the artist, was selling clay horses, not as perfect as the older woman's bowls, but I liked that they were each different and wild looking. I decided, quickly, while Iris and Marshall were looking away, to buy three horses, one for each of us. It would be nice to give them something, too, so we would all remember.

By the time the shuttle bus brought us back down to the parking lot, we were all hot and tired. I'd stuffed the horses in my backpack, deciding to wait until the end of the trip to hand them out. We refilled our water bottles and were heading for the minivan when Dory suddenly said, "I'm going to buy something else," and headed toward the line of parking lot vendors.

"What?" Iris said. "Mom, I've got a headache!"

"I'll just be a minute."

"Well, can we at least get in and turn on the air-conditioning?"

"Go ahead," she called back.

I got in the driver's seat and turned the ignition so the a/c came on, but I sort of hated doing it, especially out here where some people didn't even have electricity, for God's sake. But we *were* hot, so we polluted the ancient environment in order to cool ourselves off. Still, it felt awfully good when the air started blowing. It's not easy to be righteous.

Dory came back with a vase that must have been at least two feet tall and a foot wide. We all stared at her: There was no room for that thing is this car.

"Mother, are you nuts?" Iris said.

"Isn't this the most beautiful thing you've ever seen? And the artist is a wonderful man. I took his name so I can contact him. He said he could send me slides of his other pots."

"Why didn't you tell him to send you this one? We don't have room for it in here."

"Oh, sure we do," Dory said. "There's room in the backseat."

"No!" Marshall was getting into the act now, too. "Iris already has her junk spread out all over the place. I hardly have any room."

"Well, Iris, couldn't you condense things a little bit? The pot could sit right here between the two of you."

Iris and Marsh went more or less ballistic over sharing their limited space with an object the size of a five-year-old, but what could they do? Dory had bought the damn thing—it had to go somewhere.

As Dory pulled back out onto the highway and headed north for Santa Fe, the rage from the backseat was practically combustible. Marsh and Iris were mad at their mother, at each other, and even at me, the person who did not have a giant jar wedged in next to her knees. Dory's attempts at conversation were soon directed only to me.

"I thought we'd take a back road up to Santa Fe. It's on that map there—they call it the Turquoise Trail and it runs through some lovely small towns, some of them almost ghost towns now."

I opened the map on my lap. "It goes over some mountains."

"I know. See that town called Madrid? It was almost a ghost town until a group of artists took it over and now it's supposed to be a cute little place. I thought we'd stop there for dinner."

"Looks kind of far," I said.

"Oh, no. Not more than an hour," Dory said.

Two silent, hungry hours later, we pulled into Madrid, a very small town, which consisted of half a dozen stores selling jewelry, pottery and weavings, a pizza parlor, and a small café. Without asking advice, Dory parked in front of the café, turned off the motor, and slumped back in her seat.

"Well, that was longer than I thought. And more confusing. But we're almost to Santa Fe now." She dared to glance into the backseat. "Anybody hungry?"

"Is *this* where we're eating?" Marshall asked. "It doesn't even look open."

Iris slammed the car door, marched up to the café, and turned the door handle. "It's open. Let's, for God's sake, eat."

The café was small but pleasant in a rundown, hippie-dippy way. Indian bedspreads were strung across windows and flung over shaky tables. Mismatched chairs and stools were painted red and yellow. Strings of chili peppers hung from the walls, which also displayed brightly colored paintings of vegetables.

For some reason it reminded me of Franny—she would have liked a place like this—a hodgepodge that was perfectly happy with itself. Not for the first time, I wished she was here with me. Maybe even more than I wished for Chris.

The café seemed to be deserted, but after a minute a young woman came out from behind a curtain, her dark hair cropped close to her head, a big white apron tied over a tank top and shorts.

"Oh, hi! I was just closing up. Did you want to eat?"

Iris and Marshall groaned.

"Well, yes," Dory said. "It's only seven o'clock—isn't that early to close?"

The girl smiled. "Not around here. We usually get visitors through at lunchtime and a few locals late afternoon, but by this time of day it's pretty dead."

"Oh, well . . ."

"It's okay—I'll stay open. I've got food. What do you think you want?"

"Could we see a menu?" Iris asked rather snippily.

"You could if I had one. This is what's left: two servings of eggplant Parmesan, enough tuna for a sub or two, plenty of cheese, tomatoes, and lettuce. I could make you a salad. Or I could cook up an omelet and throw an avocado in it. Any of that sound good?"

"Avocado with an *egg*?" Marshall made a face before ordering a tuna sub with lettuce. Iris asked for a salad, then glanced at me and told the girl to put some tuna on the side, too. Dory got the eggplant and I went for the omelet with avocado, which turned out to be excellent.

"Miss, do you have coffee, by any chance?" Dory asked.

"Name's Savannah. But I'm sorry—I don't have any more water."

"You don't have *water*?" Iris said.

Savannah shook her head. "There's no water piped into Madrid—not drinking water, anyway. We buy it, but I ran out today. There's some iced tea left, though."

"This town is weird," Iris said when Savannah disappeared behind the curtain. "The only restaurant in town closes at seven o'clock and they don't have any water. Trust you to pick this place." She glared at her mother.

"I think it's charming," Dory said. "And besides, she's being very helpful. In a bigger town they might have just said, '*We're closed—go away.*'"

"A bigger town might have *water*," Iris said.

Dory looked down at her plate and let her fork drop. "Iris, I'm really getting tired of your attitude. Even I can only take so much."

"Even *you*? Like you're some kind of saint?"

Fortunately Savannah came back out then, iced tea pitcher in hand, and poured us all a round.

"You have a long drive today?" she asked.

"From Texas," Marshall said. "And we stopped at Acoma Pueblo, too."

"Wow, you covered a lot of ground for one day. You'll be glad to get to bed tonight. I guess you're heading for Santa Fe."

Dory nodded. "I didn't make reservations anywhere, but I'm assuming we'll find a place."

"Oh, sure. Only the expensive places fill up early."

"We wouldn't want to stay in an *expensive* place," Iris said, almost to herself.

Savannah fumbled in her apron pocket, then brought out a white card. "Here's the place my parents run. It's clean and there's almost always a vacancy."

Dory looked at the card. "The Black Mesa Motel. I like the name."

"Black Mesa is the name of the rock behind the San Ildefonso Pueblo. It's where my parents met."

"Are your parents Indians?" Marshall asked.

"Native American," Dory corrected him gently.

Savannah laughed. "No, they're just hippies. My dad is a potter and he used to go to the pueblo a lot to study Indian methods for making hand-built pots. And one day my mother was there and they met. She was on a trip with some friends from New Jersey, where she lived. But after she met my dad, she never went home again."

"Never?" Marsh asked.

"Well, she's gone back to visit her folks, but she says she knew right away New Mexico was her spiritual home and my dad was her soulmate." She laughed. "That's the way they talk."

"Kind of cornball," Iris said.

"Yeah, they are," Savannah agreed. "Ya gotta love 'em, though." She cleared our dishes and took them behind the curtain.

Dory paid her, including a big tip. "I'm sorry we made you stay so late."

"No problem. I'll lock up right behind you."

She waved good-bye to us and took off her apron. As we climbed into the car, the sun was already starting to go down behind the mountains and the air was getting cool. I think we were all looking forward to settling into a place in Santa Fe for a few days and not having to ride in the car for a while.

"What a sweet girl," Dory said. "I'm glad we stopped there."

The minute the doors slammed closed, Iris started in. "I am *not* staying in some cheap old motel again—I don't care if it is run by *soulmates*."

"Hey! I want to go there! We could see her father's pottery!" Marsh chimed in.

"Yeah, and Mom would *buy* it. Just what we need—more pots to cram into the backseat."

"Put your seat belts on," Dory said, trying to ignore them. "I just stay on Route 14 here, don't I, Robin?"

I checked the map and showed her the route into town. We pulled out onto the shadowy old highway.

But Iris was still livid. "I'm sick of *you* making all the decisions. *You* decide where we eat. *You* decide where we stay. *You* decide we're too poor for me to go to Forest Hill School even though *you* can spend money on other stupid junk like this ugly vase, *which is pinching my legs*!" Her tirade had developed into a full screech.

"Ow!" Marshall entered the fray. "Iris kicked the vase right into my knee!"

"Well, I *can't stand it anymore*!" Iris said. She kicked the vase so hard I could feel it hitting the back of my seat.

"Iris, if you break that pot . . ."

"I hope I *do* break it. It would serve you right!"

Dory unbuckled her seat belt so she could turn far enough around in the seat to see her daughter. "Iris! Get hold of yourself. What is wrong with you?"

"What's wrong with me is *you*! Why did Daddy have to die? He wouldn't make me do things I don't want to do!"

"Shut up, Iris!" Marshall demanded. And then he lifted his foot and smashed it into her thigh.

Dory turned back to look at the road, and then turned around again, trying—with one arm—to keep Iris from kicking the pot, to keep Marsh from kicking Iris. I think what she wanted to do was pull the car over to the side of the road, but we were going too fast, and everything was so loud and crazy. When we came around the curve, we were too near the edge, and then everything went into slow motion. The tires went off the road and bumped over the rocky dirt. Dory swore and tried to wrench the steering wheel in the other direction, but suddenly the van didn't seem to be under her control anymore.

"Mom, stop!" Iris screamed, but this time there was nothing Dory could do. Marshall was just yelling, without words.

The van leaped sideways, heading down the slope of the hill. Dory kept stomping on the brake, but it was useless. As the van tipped, I braced myself against the dashboard and looked over at her. She was staring through the windshield with wide, terrified eyes; she'd given up trying to stop the inevitable.

Oh, my God, is what I was thinking. *This can't be happening. Make this not be happening.* The screaming from the backseat continued as the van rolled over once, twice, three times, and finally landed on its side like a wounded elephant.

Then everything was quiet.

Chapter Nineteen

For a minute I thought I must be paralyzed—I couldn't seem to move. But then I realized that the van was lying flat on the passenger side and something had fallen on top of me and was pushing me against the door. I craned my neck to the side to see what it was. And there was Dory, not caught behind the inflated air bag in the driver's seat, but lying heavily against my side, her head almost on top of mine.

"Mommy!" I recognized Marshall's voice.

"Are you guys all right?" I yelled back.

"She's bleeding!" Marshall said.

"I think I'm okay," Iris said. "What's wrong with Mom?"

I heard someone else then, someone outside the car, coming down the hill toward us, yelling, "I called for help! Don't worry, we'll get you out!" The voice sounded familiar.

"Are you okay in there? It's Savannah, from the restaurant—I saw you go off the road!"

"I think we're okay," I called back. I wasn't actually sure that was true, especially since Dory hadn't said anything yet, but I didn't want to get Iris and Marsh more scared than they already were.

"Can you get the front door open? That's the only door on this side," Savannah said. "The car won't roll any farther—there are trees stopping it."

I was afraid to move since Dory was lying against me and I didn't want her to fall. "Iris, can you climb up front and get the door open?"

The air bag had deflated by then so Iris was able to hang on to the seat back and step over her mother. She grabbed the steering wheel and crouched with her feet on the gear shift box. "Should I turn the car off?" she asked in a shaky voice.

"Yes, good idea," I said.

She did, then turned to look at her mother. "Mom? Are you okay?"

Dory groaned then, and tried to shift her weight.

"There's blood on her head," Iris said. In the backseat Marshall started to cry.

"We need to get her out of here. See if you can open the door."

Iris tried the handle, but it was stuck. "Maybe I can kick it open." With one hand on the headrest and the other on the steering wheel, she raised up her body and kicked both feet out against the door. The third kick knocked the door back and the cool, pine-scented air reminded me where we were—in the middle of nowhere.

"Great!" Savannah said. "Can you jump?"

"I don't know. My ankle hurts now," Iris said, then looked back at me. "Should I get out?"

Obviously I was now in charge whether I liked it or not. "Help Marsh climb over the seat, too. Then both of you get out of the car."

Marsh did as he was told, sobbing as he climbed past his mother. "Mommy!" he screamed at her.

Dory stirred again and this time lifted her head.

"What . . . ?" she managed, then laid her head back against mine.

"We had an accident, but we're all okay, Dory. We're getting out of the car," I said, although I couldn't imagine how the two of us were going to get out.

Iris lowered her weeping brother out of the front door, down to Savannah, then jumped down herself.

"My mommy's hurt!" Marsh reported to Savannah.

"She's bleeding from her head," Iris said. "And she's lying on top of Robin so she can't get out either."

"Don't worry!" Savannah called in to me. "People are coming to help. I called the local emergency squad and the Santa Fe ambulance both."

"They're coming to help us," I said to Dory, but she didn't move a muscle. There was a terrible thought rising in my head. I tried to push it down, but it kept bubbling back up. *Don't die, don't die, don't die, please don't die,* I told her, though not out loud. *You can't die because your children need you, and I could never find a way to help them if you died, too.*

And then I heard the siren, and the voices, and I hoped it meant we were safe. All of us. I could hear a ladder being hoisted up to the open car door.

"The Madrid Emergency Squad is here," Savannah called in to us. "They'll be able to get you out and help you until the ambulance arrives."

My God, I thought, *what would have happened if Savannah hadn't been driving behind us? If nobody had seen us go off the road? We could have been here until morning before anybody noticed us.*

Within minutes a man had climbed up a ladder and inside the van. He put a thick white collar around Dory's neck, then he and a second man carefully turned her so her back rested on a board. She groaned as the two of them slowly lifted her out the door and lowered her down to the ground. A woman showed up next and helped me up from the bottom of the van, then down the ladder. My head was buzzing like crazy and I felt dizzy, especially after I got outside and saw what a wreck the car was.

Marsh and Iris were trying to get a look at their mother, but the emergency crew was busy checking her over and they were pushed back. She moaned when they touched her right shoulder and then opened her eyes. "Where are my children? Iris? Marshall?"

"We're here, Mom," Iris said. "We're okay. We're fine. Robin's okay, too."

"Robin! Oh, my God. What have I done?" Tears spilled from the corners of her eyes.

"You just had an accident," Savannah told her. "You'll be fine."

It wasn't long before the ambulance from Santa Fe came careening up the road. The Madrid people gave them a shorthand account of what had happened.

"Looks like she didn't have a belt on. Arm fractures, maybe collarbone. Head contusions. Possible internal injuries."

It all sounded awful. Marsh was huddled against Iris's side and Iris stood so close to me our hips banged together. It occurred to me again that I was in charge now; I was the surrogate mother for these two even if I was only seventeen and scared witless. Thank God, Savannah had more sense than I did.

"Tell me your names," she said, and we did.

"Okay, Robin, the hatch is sprung open just enough to pull your suitcases and stuff out. I'll put your things in my car, okay? I'll follow you to the hospital."

"What about the stuff inside the car? Dory's purse and mine . . ."

"And my drawings," Marsh said quietly.

"The vase!" Iris said. "What about the vase!"

"It's probably broken anyway," I said.

"No! We should get it out!"

Savannah put a hand on Iris's shoulder. "Let me see what they're going to do with the car." She went to talk to a policeman, then returned.

"They'll tow the car to a Santa Fe repair shop to see if it's worth fixing. Once they get it turned upright the police will take all your stuff out for you and bring it to the hospital. Okay?"

I nodded. It kept hitting me over and over that we'd been in a very bad accident, that nothing was the same now as it had been an hour ago. My head was throbbing. "I think I have to . . ." was all I got out before I turned around and threw up in the dirt.

"Okay, her on the other stretcher," the EMT called, pointing to me.

"No, I'm okay," I said. "You should look at the kids."

"All of you, then. In here with your mother."

Instead of making any of us lie down, they put us in seats with shoulder belts next to Dory's stretcher, and then turned on that awful screaming siren. Every time the ambulance careened around a corner the three of us hung onto the belts and the sides of the chairs. It wasn't fun. I was beginning to realize I must be bruised from the seat belt in the minivan because my chest ached. Marshall had stopped crying and sat quietly, staring at his mother whose face was as white as the collar around her neck.

"She'll be all right," I told him.

He looked at me, then curled his lip as if he was speaking to an idiot. "How do you know? Did you ever see anybody die?"

"No, but . . ."

"She isn't going to die!" Iris said. "She isn't!"

"You hope," Marshall said, the last word on the subject.

Once we got to the hospital, we were all taken into separate curtained-off rooms in emergency. My curtain wasn't closed all the way and I could see doctors and nurses running in and out of

Dory's room, bringing all kinds of equipment and looking very serious. I hoped Marshall couldn't see it from his room.

As I lay there waiting for someone to come in, it dawned on me that I probably wouldn't make it to Phoenix, Arizona. Not on this trip, anyway. I tried not to feel too sorry for myself, since the Tewksburys were obviously more hurt by the accident than I was, but still I thought, *why couldn't this have worked out for me?*

Finally a nurse came in and asked me a bunch of questions. Some of them I didn't know about: insurance and who everybody's doctor was. I said Dory would be able to tell them all that once she felt better. I took it as good news that the nurse didn't say, "Her? She'll never get any better." Then I had to sign some papers. A policeman came in and asked me how the accident happened. I told him about the argument, how Dory had taken off her seat belt to deal with the kids in the backseat, how all of a sudden the car had run off the road.

He shook his head. "*Kids,*" he said, in a way that sounded like he'd do away with the whole species if he could. "By the way, I left your belongings that were in the car at the front desk. I can't believe that big pot didn't break getting flipped over like that." *Great,* I thought. *It was the damn pot's fault to begin with.*

Finally the nurse came back and took my blood pressure. "So, you doing okay? Anything hurt you?"

"I'm kind of sore where the seat belt was," I said, "and my head hurts," I said, pointing to the spot. "I think I bumped it on the door."

She unbuttoned my shirt and felt around my rib cage. "That hurt?" she asked.

I twisted away from her touch. "A little."

"Yeah, you're bruised but not broken." Then she looked into my eyes with a little flashlight. "Not dizzy, are you?"

"Not anymore. I was right after the accident."

"You got a goose egg up there, but I think you're okay. I'll get you an icepack to hold on it. Otherwise, you look fine. Soon as I tape your sister up . . ."

"My cousin. Is she hurt?"

"Not much. Sprained ankle. She'll be on crutches for a few days."

"And the little boy? Marshall?"

"Not a scratch on him! Lucky kid. Oh, there's somebody in the waiting room who said to tell you she's here—Suzanna, I think she said."

"Savannah?"

"That's it."

They let Marsh come and sit in my room with me while they explained the physics of crutches to Iris.

"Your head hurt?" Marsh asked.

"A little. The nurse said you're fine, though. Not a scratch!"

"Yeah." He looked at me. "What do we do now?"

What I felt like saying was, *I don't know! How am I supposed to know?* But I didn't think it would be right to let a worried ten-year-old know I was scared, too. "I guess we wait until we find out how your mom's doing. That's the first thing."

He nodded.

When Iris could maneuver around on the crutches, they sent the three of us out to the waiting room where Savannah was sitting reading a battered-up book called *Enormous Changes at the Last Minute.* Which sounded like the biography of my life this summer. She jumped up when she saw us.

"You guys don't look too bad, considering what the car looks like. Is your ankle badly hurt?" She helped Iris into a chair, then took the crutches and leaned them against the wall.

"No. I guess I sprained it when I kicked the door open."

"And Robin has a bump on the head," Marshall told her, "but I'm fine. I didn't even get hurt."

"Well, that's one good thing, huh?" Savannah put an arm around Marshall, and, to my surprise, he allowed it. "Listen, I'm going to stay with you until you hear about your mom, and then I'll take you all back to the motel. I called home and my mom said there are several vacant rooms, so there's no problem."

Marshall looked worried. "I want to stay here with Mom."

"I know you do," Savannah said, "and we *will* stay here until we know she's okay, but there's no place to sleep here, and there's plenty of room at the Black Mesa Motel. You'll like it there. Really."

"Thanks," I said, sinking into a chair. It was nice to have somebody else make a decision for us. I leaned back and let the ice numb my brain. There was a big television mounted on the wall which was turned to the late news—most of it sounded bad, something about rising oil prices and a falling stock market. "Can we turn that off?" I asked.

Savannah shook her head. "I already tried. It seems to be on permanently. Do you want me to read you a story? Maybe I can drown it out."

She had a good reading voice, and I think I would have liked the story if I'd been able to concentrate on it. I closed my eyes and let her voice run over me like water.

It was almost midnight before a doctor came out to talk to us. Marsh had fallen asleep with his head on my lap and Iris was stretched out across four chairs.

"Are you the Tewksbury family?" Everybody sat up immediately, and all of us, Savannah included, said yes.

"My name is Dr. Ellis." She shook Savannah's hand, then mine.

"Is Mom all right?" Iris asked, getting right up in her face.

"Your mother will be fine, but she has to stay here for a while. A week or so. There are two broken bones in her upper arm and her collarbone is pretty bruised. Two ribs are broken. She has a concussion, which I think is mild, but we want to keep an eye on that for a few days, too. She's pretty banged up, but she'll be good as new before you know it."

It was funny, how the kids reacted. Marsh was so relieved, he started jumping up and down. But Iris, who'd been her usual tightly wound self up until now, suddenly fell apart. Tears streamed down her cheeks.

"Can we see her?" she asked.

"For a minute, yes. But she needs to rest. Do you have a place to go tonight?"

"They're staying with me," Savannah said firmly. "I'm a friend of the family."

I was glad to hear it. We needed a friend right now.

Dory was too dopey to even know who was in her room. She opened her eyes and smiled at us, but then went right back into dreamland. Still it was good to see her looking relatively normal again. Her arm and shoulder were in a plaster cast that was held up by a pulley of some kind, but her face was the right color and, wherever she thought she was, she seemed happy there. Marshall gave her a kiss on the cheek and Iris, who'd stopped crying, twirled her mother's wedding ring around her limp finger.

"She never took it off," Iris said.

We tiptoed out and followed Savannah downstairs.

I remembered as we passed the front desk that our things from the car were there, and we stopped to get them: a garbage bag full of purses, books, CDs, and drawing supplies. And an enormous Acoma vase, unbroken.

"What a beautiful pot. I can't believe it didn't break," Savannah said as she handed it to me to hold in the front seat.

"I grabbed it between my knees," Iris said.

"You did?" I said. "When?"

"When the car started to roll. I don't know why. It was just something to hold on to, I guess. I protected it."

"Or maybe the pot protected *you*," Savannah said. "You never know."

"Maybe it protected all of us," I said.

"Me and the vase were the luckiest ones," Marshall said. "We didn't get a scratch."

Chapter Twenty

"I can't believe this! Are you sure Dory's going to be all right? Are you sure *you're* all right? How could this happen?"

"Mom, we're okay, really. Don't worry." I could just imagine her pacing up and down the kitchen, twisting the phone cord into complicated knots.

"Well, you're *not* okay. Dory's in the hospital with broken bones and the rest of you . . . where *are* you, anyway?"

I was standing in the Bolton-Packer family's kitchen watching Savannah's father, Roland, flip pancakes like a professional chef while her mother, Sukey, poured milk for Iris and Marshall. (They'd told us to call them by their first names right away.) Sukey was wearing a kimono with big wing sleeves that made her seem like a good fairy flapping around the room. How could I explain it all to Mom?

"We're at a motel in Santa Fe, New Mexico. We're fine. We're actually having breakfast with Savannah and her parents now—they own the motel."

"Savannah? Who's that? What motel? I'm going to have to fly out there right away—you need an adult with you."

"No, listen to me, Mom. Savannah is a waitress at the place we ate dinner last night. She was following us down the road when the accident happened."

"Why was she *following* you?" I couldn't tell the story fast enough. Mom was trying to read between the lines without even seeing the page.

I sighed. "Will you calm down and let me tell you?"

Savannah walked over and took the phone from my hand. "Let me," she said, and then began to talk to my mother in the same rational voice she'd used yesterday to help us all out of the overturned van.

"Hi, Ms. Daley. This is Savannah Bolton-Packer." She related the story of who she was, how we'd met, and the rest of last night's proceedings in an orderly fashion, and I could tell Mom must be calming down because eventually Savannah laughed at something she said. I was about to take the phone back when the good fairy grabbed it.

"Hi. Sukey Bolton, Savannah's mother. Don't worry about a *thing.* Your children are welcome to stay here as long as they need to. I love having kids around and some of mine are already grown and gone, so this is fun. We'll take them over to the hospital whenever they want to go. It's not far. What a shame their vacation got interrupted like this—we'll show them around town while they're here."

Mom must have protested that they didn't need to do that because then Sukey said, "Don't be silly! Hanging around with kids makes me feel sixteen again! Sometimes I think I'm still a teenager, one with gray hair!"

"You are, Mom, don't worry," Savannah said.

"Besides," Sukey continued, "I need something more interesting to do than sit behind a desk all day."

I already knew the Bolton-Packers did a lot more than sit at desks all day. Savannah had showed me her mother's loom with a half-finished blanket on it. Apparently Sukey's weaving sold in shops all over the area, as did Roland's black, scrubbed-looking pots, which were also displayed all over the house. His studio was behind the motel, next to a barn with two horses and several goats. And, of course, they ran the motel, too, not to mention feeding stray children who showed up on their doorstep.

I took the phone back. "Okay, do you get it now?"

"Well, they sound a little kooky, but very nice. It was a stroke of luck that you ran into Savannah."

"I know."

"I guess you won't get to California, though. Or Arizona either."

"I know." I was trying to keep myself from thinking about it. Seeing Dad and David in Arizona was what had made me want to take this trip to begin with. I'd gotten so close—one state away—but now I wouldn't make it. All morning I'd been fighting off that *it's not fair* feeling—it never makes you feel any better, anyway. It wasn't fair that Chris left and went to Italy. It wasn't fair that Allen Tewksbury got hit by a taxi. It wasn't fair that Dory ran off the road and wrecked the van and broke her bones. It wasn't fair that Iris and Marshall were too freaked out to sleep last night. And it wasn't fair that I wouldn't get to go to Arizona. So what? I mean, you could look at it like, *nothing's fair.* But that's pretty depressing. So I was trying not to look at it at all.

"I'm sorry, honey. I know you were looking forward to seeing him and meeting your brother. Do you want me to call your dad and let him know what happened? Or do you want to call?"

"Would you call? I mean, I hate to tie up the phone here . . ." That wasn't it, of course. I was just suddenly afraid to call. What if I could hear relief in Dad's voice when I said I wouldn't be showing up? Or what if it was obvious he really didn't care one way or the other? I felt too fragile right now; I couldn't take the chance.

"I'll call him this morning. When will you hear about the car?"

"Roland is going to check about it this afternoon."

"Roland?"

"Mr. Packer."

She sighed again. "Well, I guess there isn't much I can do from back here. I'll call you tomorrow to see how Dory's doing and if the car can be fixed. If it can, I'll have to come out and help you drive it back."

Even though it was great to talk to Mom and to know she was ready to come out at a moment's notice, I didn't really want her to come now. The thing was, with Dory I'd always felt more or less *equal*—like I wasn't one of "the kids." But if Mom showed up, she'd definitely be in charge. I'd be demoted in front of Iris and Marsh.

They knew me now and they trusted me, as much as they trusted anybody. And after last night, I had the feeling the worst might not be over with them. I guess I wanted to be the one to help them get through it.

Exhausted as we were last night, none of us could get to sleep. Sukey had set up a cot in our room so we could each have our own place to sleep, but the lights were barely out before Marsh was standing next to my bed asking to climb in with me. He scooted around like a puppy trying to find a comfortable position, and just when he'd settled down, Iris sat up.

"I can't sleep either. Is there room?"

How could I say no? After what we'd already been through, sleeping in one bed should have been simple. Except that Iris's ankle was sore, and my head hurt, and just when I'd finally dropped off to sleep, Marsh woke up screaming. I knew it must be because of the accident—he hadn't awakened like that since the beginning of the trip.

I tried to rub his back like I'd seen Dory do, but he wrenched away from me and flung himself out of the bed onto the floor, sobbing.

Iris pulled the blanket over her face and yelled at him, "Marshall, shut up! It's the middle of the night!"

"That's not going to help," I said. "What does your mother do when he gets really upset like this?"

She lowered the blanket a little. "I don't know. She sings to him sometimes."

"What does she sing?"

"I don't *know*! Dumb songs. Why does he *do* this? My ankle hurts and I want to sleep!"

"Iris, he's your brother. He's scared because of the accident. Don't you get that?"

"I *get* it, Robin. I just don't want to get sucked under with him. Do you get *that*?" She turned her back to me.

They kept surprising me, these little hints of Iris's humanity. I ran my fingers through her sloppy ponytail. "I know. It's been a horrible day. But we need to get Marsh to calm down, and you know how to do it."

She groaned. "I don't know the songs. Silly stuff, like camp songs and things."

"Like *what*? You must know one or two of them."

Iris sighed deeply, then hoisted herself into a sitting position, rubbing her eyes. "*My paddle's clean and bright. Flashing with silver,*" she sang tunelessly.

I remembered it from years at Girl Scout camp and joined in. "*Follow the wild goose flight. Dip, dip, and swing. Dip, dip, and swing it back, flashing with silver. Follow the wild goose flight. Dip, dip, and swing.*" I sang it again, myself; it seemed like Marshall's crying was winding down a little.

When I stopped singing, he said, "Again."

"Do it with me, Iris. In a round," I said.

"Are you crazy? I'm *tired*!" she said.

I gave her a look and began singing; she started her part when I was halfway through and we sang it three or four times. Marshall was breathing normally by then, but he was still lying on the floor.

"Why don't you get back into bed?" I asked him.

"Sing another one," he ordered. "Sing 'Comin' 'Round the Mountain.'"

Iris rolled her eyes. "Get up here on the bed first—then we'll sing." She was getting the idea anyway.

Marsh climbed back up next to me, and Iris and I started in. By the time we got to verse four, "*Oh, she'll have to sleep with grandma when she comes,*" he was breathing steadily. We carefully eased ourselves back down onto the bed as we came around the mountain for the last time. Marsh and Iris were both fast asleep within minutes, but I lay awake for a long time. I felt so responsible for the kids sleeping on either side of me. But I was also really glad to be in charge. I was glad Mom wasn't coming out to help me. And I was even glad Chris wasn't there for me to lean on and complain to. I had no choice but to *do* this. It was frightening, but it also made me feel strong. And, in an odd way, it even made me like them more, maybe even love them.

"No way!" Marsh was talking through a mouth stuffed full of cinnamon pancakes. "You have five brothers?"

Savannah nodded.

"And no sisters?" Iris gave her a look of horror. "That's awful!"

"I don't mind. We all get along."

"Where are they?"

"Two older brothers live in Albuquerque, where they went to college. One goes to University of California at Berkeley—he stayed there for the summer. And the two younger ones, Tony and Cesar, who knows? They're teenagers."

"Tony's down in the barn with Ruby and Eleanor, his horses," Sukey said. "Cesar's sleeping late, as usual."

Roland sat down next to Savannah and put a lazy arm around her shoulders. "Savannah is our only daughter and she goes the farthest away from us. Now, I ask you, is that fair?" He shook his head.

"I'll come back when I'm done with school. Probably." She smooched Roland's cheek.

"Where do you go to school?" I asked. I'd been thinking waitressing was Savannah's occupation, but obviously it was only a summer job.

"University of Washington in Seattle."

"Why did you want to go there?" I asked. All I knew about Washington was it rained a lot and they grew apples.

"I'm studying art history," she said. "I'm mostly interested in Indian art, or Native American art, as the college catalog says. I already knew a lot about the Indians around here and I wanted to learn more about the art of the Northwest Coast Indians. So, Seattle was a logical place to go."

I wondered where the logical place was for *me* to go. Chris thought his place was Georgetown. I'd figured on just going to the University of Iowa, but maybe a different school would be better.

Not that I knew what I wanted to do yet, but over the past few weeks, dealing with Iris and Marshall, I'd started to think it was something I was good at. Talking to kids and helping them figure things out. Maybe it came from all those years of having Franny around, needing me. Anyway, I thought I might like learning more about psychology or sociology. At least it was a place to start.

Sukey started cleaning up the dishes while Roland went out to the front desk to check out people who were leaving.

"We'll help you with the dishes," I offered, giving Marsh and Iris looks. I was pretty sure they weren't used to doing any housework, but they shuffled to their feet and picked up their plates, even though it was hard for Iris to do with crutches. Sukey had already made other plans for us, though. Savannah, she said, would drop us off at the hospital on her way to work. We could call the motel whenever we wanted to come back and somebody would pick us up.

I hadn't really gotten a good look at Santa Fe the night before. It was dark and we were all pretty crazed after the accident. Driving over to the hospital I had a chance to take it in a little better. It was beautiful even with tourists standing around everywhere. I wished we could spend the day exploring the colorful shops with their banners out front, the downtown square where the Indians laid out their jewelry on blankets.

"I love the way this town looks!" I said. "*Everything* is made out of adobe."

"It is a special place," Savannah said. "I don't have to work tomorrow. I'll take you on a tour if you want."

"That would be great!" I said. Iris and Marshall were quiet. "I mean, assuming Dory is okay."

Savannah glanced back at them. "Would you guys be interested in seeing the San Ildefonso Pueblo where my parents met? It's not far out of town and it's a very cool place."

Marshall sat up. "Yeah! Will there be real Indians there?"

Iris gave him a disgusted look. "Who else would live in an Indian pueblo?"

"Native Americans," he said with a straight face. Even Iris laughed.

Savannah let us out at the main entrance to the hospital and drove off. Just inside the front door Iris spied a rest room.

"One minute," she said, disappearing inside.

"Do you need help?" I said, thinking about the crutches.

"No, thanks."

Marshall and I waited outside. I wasn't really even listening for anything—I'd kind of given that up the last few days, but I heard it, anyway. No water running or anything—if Marsh hadn't wandered down the hall, he'd have heard it, too. Iris had decided not to hide anymore. Could the accident have had something to do with this, too?

"Ready," she said when she came out. I expected her to give me one of her frosty stares, but she didn't even look at me. Her face was pale.

I couldn't say anything in front of Marshall, and certainly not in front of Dory, the condition she was in, so I just smiled at her. "Feel better now?"

"Yeah," she said quietly.

Well, so much for psychology. I had no idea what I was supposed to do now. Anybody who would throw up the best pancakes on earth was beyond me.

When we got to Dory's room the doctor we'd seen the day before was just coming out. "This will get her spirits up!" she said. "Mrs. Tewksbury, your clan is here!"

It was sort of a shock to see Dory. She was sitting up in bed, but her hair was sticking out weirdly around a bandage on her head, and one eye had turned black and blue. Her shoulder and arm were still in traction and her hospital nightgown was twisted around her like soft-serve ice cream. Basically, she looked like hell.

Marshall didn't care. He flung himself down onto her good side and hung on tight.

"Be careful, Marsh," I said. "Your mom's kind of fragile."

"I'm okay," she said, though she was obviously wincing under

Marshall's weight. He'd brought her a drawing of Sukey's kitchen and was trying to explain it to her, but Iris interrupted.

"Savannah sent some oranges," she said, setting a plastic bag on the sheet by her mother's legs, then backing off.

"I'm so glad to see all of you. But, Iris, why are you on crutches? They didn't tell me you were hurt!" Dory stretched her good arm out toward Iris, but Iris didn't come any closer.

"It's just a sprained ankle. No big deal."

"She just has to stay off it for a few days," I explained.

"Thank God, none of you were seriously hurt. I could never have forgiven myself! I'm just so sorry about everything. I wrecked our whole trip!"

"I don't care," Iris said. "I want to go home, anyway."

"We don't have to go home right away, do we?" Marsh said. "I like it here. And Savannah's going to take us to see a pueblo tomorrow. Like Acoma, only different."

"Is that where you're staying? With Savannah's family? I thought that's what I remembered hearing last night, but I was so woozy."

I nodded. "Savannah's parents are really nice. We're staying in one of the motel rooms, but they want us to eat with them. They have a lot of kids, anyway."

Iris plunked herself down in a chair halfway across the room. "Hard to believe six kids could have ever lived in that house. It's way too small."

"Savannah told me Roland built it."

"I know. She's so *proud* of them. She acts like she's *their* parent."

"Iris," Dory said, sounding stern for a moment. Then she changed her mind. "Come a little closer. I can hardly see you way over there."

"I look the same as I did yesterday."

But you're acting even worse, I thought.

Dory sighed. "Dr. Ellis says my arm has to stay in this contraption for a week, and I'll be in a cast for three months after that. At least the concussion was mild. Robin, be sure to tell Savannah's parents to keep track of the expenses—your food and everything—and I'll pay them before we leave."

"I will," I assured her.

"I won't be able to drive back to Chicago, though."

"If there's even a car to *drive,*" Iris said.

Dory winced. "Will you guys ever forgive me for this?"

"It was Iris's fault!" Marsh said. "If she hadn't been arguing with you . . ."

I waited for the inevitable screams of protest from Iris, but she was silent, staring at her lap. It was Dory who interrupted Marshall.

"No! It was certainly not Iris's fault. I was the one who took off my seat belt. I was the one who wasn't watching the road. It was *my* fault, Marshall, not your sister's."

"Yeah, but she was annoying you!" Marsh insisted.

Dory gave a little laugh. "Sweetheart, if I had an accident every time Iris annoyed me, we wouldn't have made it out of Iowa City."

Even Iris had to smile at that. She looked relieved, too. Then suddenly her face brightened. "Guess what?" The pot didn't break! The jar thing from Acoma."

"Yeah," Marsh chimed in. "Me and the pot were the only things that didn't get a scratch."

"Wouldn't you know? That damned pot," Dory said. "I don't care if I never see it again."

"I saved the pot," Iris said.

"You did?"

"She held it between her knees," I told Dory.

"Why? I thought you hated it."

Iris shrugged and crawled back behind her disdainful mask. "I like it now. I want to keep it."

And that's how we spent the next few hours, Marshall hanging on, Iris pushing away, me somewhere in between, still trying to figure out how to tie everyone together.

Chapter Twenty-one

Whether from exhaustion or just the need to escape from one another, my cousins and I were each in a separate bed and asleep by nine-thirty. When I woke at seven, Iris was still sleeping, but Marsh's bed was empty. He wasn't in the room at all. I dressed quickly to head over to the Bolton-Packer quarters to see if he was making a pest of himself this early in the morning, but as soon as I got outside I saw him walking up from the barn in back of the motel.

"How come you're up so early?" I asked.

He shrugged. "I just woke up. You guys were still snoring, so I went to see the horses. They've got two, Eleanor Rigby and Ruby Tuesday."

I laughed. "They told you their names?"

Marsh was not in a joking mood. "No. Tony was down there—he takes care of the horses. I helped him with Eleanor."

"Wait until Iris hears. She'll be down there begging to ride."

The anger that flashed across Marshall's face startled me. "I wish she wasn't here! I wish she wasn't even my sister!"

"Whoa! Marsh, I know you're not exactly best buddies, but . . ."

"I hate her." He glared, daring me to try to talk him out of it. I kept my mouth shut.

After a minute he broke his stare. "I don't always hate her. But I hate her when she gets crazy and mad, like she is now."

"Does it scare you?"

"No!" he yelled. "It just makes me mad and crazy, too. It's like the chicken pox or something that I catch from her. I just want to be normal again like we used to be."

"Don't you think Iris wants that, too?"

"Who knows what she wants," he said, but his voice was a little calmer. He scratched his sneaker in the dust. "Let's stop talking about it, okay? I don't want to be mad at you, too."

Just then the door of room number 5 opened and Iris walked out in her T-shirt and underpants. "You guys just went off and left me in here all by myself! I wake up and you're both gone, for godsakes!"

"Jeez, Virus. What did you think—we walked back to Chicago without you?"

"Well, where did you go?"

"We were right outside. You don't have any pants on," I reminded her. "And aren't you supposed to use your crutches?" I pushed her back inside and Marsh followed me.

"I don't need the crutches. My ankle's okay. How come you went outside?"

"I went to look for Marsh, that's all," I told her. "He went down to see the horses this morning."

"Without me?"

"You were asleep, dipwad," Marsh said.

"I want to go see the horses, too!" She seemed on the verge of tears over this nonevent.

"Well, get dressed and we'll walk down there after breakfast," I said, but Marshall's harsher comment drowned me out.

"Why don't you leave the poor horses alone? You'll just infect them with your craziness, too."

I should have seen it coming, but Iris was so fast, I wasn't prepared. Her fist shot out right in front of me and landed squarely in the middle of Marshall's face. His head flew back like his neck was on a spring, and the look in his eyes raced from surprise to anger to anguish in five seconds flat. He started to howl as blood poured from his nose.

"You broke my nose! Look what you did, you stupid bitch! You broke my nose!" His hands were cupped to catch the blood flow, but that left his feet free to kick out at his sister. He landed one on her kneecap that buckled her and she fell sideways onto the bed.

"Ow, that's my bad leg, you idiot!"

This time I could see the retaliatory strike coming and I stepped between them, pushing Iris back down on the bed. "Iris, don't you dare hit him again! He's already bleeding all over himself."

I grabbed Marsh by the shirt, dragged him into the bathroom, and sat him on the toilet seat so I could see how much damage had been done. He was screaming like crazy, totally enraged at what had happened.

"I hope you bleed to death!" Iris yelled.

"Iris, shut up before *I* kick you," I yelled back.

There was a knock on the door, but before I could answer it, Savannah and her mother rushed in.

"What happened?" they asked, looking at the three of us.

Iris and Marshall became suddenly mute, Iris crawling back under the bedcovers, Marsh sniffing up blood and tears.

"We had a little accident," I said. "Marsh got hit in the nose."

"By her!" he said, pointing at Iris.

"Okay, it's over now," I said. "Let's just make sure your nose is okay."

"Let me look," Sukey said. "I used to be an EMT—I know a little bit about these things." The blood had slowed to a trickle and

I cleaned Marsh's face with a washcloth while Sukey gently moved his nose from side to side.

"Does that hurt?" she asked. He nodded, but obviously he wasn't in all that much pain anymore. "It's not broken. The cartilage is fine. You probably just burst a vessel in there. Savannah, go make up an ice bag for him to hold on it."

Now that the screaming had stopped, I was embarrassed that Sukey and Savannah had seen our dysfunction in action. They would probably think I couldn't handle my cousins alone, that I was too young to take care of them. Maybe I was. A few weeks ago I wouldn't have cared—who wanted to take care of them, anyway? But now I was so tied up with them, and I wanted so badly to be the one to help them through this stuff. I couldn't bear the idea of sending them back to Chicago kicking and screaming and hating each other, when it seemed like they were really just sad and scared and needy. And even though I didn't have a clue how to go about helping them, it was beginning to seem like my mission in life.

Of course Sukey and Savannah didn't make a big deal out of the fight. Sukey said something like, "I've raised six kids—this is not the first time I've seen a sibling-inflicted bloody nose."

By the time we finished our unusually quiet breakfast and piled into Savannah's car, Marsh's nose was fine. I talked Iris into taking one crutch along so she wouldn't tire her ankle out too much, even though she swore she didn't need it. We stopped at the hospital first to check on Dory who seemed a little less cheerful than the day before.

"I can't wait to get out of this traction thing," she said. "I can't do anything except lie here and listen to stupid television programs."

"Lucky!" Marsh said.

The kids were fairly quiet while Dory talked to Savannah about the arrangements for us at the Black Mesa. I kept waiting for

Marsh to tell his mother about Iris's punch and the bloody shirt I'd thrown in the trash. I think Iris expected it, too, but he didn't say a word. I could have kissed him, although that might have endangered my own nose.

Dory was glad Savannah had planned a day of activities for us. "I'd be more upset if you had to spend all week sitting around this hospital waiting for my arm to heal. Go have fun and tell me about it tomorrow."

Amazingly, considering the way the day had started, we did have a good time. I think I'd even say a great time. And the kids would probably agree. Savannah had lived in Santa Fe all her life so she was a perfect guide. First we walked around downtown where the buildings are all made of adobe and not more than two or three stories tall. There's a shady park in the center of town called the Plaza and on one side of it is a long, covered walkway where Indians put their crafts out on blankets to sell—leather goods and pottery and beautiful jewelry.

I tried on a silver ring with small pieces of turquoise set around a circular design. It reminded me of the bright sun we'd spent so much time underneath on this western trip. For a moment I thought I might buy it.

"Do you like it?" I asked Savannah and Iris.

"It's lovely," Savannah said.

"Yeah, you should get it," Iris said. "You never buy yourself anything!"

I could have bought it—I had enough money along, and I'd hardly spent any of it, but it was awfully expensive for a ring. I never buy myself things like that—things I don't actually need. I just couldn't do it.

I put the ring back on the blanket and watched it sparkle at me.

"You aren't getting it?" Iris said.

I shook my head.

"But you like it, don't you?"

"I love it, but that doesn't mean I have to have it."

"You're funny about money," Marsh said, then put up his hands to block my retort. "I know, you were raised that way, like my mom." He shook his head over the oddity of Iowa childhoods.

We got ice-cream cones and sat on the Plaza for a while, watching men in cowboy hats and long ponytails, women in short skirts and big sunglasses, in-line skaters in tank tops and knee pads, old people with big dogs, bicyclists with tattoos, and little kids riding in racing strollers. It seemed like every kind of person on earth had a representative right there in that little park.

Then Savannah drove us up to the Museum of International Folk Art, which she said was her favorite place in all of Santa Fe. You could see why. Each room was filled to its high ceiling with folk art pieces from all over the world: embroidered cloths from India, paintings from Africa, dolls from before the Civil War in America, huge bride sculptures from Mexico—so many things it was impossible to see them all. Best were the enormous dioramas in which tiny figures made of wood or clay or even bread dough depicted scenes of village life in various countries.

After lunch we headed up to San Ildefonso Pueblo. For some reason I felt nervous about it; I remembered James at Acoma and the way he looked at us like intruders. But I needn't have worried—Savannah knew people at San Ildefonso. Her father had studied pottery there with a man named George who was very friendly. He showed us around his studio and the public parts of the pueblo. George's pottery was all black, too, although each pot was part matte and part polished so that, from up close, you could see a design. He explained that every pueblo's pottery was somewhat different, and that this was the traditional pottery at San Ildefonso.

George showed us how he starts making a pot, with coils of

clay that he builds up layer by layer. It was hard to imagine the time it must take to go from the rough coils to the finished black pot.

"How do you get it all smoothed out?" Marsh asked. "Especially inside the pot?"

"I have tools to help me," George explained, showing Marsh some small wooden implements he used. "But I use my hands, too. Here, you try to smooth inside this one," he said, handing him a half-finished pot. Carefully, Marshall took two fingers and reached inside to caress the clay.

"I like the way it feels," he said.

George nodded. "So do I."

Marsh was so intent on what he was doing, the rest of us went outside in the sun for a while and just let him work.

We walked around the small cemetery and then rested under the huge cottonwood tree in the middle of the courtyard until Marsh was ready to go. I was happy to see that he didn't need any prompting to thank George for letting him work on the pot.

On the ride home, Marsh was ecstatic. "He is so nice. I wish I could live in a pueblo. I wish I was an Indian!"

"God, Marshall, get a grip," was Iris's comment, but Marsh was too happy to let it bother him.

After dinner with Savannah and her family, Iris left the table quickly. I didn't follow her, but I was fairly sure that the generous amount of macaroni and cheese she'd just wolfed down was being quickly deposited into the septic system. The problem seemed to be getting worse, and I decided the next day I'd have to find a way to talk to Dory about it.

Meanwhile, it wouldn't hurt to mention it to my mother.

While Savannah and Sukey were looking at Marshall's drawings (and giving him lots of praise), and Iris was proudly showing Roland the pot from Acoma as though she'd made the purchase, if not the pot, herself, I took my phone card and sneaked out to the pay phone.

"Roland says the car can be fixed," I reported to Mom first. "There was a lot of damage to the body, but the engine is okay."

"Well, that's good news," she said. "I've come up with an idea for driving it back here that I think you'll like."

"You're coming out?"

"Well, the thing is, I can't really take that much time off right now—several other nurses are on vacation and we're short staffed as it is. So, I asked Franny what she thought about flying out to New Mexico and helping you drive the car back. You can imagine her reaction."

"Franny's coming out?" This was the best news I'd had in weeks. "That's great!"

"I thought you'd like the idea. I talked to Dory this morning, and she'll pay for Franny's plane fare and your hotel rooms and everything on the way back. She said she's glad you'll be able to have at least a few good memories from this trip. She made it sound like the kids have been quite a handful."

Where to start? "Yeah, I wanted to talk to you about that. I'm pretty sure Iris is bulimic."

"What? Dory didn't say anything about that!"

"Dory doesn't want to hear it. I tried to talk to her about it and she said all teenage girls are worried about their weight. For a while I thought it was getting better, but since the accident she's worse again."

"Has she lost much weight?"

"Maybe five or six pounds. I don't think she really wants to be doing it. It's like she can't help herself."

"I suppose it's some kind of reaction to Allen's death."

"I want to help her, but I don't know what to do about it."

"Honey, Dory told me you've been an incredible help to the kids, that Marshall adores you, and he's much better than he was when they left Chicago."

"Yeah, well, she hasn't seen them much since the accident. They're both pretty looney again now."

"Robin, you won't be able to solve all their problems in a few weeks. These children have been through a huge trauma. It's amazing you're having any luck with them at all."

"You know, the funny thing is, as awful as they are sometimes, I actually like them. Even Iris, who's a terror. I don't even know why exactly, but, when this is over, I'm going to miss having them around."

"I'm sure they'll miss you, too."

"Anyway, Dory shouldn't worry. My memories from this trip will be good ones, very good ones. Even if we didn't make it to California, I got to see things I never knew existed."

"I'm glad, honey. I guess seeing the country got your mind off Chris once in a while, huh?"

"Yeah, I guess it did." Even to Mom I didn't dare admit just how *off Chris* my mind had gotten. There was so much else to think about!

Chapter Twenty-two

"I wish this day wouldn't end," Marshall said. Iris and I had been reading while Marsh drew in his book. I looked at the clock—it was almost eleven.

"It's been a good one," I said, pleased he seemed to have forgotten the early morning fistfight. "But it's late. We should turn out the light."

Iris threw her book overboard and flopped down on her pillow. "I'm ready."

I clicked off the lamp between our beds. "Marsh, can you get the one over by you?"

He was silent a minute and then he said, "No."

"What do you mean, 'No'? It's late."

"I don't want to go to sleep tonight. I want to stay up."

"Oh, Lord," Iris said. "Do you always have to make trouble?"

"Me? All I want to do is stay up—that's not making trouble."

"Okay, okay," I said. "Let's not argue about this. Marshall, you have to go to sleep or you'll be too exhausted to do anything tomorrow."

"So? Savannah has to work tomorrow. We'll just go to the

hospital and then hang out around here. I can sleep in the afternoon if I want to."

By now I knew that arguing with Marshall was not the best way to get him to come around. He was too stubborn to give in. "Okay, you can stay up. But you can't keep Iris awake. That light has to go out."

"Then how will I draw?"

"We'll go into the bathroom and close the door."

"Are you staying up, too?"

"For a while. I'll write a letter."

I figured Marsh would give out before I did, and I could at least stick a pillow under his head and cover him with a blanket before I went to bed myself. Besides, I'd been thinking about the last letter I'd written to Chris, all about good-looking cowboys and Iris and I becoming girlfriends. I'd been so angry when I wrote it that it wasn't very honest. Even though he'd been cavorting with Gabriella, he'd at least told me about it, and he didn't deserve the phony-baloney reply I'd sent.

Iris grumbled at us as we got our materials together and took pillows and blankets into the bathroom. "You two are insane— that's all there is to it."

We closed the door on her and grinned at each other. "Toilet seat, bathtub, or floor?" I asked him.

"Can I sit in the bathtub?"

"Be my guest."

Marsh took off his shoes and arranged the pillow and blankets just so, scrambled into the tub with his drawing materials, and let out a sigh of contentment. For my part, I found myself once again sitting on a toilet seat, trying to figure out just what words were the perfect ones to send to Chris. I decided to make a stab at the truth, if only I could figure out what it was.

•

Dear Chris,

A lot has happened since I wrote you a few days ago, but first I want to go back to the last letter I got from you. Even though I pretended I wasn't bothered by it, I was. It was all about hanging out with Gabriella and a bunch of other girls and drinking and dancing and sweating. You were talking about caffes and corsos and piazzas—things I've never even seen, and it made me feel terrible. I don't think you meant it that way, but to me it felt like you were giving me the reasons we could never have the same relationship we used to have. It seemed like you had grown up and left me behind.

But now I realize you haven't really left me behind, because this summer has been full of new experiences for me, too. I'm not learning a new language or meeting foreign students like you are, but I am learning other things: why people choose to live the places they do, how mountains look when you're driving right through them, what kind of salve to put on a rope burn, how Indian pottery is made, and how to talk to a ten-year-old who's ready to explode. This trip hasn't always been easy, and it certainly hasn't always been fun, but it's always been amazing.

We're in Santa Fe, New Mexico, now, and we'll be here for a while. This is the end of the journey . . . at least for now. Our car ran off the road and flipped over about an hour from here. Dory was the only one who really got hurt, and she'll be okay—she has some broken bones. The van was pretty busted up and we're waiting for it to be fixed. Dory and the kids will have to fly home when she gets out of the hospital. Franny is coming out here to help me drive the car back to Iowa, and then Mom and I will take it up to Chicago.

I know that all sounds like terrible luck, and in a way it is. But I'm beginning to see that there's often a good side to bad luck. We're staying with a family who owns a motel here and they've been wonderful to us. Savannah, who's twenty, has shown us all around the city and taken us to the San Ildefonso Indian Pueblo where she has friends. I love the west. I'm thinking that, if Mom says we can afford it, or if I can get some scholarship money, I'd like to go to school out here. As long as we won't be together anyway, there's no reason for me to stay in Iowa.

I guess pretty soon you'll be leaving Rome and starting to travel around Italy. I know how much fun that will be. I mean, now I really know it, and I understand why you had to go on this trip. I'm glad you did—if you'd stayed in Thunder Lake, I would have too, and I never would have seen New Mexico!

Okay, I admit I'm jealous of Gabriella. But by next year I'll probably be jealous of somebody else. There are going to be so many changes in our lives the next few years, but I think most of them will be good ones.

I know you will have changed by the time you get back to Iowa, and I hope you'll still love me. I still love you, Chris, but I think I've changed, too.

From Santa Fe to Rome, all my love,
Robin

I folded the letter and addressed the envelope before I looked over at Marsh. His head was bobbing and falling toward the side of the bathtub. Surely he'd be willing to get into bed now. After all, the tub couldn't be very comfortable.

"Marsh," I whispered. "Let's go to bed."

His head jerked up. "No. I'm not tired." He batted his droopy lids.

"You're asleep already. Come on!"

I tried to take his hand to help him out, but he pulled away. "No! I don't want to go to sleep!"

I sat down on the edge of the tub. Something more was going on than just his usual argumentativeness. "Why not?"

Suddenly, tears began to stream down his face. "I don't want to, Robin—don't make me! I'll have bad dreams again! I know I will! Don't make me go to sleep!"

He let me take his hand then, and I pulled him up to sit beside me on the tub. He was so overtired and upset he leaned his head against my shoulder and sobbed. "I hate the dreams! I hate them!" I let him cry until he shuddered and fell heavily against me, already more asleep than awake.

"Would it help to tell me about the dreams?" I asked quietly.

He shook his head. "Don't want to talk about them."

"Okay. But you should lie down now—in my bed if you want. You don't have to go to sleep, but if you do, I don't think you'll have the dreams tonight."

"How do you know?" He looked up at me, his face soggy and pleading, as if he hoped I might really have the inside scoop on his nighttime brain waves.

"I don't know for sure. But if you do, I'll be right there and I'll wake you up."

He continued to cry a little, but he was too exhausted to fight it anymore. I put my arm around his shoulders and led him back to the bedroom. He crawled between the sheets, snuffled for about thirty seconds, and before I'd even fluffed my pillow, he was fast asleep.

We were all thankful to wake up and realize it was morning and the night had passed without interruption. Savannah dropped us at the hospital before she drove down to Madrid for the day, and Iris ducked into the bathroom again as soon as we got inside. Since she'd only had a piece of dry toast for breakfast I couldn't imagine what she hoped to bring up. I had to talk to Dory about this.

Savannah's brother Cesar was scheduled to pick us up at noon, but by ten thirty the kids were bored sitting around the hospital room. I saw my opportunity.

"Why don't you guys go down and look around the gift shop?" I suggested, knowing they could never resist the idea of shopping. I'd had Dory's purse since the accident and had taken a twenty-dollar bill out this morning for just this purpose. I wiggled it in front of their faces.

"That's all you're giving us?" Marsh said.

Iris grabbed it. "It'll do."

"That's ten for each of you," I reminded her.

"Yeah, yeah," she said, walking out the door.

"Let me hold on to it," Marsh said, following her.

"Yeah, that'll happen."

They squabbled all the way down the hall to the elevator, and then they were gone. Dory was staring at one of those dumb judge shows on the TV that hung from the ceiling. "Can we turn this off a minute?" I said. "I really need to talk to you about Iris."

She clicked it off and looked up at me with an expectant frown. "What's she doing now? Tormenting her brother again?"

"Well, sure, that. They both torment each other, but that's not what I'm worried about. Dory, I think Iris is bulimic."

She gave a little laugh. "Bulimic? No, Iris is just . . ."

"Dory, I know she's bulimic. I hear her throwing up meals almost every day. Earlier in the trip I even saw her doing it." Dory's face went slack and she pulled the sheet up higher on her chest. For a minute I thought she was going to pull it up right over her head. "She knows I know about it. She begged me not to tell you. For a while I thought she was over it, but since the accident, it's gotten worse again. I don't know what to do."

"Why? Why would she do something like that? Iris is a smart girl—she knows better."

"I talked to Mom about it last night. She thought it might have something to do with Uncle Allen's death."

"But she's taken it better than any of us. She's so strong—she's gotten me through this. It's Marsh I'm worried about, with his nightmares and those drawings . . ."

"I think Marsh is actually okay, Dory. I mean, I've been thinking about it. He's been upset, but I think the drawings and even the nightmares are the way he's getting the fear out. He can talk about Allen's death and feel sad about it. All Iris can do is make nasty comments."

Dory looked at me skeptically. "You think I'm worried about the wrong child?"

"I do, yeah."

Dory sighed and shifted her weight so she could look out the window. "Well, Robin, I don't mean to sound ungrateful, but I do think I know my children a little better than you do."

What could I say to that? Only this: "Dory, she throws up her meals. That I know for sure."

Dory's good arm came up to shield her face. I thought she was just rubbing her forehead, but then I saw the tears cascading down her cheeks. "Oh, God, I don't know what to do for them! Most of the time I'm so upset I feel like throwing up my own dinner. How can I help them, Robin? We're all screwed up!"

I handed her a tissue and sat gently on the side of the bed. "I don't know what to do either. But I think you need to stop pretending Marsh's nightmares are the only problem. I think you should start talking to one another instead of telling me everything."

Dory nodded. "You're right, you're right."

"Tomorrow I'll let the kids come by themselves, okay? Maybe you can figure out how to talk about things."

"Okay." She took my hand in her good one. "Robin, you've been a buffer for us this summer—you've kept us from rubbing each other raw. I hardly know how we'll get along without you. I imagine you'll be glad to see the last of us, though."

I leaned over and gave her a soft kiss on the cheek. "I wouldn't trade this trip for anything, Dory."

The kids returned a few minutes later, giggling in an oddly conspiratorial way for the two of them. They had their hands behind their backs and their mouths stuffed with gum.

"All we got was gum," Marshall said, barely able to speak around the wad in his cheek.

"You bought twenty dollars worth of gum?" I said, incredulous.

"Well, we got some other stuff, too, didn't we, Marsh?" Iris said, smiling at her brother. Dory and I were speechless in the face of the two of them acting so good-natured.

"Don't you wanna know what we got?" Marsh asked.

"Yes, show me," Dory said.

Simultaneously they both brought their arms from behind their backs and thrust their purchases at their mother. Marsh held out a box of chocolate-covered cherries and Iris a vase of tiny red roses. "We bought stuff for you!" Marsh announced proudly.

"Oh, my God!" Dory took the candy and put it in her lap, then grabbed the flowers. She kept looking from the gifts to her children as if she couldn't believe the two had any connection. "You bought things for me?"

"There wasn't much good stuff down there," Iris confessed. "But we decided on the way down that you deserved presents more than we did."

Dory put her good arm out to her children and they allowed her to pull them into an awkward hug. "My angels!" she said, exaggerating the case just a bit.

Chapter Twenty-three

Cesar was waiting for us when we came down the hospital steps at noon. I'd talked to him at breakfast a few times, but he was usually late for something and in a hurry. Today, though, he seemed calm as he sat behind the wheel reading *Guitar* magazine.

"Hey," he said when we crawled into the car. "How's your mother doing? Or your aunt or whatever."

"My aunt, their mother. She's better. She can get out in a few more days," I told him.

"You leaving then?"

"Well, I guess they are," I said, motioning to the backseat. "I have to wait for the car to be fixed and for my friend Franny to fly out here so we can drive it back to the Midwest."

"Just you two girls? Can I come too? I'll fix your flat tires." I knew he was teasing, but I made a face at him anyway.

"I think we *two girls* can manage it on our own."

He smiled. "You're lucky. I'd like to drive across the country. See something different than New Mexico every day."

"I think you're lucky to live here. This is my favorite of all the states we've been through," I told him. "I love Santa Fe."

"It's okay," Marsh said. "But my favorite was Wyoming, on the ranch."

"Me, too," Iris agreed, confirming the weird partnership they'd entered into in the hospital gift shop. "That reminds me, Marsh says you have two horses. Do you think I could ride one sometime?"

Cesar shrugged. "That depends on Tony—he's the horse whisperer."

"He is?"

"He thinks so. How old are you?"

Iris paused before answering and I turned around to stare at her. "Thirteen," she admitted.

"That's in your favor. Tony's fourteen. He'll probably let you ride."

"How old are you?" Iris asked him.

"Seventeen," he said.

"Same age as Robin! Too bad she already has a boyfriend."

Cesar looked over at me and grinned. "Oh, yeah? That is too bad."

I turned to look out the window, but not before my evil cousin spied my face. "Oh, look, we made her blush," she said.

Why is it so difficult not to feel mortified when your face betrays you like that? From Iris betrayal is no surprise, but you should be able to trust your own body. Thank God, Cesar didn't say anything. Although, when I finally looked over at him, he was still grinning.

To turn the conversation away from myself, I started telling him about the rodeo at the Lazy River Ranch. Iris and Marsh were happy to embellish my stories with their own, and that took us all the way back to the Black Mesa Motel without any more embarrassing incidents.

As we parked behind the Bolton-Packer residence, Cesar said,

"Oh, yeah, I forgot to mention—there's a surprise waiting for you inside."

"For me?" I said.

"Yeah. It came right before I left to pick you up. Check with Sukey—she had it last I knew."

"What is it?"

"Probably a letter from what's-his-name," Marsh said.

I shook my head. "Mom would have said if she'd sent one on."

"I think it's bigger than a letter," Cesar said. "Go in and see!"

We all piled out of the car and ran into the house. There, sitting at the kitchen table with Sukey was my dad, with less hair than I remembered and a little blond boy perched on his lap. Across from him sat Allison, who I'd only seen once before, when she was six months pregnant.

I stopped just inside the door and stared. Marsh and Iris stopped and stared, too, even though they had no idea who these people were.

"Robin! There you are!" Dad stood up holding David in his arms, patted my shoulder, and kissed me on the cheek. I kissed the air next to his left ear and felt his stubble rake my jaw. The two of us were never very comfortable with hello and good-bye.

"I can't believe you're here!" I said.

"Well, gee, kiddo, you came three quarters of the way—we couldn't very well let you turn around and go home again without even seeing you. Besides, David was anxious to meet his big sister."

Allison had come over to me by that time, too. She put her arm around my waist lightly. "As soon as we told him his sister was coming to visit him, he couldn't talk about anything else!" she said. "We didn't want to disappoint him."

David stared at me, his eyes big as walnuts. He didn't act like he couldn't stop talking about me.

"Hi, David. I'm glad to finally meet you. I'm Robin."

He burrowed into his father's shoulder and stuck his thumb in his mouth.

"He's a little shy," Allison explained. "He'll warm up when he gets to know you better."

"We can only stay one night, I'm afraid," Dad said. "It's hard for me to take off work in the middle of the week like this, but I told them it was a family emergency. I was afraid you might be gone by the weekend."

"I'm so glad you came," I said, noticing how comfortable David was leaning into my father's chest, obviously a familiar spot for him. A little stab of jealously poked me, but I pushed it aside.

"And you must be Dory's children," he said.

"Iris and Marshall. This is my dad, in case you haven't figured that out yet."

"I'm glad to meet you," Dad said.

They looked at him suspiciously.

"I was so sorry to hear you lost your father last year. That must have been very difficult for you."

Still they stared. I was half afraid Iris would say, "We didn't lose him—he *died*!" But maybe that's just what I was thinking. I'm the one who lost my father.

Finally Marsh said, "Did we ever meet you before?"

"No, but I used to know your mother."

"When?"

"Oh, a long time ago."

Dad looked uncomfortable, but Allison stepped forward and bent over at the waist to speak to Iris and Marsh, even though she was the same height as Iris and only a few inches taller than Marshall. "I thought we could all go out for dinner later. How would that be? Any place you want to go."

"Could we go someplace they have French fries?" Marsh asked. "We haven't had any in ages."

Iris rolled her eyes but remained silent.

Dad laughed. "I'm sure we could find someplace like that. David likes French fries, too, don't you, Davy?"

At last the little boy grinned, a beautiful smile that scrunched up his eyes and dimpled his cheeks. "I wike Fench fwies." God, this child was my brother.

It was a strange day. Dad, Allison, David, and I walked downtown to get lunch. Sukey offered to fix something for all of us, but Dad said that wasn't necessary. When we left Iris and Marsh were sitting at the table spreading peanut butter on crackers and giving me the evil eye. Cesar, who was pouring their milk, winked at me and didn't spill a drop. I had already decided not to think about whether or not he was cute. He probably was, but I had too much else on my mind already.

"David, do you want to hold your sister's hand?" Dad asked the poor kid on our way into town. David looked at me nervously and shook his head.

"He doesn't even know me yet, Dad. Give him a chance."

The boy looked up at me from his post, glued to my father's leg, and said, "My daddy." The first words my brother spoke to me and they were full of sibling rivalry already. Dear God, would we become Iris and Marshall?

"Remember what we talked about, Davy?" Allison said. "Daddy has two children. He's your daddy, but he's Robin's daddy, too."

"And I love you both," he said, looking meaningfully at first David, then me. We'd only walked three blocks and already I was exhausted by the level of emotion this reunion entailed. If David had asked me right then to relinquish my share of Jerry Daley so he could have full ownership, I would have agreed to it. It would have been simpler for everybody.

Because Davy really needed a nap after lunch, we all sat through an awful cartoon movie. The toddler conked out after ten minutes while the rest of us stared at a screen full of talking cockroaches for another hour and a half. If they knew the kid would fall asleep anyway, why couldn't we have gone to something decent? I didn't even get to watch him sleep—which would have been a chance to look at him as much as I wanted to without freaking him out—because Allison was seated between me and Dad, whose lap was obviously David's personal futon.

After that, Allison wanted to look at some of the shops, so Dad and I offered to take David to the Plaza where he could run around a little. There was a group of kids playing guitars under a tree, which seemed to intrigue Davy. He stood watching them for a while until they stopped playing and tried to talk to him—then he came running back to us. Dad eagerly let him crawl back into his favorite spot, even though Davy's sneakers left grassy stains on Dad's pants.

"I'm so glad I could get you two kids together," he said, his grin spreading out to his ears. "I want you to get to know each other. It's my goal that you not be strangers."

I wondered if Allison had the same goal. I kept thinking there was so much I wanted to ask him, so many things I didn't know about my own father. *What does your house look like? Do you like your job? What kind of books do you read? Does Allison make dinner every night or do you cook? What do you do for fun on the weekends? Is it always hot in Phoenix? Is your house air-conditioned? Do you have cactus growing in your yard? Are you and Allison going to have more children? Do you ever think about my mom? Do you ever think about me?*

But you can't just start asking somebody questions like that, even if he is your father. So all I said was, "Do you like living in Phoenix?"

"We love it," he said. "Ally grew up there, you know."

"No, I didn't know that." Apparently, I didn't know much.

"Yeah, it's her home. And I've settled in there. It's my home now, too."

The man sitting next to me on the bench seemed like a complete stranger. Where was that nervous guy who used to try to keep my mouth busy with burgers and milk shakes so I wouldn't talk too much? Had I *ever* sat on his lap?

Dad was so excited about being a husband and father this time around he couldn't stop talking about it. He even wanted me to be a part of it. I kind of wanted that too, except I couldn't figure out how to do it. This was a complete family already—mother, father, and child—when you added in a half sister or a stepdaughter it got too complicated. "We'll get you out to our place one of these days," Dad said. "Soon! So David still remembers you." He gave his son a hug. "So you can have a big sister!"

David eyed me uncertainly. He was probably wondering why he needed a sister anyway. I was wondering if that was what all this family stuff was *really* about. Getting a sister for David, not a father for me.

For dinner Sukey had suggested a restaurant she knew about that had a cowboy theme and fat French fries. Savannah had been invited, too, to thank her for all she'd done for us, so we took two cars. Marsh and Iris climbed in with Savannah, and Dad's family got into his car, and I stood there between them, unable to choose which direction to go. I felt more a part of Savannah's family than Dad's, and certainly closer to Iris and Marshall, after all we'd been through. But I knew I was expected to go with Dad, that I should be glad they wanted me with them, accepted me. Reluctantly, I climbed into the backseat next to Davy's car seat.

By the time we finished our burgers and fries, Davy had warmed up to me, and to Marshall, too. Since Iris was as silent as humanly possible, he probably wasn't even aware of her existence.

David had watched gleefully as Marsh stole French fries off my plate from across the table. Since Davy was seated right next to me, he tried the same maneuver. We got into a little game with the two of them ganging up to ravage my plate, and me pretending to be outraged. Davy got the giggles after Marsh gave him a high five. When I ran low on fries, I grabbed a pile from Iris's plate, since, of course, she wasn't really eating them, anyway. Allison was a little dumbfounded by her angel and his new pal flinging food around the table, but Dad seemed thrilled with the camaraderie between the three of us. He kept saying, "Are you teasing your sister?" as if teasing were the greatest compliment that could be paid. Which, I guess, from a two-year-old, it might be.

On the drive back to the Black Mesa Motel, there was no question of where I'd sit. David demanded that "Wobin" sit on one side of his car seat and "Marthow" on the other. Iris flew into the front seat of Savannah's car as if she couldn't wait to escape the rest of us. Dad's family had taken a room at the Black Mesa for the night, too, and Marsh and I walked them to their door, each holding one of David's hands.

"I guess we should say good-bye to you tonight," Dad said. "We have to get on the road real early tomorrow. Allison's on a committee about building a new elementary school and there's a meeting tomorrow night, so we have to get back for that."

"I would just skip it," Allison explained, "but this is the week we talk about the various sites we've visited and I have to report on my site. It's pretty important."

"Oh, sure," I said. But what I was thinking was, *One day? You came all this way, and we haven't even had a decent conversation yet, and you're leaving already?*

"I wish we had more chances to see you," Dad said. He looked like he meant it, like he felt bad about the quick visit. Then he said, again, "I want you and David to get to know each other."

"I know, Dad. Me too. I've been kind of thinking I might like to go to college out here," I said, letting the idea I'd been playing with escape into public for the first time. Why shouldn't I go to school someplace interesting? I didn't have to stay in Iowa. Isn't part of education seeing different things and meeting new people?

"Really, Robin? That's wonderful!" Dad's eyes got sort of damp looking and I was afraid he was going to start crying.

Once again, Allison came to the rescue. "Davy and I are going to say good night now. He needs to get to bed."

"No bed," he said, but he could tell Allison meant business. Marsh gave him another high five before he ran off to our room, and then Davy even let me give him a kiss on the cheek.

"'Night, Wobin," he said, letting his dimples show once more.

"Good night, David. I'll try to come and visit you sometime. Okay?"

He nodded. "Vithit me!" he demanded. Allison gave me a quick hug and hustled Davy into their room.

And then I was standing in the dark, alone with my dad. I smiled shyly. "I guess I better go, too."

His words rushed at me suddenly. "Tell your mother I want to help pay for your college. I don't have a lot of extra money, but I can help. I want to be part of it, Robin. I want to be part of your life."

If you'd told me before the trip that my father was going to make this proclamation, I think I would have been thrilled. At last I was going to have a real father. But that just wasn't the way I felt at the moment. His words hit me like a handful of pebbles and what I felt like saying was, *"Isn't it a little late now?"*

But I didn't. I said, "Thanks, Dad." I put my arms around his shoulders in a lightweight hug and let him brush his cheek against mine once more. "Thanks for coming. Tell David I love him."

Chapter Twenty-four

The morning after our dinner out with Dad, Iris was in a fury. I woke up to her standing over my bed with her hands on her hips. "How nice of you to rub it in our faces, Robin, that you have this great father and we don't!"

Apparently my sleeping later than usual had given her a chance to indoctrinate Marshall into this cuckoo line of thinking, too. "Yeah," he said, frowning at me, "how do you think this makes *us* feel?"

"What?"

"We know we'll never be a normal family again—you didn't need to remind us," Iris said, glaring at me.

I sat up on the edge of the bed and tried to make sense of what was going on. "First of all, I didn't even know they were coming—they just showed up. And second, if you think what you saw yesterday was a 'normal family,' you're blind. I haven't seen my father in three years, I barely know his wife, and I've never laid eyes on David before. How is that normal?"

Marsh wasn't sure; he looked at Iris for the answer. "It's normal because your father isn't dead," she said. "You don't have any idea how we feel, and you don't care either."

Suddenly I was really sick of Iris, sick of her rag-mop hairdo, her whiny voice, her skinny barfing body, and her crappy attitude. Where did she get off, anyway?

"You, my dear cousin, have no idea how *I* feel, or how I've *ever* felt, for years and years. Whereas, I have been doing my damnedest all summer to care about the two of you. But right now, I have to admit, I don't care. Not one little bit." I stomped over to my open duffel bag to see if I could find something to wear that wasn't filthy.

Iris tried to hide her shock that I was actually fighting back—I guess she thought having a dead father would easily trump anyone else's emotional baggage. Marsh, however, took a few steps back from his sister, no longer sure whose side he was on.

"At least you *have* a father," Iris said sullenly, trying to win back her advantage.

"Look," I said. "You had a father for twelve years; Marsh had one for almost ten. I barely had one at all, even though now that I'm practically grown up he wants to get to know me. I'm not saying one is better than the other, but my relationship with my father is certainly nothing to brag about and nothing for you to be jealous of. I know you're unhappy, Iris, but I wish you'd stop trying to blame it on everybody else in the world!" I grabbed a T-shirt and the least crummy pair of shorts I had, and slammed into the bathroom.

When I came out they were both looking glum, although Iris was quick to put a polish of anger over it for me.

"I don't have any clean clothes," I said. "Make a pile of anything you want washed and I'll stay here and do laundry this morning while you go see your mom."

"Ha. You probably just want to stay around here to flirt with Cesar some more."

I did have an ulterior motive for not going along, but not the one Iris suspected. I thought Dory ought to talk to her daughter without me around for Iris to deflect her anger toward. Marsh would be there, of course, but maybe it would be good for him to know that he wasn't the only one having problems since their father's death.

I was relieved to see the two of them ride off with Savannah—we definitely needed a break from one another. While the clothes were spinning in Sukey's machine, I sat outside under a cottonwood tree and looked at some magazines that were lying around for the guests; they were full of beautiful pictures of the New Mexico landscape. I was examining a particularly gorgeous photograph of a place called Ghost Ranch when Cesar came up behind me and looked over my shoulder.

"That's my favorite place around here," he said. "Georgia O'Keeffe lived there for years—you know, the painter?"

"Sort of," I said. "Didn't she paint big flowers?"

"Yes, but she also painted those mountains. Do you want to go see them? I don't have to work this afternoon. I could take you—and the kids, of course."

I grimaced. "The kids probably won't be speaking to me at all by then. But I'll ask them. How far is it from here?"

"Not too far—an hour and a half. Worth the trip. I'll show you O'Keeffe's paintings of the place. We've got a book."

We sat looking at the paintings until it was time for Cesar to pick up the kids at the hospital. I loved the colors in her work, the pinks and reds and almost blacks, and the curvaceous lines that made the hills seem to be living, breathing beings. I was looking forward to seeing the place she'd lived and painted.

I was folding our clothes and stacking them in piles by each suitcase when I heard the car doors slam. Iris headed straight to room 5, like a tiger who'd sniffed out a deer.

"You told her! You promised me you wouldn't, and you did!"

"And you told me you were going to stop throwing up. And

you didn't." I was carefully smoothing the wrinkles out of one of Iris's tiny shirts, but she grabbed it away from me.

"I'll never trust you again!"

I sighed. "Iris, will you cool it with the self-righteousness for a minute? You're in trouble here and somebody has to figure out what to do about it. It's not a secret I could keep; your mother had to know."

But Iris was not giving in that easily. "You've got her all crazy about it now. She says I have to go see another shrink and a nutritionist and God knows who else as soon as we get home. I knew she'd go apeshit." She threw the clean shirt on the floor and stomped on it with both feet.

"Well, of course she's upset. You're doing something dangerous, Iris. You've got to stop it!"

"I can't stop it! Why can't you get that? And it's not about wanting to be skinny either. You think you're so smart, but you don't even know why I do it!"

"Do *you* know why you do it?"

"Yes! Sometimes. I don't know exactly, but I know that sometimes I just can't stand to have food inside me—it makes me feel . . . soft and . . . weak. I don't need food the way other people do."

"Listen to yourself, Iris. Everybody needs food. You can't continue to live without food!"

"Maybe I can and maybe I can't." She tilted her head up defiantly.

If I'd had a moment or two of regret about breaking her confidence to Dory, it was gone now. Iris needed more help than I could possibly give her.

I told her I was going to Ghost Ranch that afternoon with Cesar; she and Marsh were welcome to come along if they wanted.

"Marsh and I have plans. Tony is letting us ride Eleanor and

Ruby. So you can go off with your new boyfriend and do whatever you want to. Don't let *us* get in your way."

"Oh, Iris, you know he isn't my boyfriend. I barely know him. Can't you at least *try* to be a civil human being?"

Her answer was to walk out the door and slam it behind her.

I guess it was on the drive to Ghost Ranch that I realized I'd have to come back to New Mexico again; it wasn't just a wish—it was a necessity. The shapes and colors were as vivid as Georgia O'Keeffe's paintings: thick blue sky, swirling white clouds like ghosts themselves, dark gnarled trees standing out against the reds and pinks of rugged buttes. As we were driving we watched black clouds gathering in the distance just beneath the fat white ones. They seemed to sit on the tops of the hills.

"Storm in that valley," Cesar said. "Keep watching—you'll see lightning."

Sure enough, the zigzag of white electricity cut through the dark clouds again and again. I couldn't stop looking. "Will the storm come here?" I asked.

"Nah. It's just a local storm. You see them a lot in the afternoons in the summer. They look like a big deal, but they run through fast. In twenty minutes it'll be clear over there again." And, of course, it was.

As we turned into Ghost Ranch, I couldn't keep my jaw from sagging open. We were in a long valley, surrounded on three sides by glorious red mountains. "How can you want to leave this?" I asked Cesar. "I've never seen anything so beautiful in my life."

He parked the car and gazed at the view with me. "I know it's beautiful, but I've seen this beauty so often, I want to see a different beauty. I want to be as surprised by something as you are by Ghost Ranch."

That I understood. I was beginning to see that if you tried to put yourself in another person's head, their feelings often did make sense. Unless they were Iris.

Cesar insisted we climb the trail known as Chimney Rock, which ended on a high plateau from which you looked across at two large "chimney" rock formations, and beyond them Abiquiu Lake and the Pedernal, a dark butte also painted often by O'Keeffe. Cesar knew a lot about the geology of the place, but I found it hard to take in much information—I was too overwhelmed by what I was seeing. It seemed to me it would be hard to live here and *not* want to paint.

By the time we climbed back down we were starving. Cesar opened the trunk and took out a cooler. "There's no place to eat around here, so I always come prepared." We sat at a picnic table and he pulled out two tuna salad sandwiches, two ripe tomatoes, a carton of Sukey's potato salad, a dozen chocolate chip cookies, and a jug of lemonade.

We polished off the sandwiches and tomatoes without pausing to breathe. Cesar smiled at me. "Okay, I think we can slow down now. Nobody's going to steal our cookies."

He made me laugh, which I hadn't done all that much of this summer. But what I appreciated most about Cesar was that, when he asked you a question, he actually listened to your answer.

"So, Iris is mad at you because you have a father and she doesn't?"

"Something like that. She's mad that her father died and she blames the world for it. I think she's really mad at her father for dying, but she knows that's ridiculous."

"Maybe mad at herself, too," Cesar said. "I think that happens—people feel guilty that they didn't appreciate the person enough while he was around."

I nodded. "That makes sense. Anyway, I'm in the path of her fury at the moment, even though my dad's been AWOL for most of my life."

"You sound kind of angry yourself."

"Do I? I didn't think I was until I saw him here, with his wife and son. I guess I didn't know what I was missing. It would have been nice to have him around when I was young. Now I think I definitely missed something."

Cesar handed me a cookie. "I can't imagine growing up without Roland around to give me grief."

"Your dad's great!"

"Yeah, he's a good guy. I guess what I really can't imagine is growing up with only one other person around. Just you and your mom."

I nodded. "It can be intense sometimes. But my best friend, Franny, comes over a lot, too. And, of course, Chris."

I'd filled Cesar in on the basics of my relationship with Chris on the ride down in the car. Now he stared at me like he was putting together a puzzle. "Most of your relationships are intense, aren't they? Your mother, your cousins, Chris."

I thought it over with a big bite of potato salad. Cesar didn't know Franny, yet, but she could have fit into that lineup, too. "I guess you're right. I started out thinking I didn't give a damn about my cousins—I thought they were snotty and unfeeling. But now I've gotten all knotted up in their dramas. It's easy to like Marshall, but I actually like Iris too now, even though she makes me so crazy sometimes I'd like to shake her. I guess I admire the ways in which they're both trying to be strong, even though it backfires on them half the time."

"You're a strong person, too—that's why you admire it in them."

"Me?" I laughed. "You wouldn't think so if you'd seen me at

the beginning of the summer, after Chris left for Italy. I thought I couldn't live without him."

"So, this summer has made you strong, too."

Maybe Cesar was right. I still missed Chris, but not with that terrible ache. I missed him in an excited way now because I knew that when we met again we'd both have stories to tell each other, we'd both have changed.

"Will you stay together when your boyfriend goes east for college?" Cesar asked.

"That was the idea," I said. "But I guess you never know what's ahead of you. I'm not so worried about it now."

He smiled. "Maybe you'll come back to New Mexico for college."

"Maybe. But you'll be far away by then."

"Maybe," he said. We smiled at each other in the nicest way, as if we were making a promise that the future, when it arrived, would be fine.

Chapter Twenty-five

Finally Dory was getting out of the hospital. Savannah planned to drive us down around noon to pick her up, so we spent the morning making a welcome home cake, with Sukey's help. All the Bolton-Packers had seen Marsh's drawings by then and flooded him with compliments, so it wasn't hard for Sukey to talk him into decorating the top of the big flat cake. She offered him a selection of icing colors in little tubes, but left the picture itself up to him.

I think Iris was as worried as I was that he'd do something gross or gory—the upside-down van, maybe, with our bodies hanging out the windows—but since we weren't speaking I didn't know for sure. However, Marshall came through. His picture, only slightly squiggly due to his unfamiliarity with the use of icing as a drawing tool, was of the front of the Black Mesa Motel, the pink adobe walls with the pots of white lilies and a string of red chili peppers hanging by the front door. On one side of the building stood the cottonwood tree that shaded our room; on the other side he'd drawn in the three of us, standing in front of the horses, Eleanor and Ruby. When Sukey saw it, she ran for her camera, saying she'd never be able to eat it unless she captured the image on film. It was a masterpiece in sugar.

Roland and Cesar were blowing up balloons and Sukey was draping crepe paper from the ceiling when we left. How had it happened that after just a week with this family—a traumatic week—the Black Mesa Motel really did feel like a home to us? Even Iris liked these people—especially Tony, as it turned out. But even Roland had managed to get her laughing with him this morning when he sneaked the cake-mixing bowl out to the backyard to lick it clean before letting her wash it.

I'd been thinking about how hard it was going to be for Dory to take them home again. They were used to a crowd now—they slept with me, ate meals with Cesar and Tony, washed dishes with Sukey and Roland. Once they got on that airplane tomorrow afternoon they'd be alone with their busted-up mother who didn't seem to know how to deal with either of them.

Mom called last night to say she'd managed to arrange everybody's tickets so that Franny would arrive in Albuquerque (the nearest airport) an hour after the Tewksburys left. That way, Cesar, who'd offered to drive us all down, wouldn't have to make two trips. While we were talking I suggested that she try to get some time off in a few weeks so we could drive the car back to Chicago and stay on awhile to help Dory.

"I thought of that," she said, "but I wasn't sure you'd be willing to spend time with your cousins again so soon."

"Actually, I think I'll want to check up on them by then. I mean, they're not bad kids. They just had their lives turned upside down when Allen died."

Mom was silent for a few seconds, then she said, "Do you know how much you've changed this summer?"

"Yeah, I kind of do."

"You're growing up, my dear. Up, up, and away."

* * *

Dory was ready to go when we got to the hospital. "Get me out of here!" she demanded the minute we walked in the door. "I'm so sick of lying in this bed all day!" But you could tell that just getting out of bed was still painful for her. When she was settled in the wheelchair for the ride out to the car, the nurse handed her two bottles of pills.

"Don't be a hero," the nurse told her. "When you feel bad, you take one. For that plane ride tomorrow you should take two. Now, you're sure somebody's meeting you with a wheelchair when you get off the plane?"

"Yes, my friend Ellen . . ."

"And next week you have to . . ."

"I know—go see my doctor at home. Don't worry. I've already called him."

We thanked her and said good-bye, then followed the man from "transport" who wheeled Dory down the hall and outside. Iris carried the droopy flowers and Marsh the half-eaten box of chocolates while I took the bag of clothes she'd had on during the accident—or what was left of them.

Cesar had pulled the station wagon up in front of the door so Dory could slide right from the wheelchair into the front seat. The three of us climbed in back; it must have been obvious to Marsh that it was up to him to separate Iris and me because he took the middle seat without complaint.

Dory was so happy to be outside again—she was in a good mood, pain or no pain. And it must have infected the rest of us too because there were no battles on the drive back to the Black Mesa. Dory thanked Cesar about a thousand times, a sentiment she would repeat again and again to every person in the Bolton-Packer family until the moment she left. Since he knew she hadn't gotten to see much of Santa Fe, Cesar drove back through downtown, the scenic route, and pointed out to her various points of interest.

"Well, I'll have to come back sometime," she said, watching the stores and hotels stream by her window. "It's a beautiful town. I'm glad you guys got to see some of it this week. Thank you so much, Cesar!"

"Believe me, we all enjoyed it," Cesar said. "It's like having more brothers and sisters."

"Just what you need!" Iris said, but there was a laugh in her voice.

The welcome home cake was a big hit, of course. Dory was astounded that Marsh had done the decorating. We all ate chicken hot dogs for lunch and then big pieces of the cake, which was unanimously pronounced delicious. Marsh and Iris fought over the part with the horses, of course, but Sukey found a way to slice the cake so they could each have one. We were becoming almost raucous—even the normally silent Tony was talking—when we all realized at the same time that Dory had become ominously quiet. Her unbroken arm was propped on the table, holding up her head, and her mouth was clenched in a tight line.

Our good moods all wore off along with Dory's pain pills. She was very tired, she said, and handed out one more round of thank you's as Sukey gave us the key to room number 6, which adjoined ours and which would be Dory's for her last day in New Mexico. Marsh had decided that he'd stay on the fold-out bed in our room for one more night. Even though he'd been free of nightmares for several nights in a row, he didn't want to take the chance of waking his mother. I guess Dory was too exhausted to realize what a sacrifice this was for him—he'd missed her terribly, especially just before he went to bed, and if he did have a nightmare, Iris and I were poor substitutes for his mother. Anyway, she didn't thank him, and I could tell Marsh was hurt not to be getting credit for his brave decision. I smiled and gave him a thumbs-up sign, but maybe he wasn't sure anymore, since my feud with Iris, if he should accept my smiles, so he just turned away, pretending he didn't see me.

Dory took a long nap that afternoon. Iris went down to the barn with Tony and Marsh hung around outside, drawing, while I helped Sukey clean up the mess we'd made in the kitchen. We'd all just congregated back in our room when Dory woke up, cranky, and called us in to her bedside.

"Hand me my sweater, would you, Robin? And Iris, get me a glass of water."

I fetched the sweater, and Iris went to get the water, but not with a generous heart. She thrust the glass under her mother's nose.

"Just hold it a minute, will you? I have to get a pill. Marsh, hand me the bottle on the dresser," she ordered.

"Is this what it's going to be like at home?" Iris said. "You ordering us around like we're your servants?"

Dory took the pill bottle from Marsh and glared at her daughter. "I will need your help, if that's what you mean. Yes. Did you think I was going to be good as new the minute I got out of the hospital?"

"No, but I didn't think you'd be so crabby."

"Well, welcome to the new me, Iris." She slugged the pill down with half a glass of water, then shook her head and handed the glass back to her daughter. "Ugh, I hate these things."

"Does your arm hurt?" Marsh asked her.

Dory thought for a minute, then said, "Yes, it does, Marshall. And my ribs hurt and my head hurts. And my brain hurts, too, when I think about how I have to pull this family back together. Tomorrow at this time we'll be on our way home, and I'm scared to death of all I'll have to deal with when we get there."

"Why are you telling us?" Iris asked, although her tone was much more subdued now.

"Because this is the way it's going to be from now on. I've given it a lot of thought the past few days. I've been treating you both as if you were breakable, and you've started to believe it yourselves. So now we're trying something different. You're both old enough to take some responsibility. I can't do it all by myself—you have to help me and help each other, too."

"Like what? I have to change Marshall's diapers or something?" Iris never knew when to keep her mouth shut.

Marsh, who was already a little freaked out by his mother's new attitude, exploded and ran at Iris with his fists up. "I do not wear diapers, you moron!"

"*THIS IS EXACTLY WHAT I MEAN*!" None of us had ever heard Dory speak so loudly, so angrily, before. Both kids stopped and stared at her.

"I've *had it* with the bickering and the battering that goes on between you two. There won't be any more of it. Do you understand me? *Do you*?" Both heads nodded.

"There's going to be one unbreakable rule from now on: No More Secrets. If you're angry or scared or sad or upset in any way, you'll talk about it. You'll tell me and you'll tell your sibling. And you'll tell your therapist, too. Same goes for me. From now on, when we feel lousy, we aren't going to hide out or slug people or throw up our dinner, or run off the road. We're going to talk to one another about what's going on in our heads and our hearts. We're going to get through this together."

I could tell Marsh was on the verge of collapse, his mouth turning down, his chin caving in. I was about to try my luck putting an arm around him when he suddenly ran to his mother's side and buried his face in her neck. She winced at the pain, but took her good arm and gathered him in.

"I hate to yell at you guys. You know that. But things have to change." She looked into Iris's eyes. "Your father is gone, but we're not. We have to start thinking about how we want to live the rest of our lives, not just survive them. Will you help me, please?"

Tears spilled down Iris's cheeks onto her pink T-shirt. I figured she hated for me to see her like this, so I quietly backed away into our room, leaving the family alone. I closed the door behind me, but not before I heard Iris say, "Mommy, I'm sorry."

Chapter Twenty-six

After that, the evening passed quietly. But it wasn't like we weren't speaking to one another—it was more like we were waiting for a little time to pass and trying to figure out a new way of talking. We all said good night to one another like normal people might.

In the morning Roland drove Dory and me to the repair shop. The part had finally come in for the minivan and the work was supposed to be finished on it by tomorrow, so Dory had to flash her credit card one more time and tell the manager I 'd be picking up the car. It was strange to see it again. Even though the bodywork had already been done, we couldn't look at it without feeling a little sick.

Dory shook her head. "I hope I can bear to drive it again." She looked at me. "Oh, dear, Robin, can you drive it?"

I nodded. "I think I'm like that vase you bought. If I didn't break so far, I can probably make it the rest of the way."

The kids had packed their suitcases right after breakfast so they'd have time for a last drive through Santa Fe with Savannah. When we got back from the repair shop, I helped Dory pack, then we sat outside under the cottonwood tree to wait. In a minute Sukey came out with a plastic bag in her hand.

"I made you some sandwiches," she said. "And wrapped up some pieces of your cake, too. Airplane food is so awful."

"Oh, Sukey," Dory said, tearing up. "No, you've done so much for us already!"

Sukey waved away her protest. "I meant it when I said I loved having the kids here—they're terrific. You know, people stop through here for a night or two, but they don't become family. You guys are family now." She saw Dory blinking back tears. "And don't you dare go telling me thank you again. You thanked me enough already to last my lifetime!"

She turned to me. "Cesar says you're thinking of coming back out here for college."

"Are you really?" Dory said.

"I might."

"Well, you better come by and say hello if you relocate out here. I'll make you a cake and decorate it myself!"

"This will be the first place I come," I assured her.

Savannah's car pulled up in front and Iris and Marshall jumped out, beaming. It had been awhile since I'd seen them both happy at the same time.

They ran over and stood right in front of me, with slightly embarrassed looks on their faces. Iris said, "Marsh had this idea . . ."

"You thought it was a good idea, too!" he interrupted.

She tipped her head in reluctant agreement. "Anyway, we decided to get you something so you wouldn't forget us." She looked at Marshall and he took a small box from the pocket of his droopy pants.

"Since you never buy stuff for yourself," he said, handing it to me.

I was so surprised I could hardly speak. "Wow. You guys . . . gee . . ." I stared at the box as if I'd never seen one before.

"Open it," Iris commanded.

So I did. In the box lay the turquoise ring that reminded me of the sun, which I'd admired last week on the Santa Fe Plaza.

"Oh, my God! I can't believe it! I never expected . . ."

"Put it on!" Marsh said.

It was beautiful. Sukey and Dory admired it as it sparkled on my finger.

"We bought it with our own money," Marshall said. Iris rolled her eyes, but she didn't poke him or call him a moron. I looked up at them and saw how pleased they were to surprise me with something they knew I wanted. What else could I do but hug them?

"Thank you, Marshall," I said, grabbing him first because he was the easiest. He hugged me right back. "This is a wonderful gift. But you know I would never forget you anyway!"

"Yeah, I know. I'm unforgettable."

"Iris," I said, then looked at her for a full second before putting my arms around her. I knew she'd resist me, and she did, but not with every muscle and bone in her body. I was willing to settle for this small miracle.

"I guess you'll never forget me either," she said in her usual ironic tone of voice.

"I'll try, though," I said, which made her laugh. "Thank you for the ring. You know I love it."

Then I remembered that I had gifts for them, too. "Wait here a minute," I said, and ran into our room, trying to remember what I'd done with the clay horses from Acoma. My backpack. I hoped they hadn't broken.

All three were fine. I decided quickly that the darkest horse—nearest in color to Okie—was for Marsh. And the white one, of course, was Silverfoot, so that was Iris's. I'd keep the reddish one.

"Presents for you, too!" I said, handing one to each of them.

"So you don't forget your wild west summer."

"These are from the pueblo at Acoma," Marsh said. "I saw them there. I can't believe you bought us presents—you never buy anything!" He looked so shocked, I had to laugh.

Iris nudged him gently in the ribs. "Just say 'thank you,' Marshall."

He glared at her. "I didn't hear you say it yet."

Iris gave me a lopsided smile and kept her eyes on her horse. "Thanks. This is really nice." From Iris that was quite a speech.

"Yeah, thanks," Marsh said. "You know we'll never forget you!"

Savannah had to leave for work so the first round of good-byes began, and then we packed the suitcases into the station wagon. The defective tent, all the sleeping bags, and a variety of souvenirs (including the unbreakable vase) would make the trip back to the Midwest with me in the car. Roland and Sukey and Tony all gathered around to say good-bye to the Tewksburys. Iris and Tony even sneaked off around the corner for a private farewell. Or maybe just to talk about horses one more time.

And then we were off for the airport. It went very quickly once we got there—check the bags, stamp the tickets, call for a wheelchair to get Dory down the long hallway to the gate. We had to tell them good-bye at the checkpoint before the gates. Iris and Marsh had done enough hugging—they were eager to get going, but Dory gave me a long one-armed squeeze and, of course, a thank-you.

"I don't want to let you go, dammit," she said. "You've been a lifesaver for me on this trip."

I told her Mom and I would be up to visit in two weeks or so.

"Two weeks? Thank God. I hope I can hold out that long!"

We waved good-bye—Cesar, too—until they turned the corner and were out of sight. Suddenly I felt like crying. It was over. Not the whole trip—Franny and I would certainly have an adventure or two on the way home. But this was the end of the Zigzag Plan.

"There's an hour until your friend's plane comes in," Cesar said. "Let's get something to eat, okay?"

I followed him silently to the food court and ordered a corn muffin and a glass of orange juice.

"That's all you want?" Cesar was getting himself a burger, fries, and a milk shake. "Don't tell me you're getting like that cousin of yours. She doesn't eat enough to keep a bird alive."

"No, I'm just feeling a little weird that they're gone. I mean, we've been so close all summer, literally so close, in motel rooms and in the van—we were never apart! And now they've disappeared, just like that."

"You miss them," he said, with a shrug. To him it was obvious.

"Yeah, I guess I do. Who'd have expected that?"

Cesar was a great person to talk to, but he was also a great person to sit and be quiet with. After a few minutes, without telling me what he was doing, he went up and got me a milk shake.

"Best medicine for melancholy," he said. Then he smiled at me in that cockeyed way he has, and I decided it was a good thing that Franny and I were leaving in two days.

Franny's plane was about ten minutes late, but it seemed like ages to me—I was so anxious to see her. Then here she came striding down the hall toward us like she was considering buying the building, her eyes taking in every pretzel seller, cigarette lounge, and newspaper stand. It was her first time out of Iowa and she wasn't going to miss a thing.

"Franny!" I screamed from the other side of the checkpoint. "We're here!"

She looked up and waved nonchalantly, as though she found herself in places like Albuquerque all the time. I grabbed her the minute she came through to our side.

"I can't believe you're really here!"

"Me either. It's like magic. I got on a big bird, it flew through the clouds for a few minutes, and here I am, a thousand miles from home. Robin, this is the best rescue mission ever—only this time you're saving me from Des Sanders."

"It's over with Des?"

"*Way* over." She looked up at Cesar. "I'm Franny. Who are you?"

"Oh, Franny, this is Cesar. He's been driving us around since the car crash."

She smiled. "Oh, like a chauffeur?"

"Not exactly. See, Robin was abandoned on our doorstep and we took her in. So, I'm kind of a . . . foster brother." His smile slipped from Franny over to me.

"I see," she said, giving me a wide-eyed look. I knew what we'd be discussing the moment Cesar was out of sight.

On the drive back from the airport, Franny wanted me to tell her everything that had happened for the past five weeks, including *details.* So I started with the Iowa State Fair, spent quite a few minutes on the mosquito attack in the Badlands, described the fossil Marsh had found, skipped lightly over dancing with Glen, gave a complete rundown on the Lazy River Ranch rodeo, explained how Denver sat right in the mountains, told her about the cow-shaped pool in Texas, the Cadillacs covered with spray paint, the lack of water at Acoma Pueblo and Madrid, New Mexico. And then, of course, Savannah, the vase, the argument, the seat belt situation, and the tumbling downhill of Dory's car. Telling the stories made me feel like I'd put a period at the end of the sentence. That trip, and all it entailed, was really over.

"And that's how we ended up at the Black Mesa Motel," I said as we pulled up in front of it.

"Now I'm really jealous," Cesar said. "Hearing about your trip makes me want to take off and go somewhere. Anywhere!"

"Well, come back to Iowa with us!" Franny said.

"I already offered to do that," Cesar said. "But I was turned down."

I knew he was joking, but he looked a little sad, too. "We'd make you square dance if you came with us," I said.

"Hey, I'd do ballet dancing for a chance to see Iowa!" he said.

"What is going on with you two?" Franny said once we were alone in room number 5.

"Nothing!"

"Oh, please—no false modesty. That guy is gaga over you."

"Don't be silly."

She shook her head. "He does not look at you like a brother, Robin, foster or otherwise. And I have to say, on first glance, I prefer this one to Chris. I know Chris has that blond thing going, but as far as I'm concerned, give me dark looks."

"Franny, will you shut up?" I slammed the window down. "What if he heard you?"

"What if he did?"

"There is nothing going on with Cesar and me. I'm still going with Chris. As far as I know."

"Cesar," she said, flopping on the bed. "He even has a good name. Oh, speaking of Chris, your mom gave me this to give to you." She zipped open her backpack and carefully removed a blue airmail letter, holding it with only her thumb and index finger, as if it were a teacup.

My stomach fell into my shoes as I took it from her. Which of my last letters had he gotten already? The braggy one certainly. The honest one, maybe. And what would he have to say about either one of them?

"I suppose you want to read it in private?"

"Would you mind?"

She sighed. "Not at all. Maybe there'll be some hot-looking young guy hanging around outside I can get to know."

"Be my guest," I said, then, as soon as she left, I started trying to come up with reasons why Cesar wouldn't appreciate Franny's finer qualities. Unfortunately, I couldn't think of any, so I sat down on the bed and opened my letter. Just looking at the familiar handwriting made my heart jump. If only I could see Chris surely things wouldn't seem so confusing!

Dear Robin,

I got your last two letters just a couple of days apart. I'm glad I waited to write you back until the second one came today. After I read the first one I was kind of angry with you, going on and on about your wonderful cousins and dancing with cowboys and everything. I should have known it was in response to my letter. When the second one came, I remembered what I'd written to you, all about Gabriella and "bonding" with my friends. I guess it sounded like I had a great new life and you weren't in it.

Maybe I wanted you to think that. I'm not sure why. I am having fun here, and I do like most of the kids on the program, but sometimes I get really lonely for Thunder Lake and for you. We have a lot of fun here, but none of these people really know me the way you do. I hope you believe that I still love you, Robin, because I do. But I have to tell you something that you won't like. I've kissed Gabriella. Only a few times, and mostly because we're both missing people. We're certainly not in love! But it happened, and I can't promise you it won't happen again.

It's so hard to be so far away from the person I love! It scares me now to think of being away from you next year. I want us to be together, Robin, but sometimes it seems like it won't work. I know this is what you were afraid would happen once we were apart, and I'm sorry I didn't take you more seriously. I always said you were the smart one.

The car crash sounded awful. I'm so glad you weren't hurt! I don't know what I'd have done if you'd been hurt and I couldn't come to see you! I'm sorry your aunt got hurt, but I guess she'll be okay. It's great you're getting to spend some time in Santa Fe—I wish I could see it with you.

In your last letter you seemed different than I remember—I guess going out into the world does that. I think I've changed too, which makes it hard to write to you. If we could talk to each other face-to-face—which we will soon—I think things would be okay again. But for now, I feel a little bit like I don't even know who I'm writing to.

Our school program is over and we're leaving tomorrow to travel to Florence, Bologna, Milan, and Venice. There's an address in Milan where we can pick up mail in about two weeks, but I'm thinking that maybe it would be better if we didn't write to each other anymore while I'm in Italy. That way, when we meet again on August 20, we won't have to sort through the things we said on paper and might have misunderstood. We can look at each other and talk about what really happened.

Does that sound all right? I'll put the Milan address at the bottom of the page, just in case you don't agree with me. Otherwise, I'll look forward to seeing you in a month. No matter what happens, Robin, I do love you.

Chris

The address in Milan was squeezed in at the bottom of the page in such small handwriting I could barely read it. It didn't matter anyway; I wouldn't need it.

Chapter Twenty-seven

Roland drove me down to pick up the van first thing the next morning. It was strange to sit behind the wheel again. Except for a few scratches, it looked the same as it had before the accident, and I had the crazy idea that, by fixing the car, we'd managed to erase all the damage—not just the broken bones, but Dory's grief, Iris's eating disorder, Marshall's fears. I knew it wasn't true, but it made me hopeful. Maybe even people who looked like they were totaled could be put back together again and made to run.

Since Franny only had one day in Santa Fe, we made it a good one. Both Cesar and Savannah came with us to tour the city, to see the museums and shops, and to eat a few last enchiladas. Franny bought herself a rope of chili peppers because she thought they were beautiful and because we had a whole van to ourselves to take things back.

"I can't believe I'm getting to see all this stuff and it's not even costing me anything," she said at least four times during the day. "I mean, I'm sorry your aunt got hurt and everything, but, God, it was lucky for me. We're going to have so much fun on the drive back!"

Whenever one of us mentioned leaving, Cesar stopped smiling. I wondered if Franny was right about him liking me as more than a friend, or if he was just feeling bad that he was "stuck" in New Mexico? I liked Cesar, and I knew that if I let myself, I could like him a lot. I had a feeling if we'd spent a few more days at the Lazy River Ranch I would have been more than friends with Glen, too. What was wrong with me this summer? I loved Chris, but I also really liked these other guys. How could both things be true?

Of course, Chris said he was still in love with me, too, and he was kissing Gabriella, so at least I wasn't the only person who was confused. We'd just have to figure it out on August 20.

Franny loved the ring Iris and Marshall had given me, so we took her to see the Indian jewelry at the Plaza. While we were walking from one display to another, she had us all laughing over her breakup with Des Sanders. "He wanted me to go out with him every weekend! And he was always calling me on the phone. Like I don't have my own life!"

"Franny, that's what you do when you have a boyfriend," I said.

"Yeah? Maybe I'd be better off getting a dog then."

"Even a dog wants a walk every night," Savannah told her.

"Every night? Isn't there some animal that doesn't demand so much? What about a bird?"

"You just haven't met the right person yet," I said.

"Maybe. By the way, I have a feeling your mother *has* met the right person."

I stopped laughing. "Who? You don't mean Michael Evans?"

"Is she going out with anybody else? I'm telling you, they've checked out every schmaltzy romantic movie in the store, and I've seen them together at the Fish Shack every time I've been there—sitting very close together. I think they're attached at the hip. Doesn't she talk about him when she calls you?"

"She mentions him, but she never said they're inseparable."

"Maybe she thinks you don't like him."

"I like him fine. I mean, I don't know him very well. It's a little weird, you know? She's my mother and she's going on dates. With a guy who looks like Ernest Hemingway's enormous twin."

"Well, I think you better get used to it. I have a feeling the bell tolls for Mr. Hemingway. The *wedding* bell."

Now *there* was something to think about. What if they got married and he moved into the house? The idea had been appalling to me when I'd first considered it in June. But now I thought, *why shouldn't my mother fall in love*? In another year I'd be leaving for college—our mother/daughter act would be breaking up, anyway. I should be happy she'd found somebody to be with. I should be, and maybe by the time I drove all the way back to Iowa, I would be.

We got back pretty late and tried to be quiet coming in so we wouldn't wake any motel clients who might be asleep. Savannah had been telling Franny about Sukey's weaving and Roland's pottery, and Franny wanted to see it, so they went inside together. There was a weird minute when I thought I ought to go with them because, if I didn't, I'd be standing outside in the dark, alone with Cesar, which might not be such a good idea. But I didn't seem to be able to move one way or the other. I stood there looking at him in the neon light from the motel sign; it gave his dark hair a blue shine and made his eyes glow. Finally, Cesar cleared his throat.

"Your friend Franny is very funny. I like her."

"Me too. She's my best friend."

Then, just when I thought we were on a safe topic, Cesar leaped into a new one. "Robin, I'm not going to be here in the morning to tell you good-bye."

"You're not? You don't usually work in the morning."

"I just . . . have things to do."

"Oh." Why did I feel so disappointed?

"So, good-bye," he said, sticking out his hand.

This was it? We were going to have an awkward handshake in the dark and then go our separate ways? I put my hand out to meet his, but instead of shaking it, he curled his fingers around it and held it so tightly I could feel his pulse beating in his palm.

"I know you have a boyfriend," he said. "But if he goes to the East Coast, and you come out west, maybe the next time I see you things will be different."

My voice had disappeared. I looked at his dark eyes and tried my best to remember what Chris's eyes had looked like.

"You don't have to say anything. But you could write me a letter when you get back to Iowa. Tell me about everything you saw on your trip. Let me know if you still think New Mexico is the most beautiful place." He smiled. "You know my address."

I nodded, looking down at our hands, still clenched.

"Good night," he said, almost whispering.

"Good night," I repeated.

And then he leaned toward me, and I leaned toward him, and we kissed each other. I was going to say I didn't know what I was doing, but that would be a lie. I knew exactly what I was doing. I kissed him slowly and sweetly, and then he was gone.

"How come you're standing out here all by yourself?" Franny asked. She fanned a hand in front of my face. "Hello? Do you read me, Houston? Come in."

"I'm here. I'm just thinking."

"Thinking about what? Chris? Cesar? Moving to New Mexico? Driving across the country with your hilarious friend?"

I linked my arm through hers and walked her back to room number 5. "All the possibilities, Franny. All the possibilities."